THE SLEIGHT before CHRISTMAS

USA TODAY BESTSELLING AUTHOR
KATE STEWART

Editor: Donna Cooksley Sanderson
Cover by Amy Queau of Q Design
Formatting by Champagne Book Design

For all the unappreciated, flabbergasted parents currently hanging by a thread from their attempt to raise decent humans. Who might, on occasion, daydream about hanging it up. Or perhaps, just once, want to call out their kids for being assholes—but would never dream of putting a voice to it.
I'm all too happy to do it for you, and so this one is for you.

Merry Christmas.

XO
Kate

THE SLEIGHT before CHRISTMAS

PROLOGUE

Twenty-One Christmases Ago. . .

B ACK TO THE FIRE, CALLOUSED HANDS PALMING THE AIR behind me, the blazing flame's warmth begins to blanket me as mouthwatering smells waft in from the kitchen. Gazing upon the brightly lit twinkling lights and glittering ornaments strung on the tree feet away, I sink into the atmosphere—this vibe in stark contrast to any memory of my own home.

A blink later, my serenity is splintered when the front door bursts open. Turning, I'm met with a tornado of snow flurries and platinum blonde hair. Instant chatter erupts from the creature as she rambles about mixed grievances and announcements while I drink her in. In the next instant, I recognize her, all the while becoming utterly fucking stupefied by the living, breathing vision of her. A fully animated version against the stationary images I've observed in passing over these last months. Images that fail in contrast to the utter . . . *chaos* that is Ruby and Allen Collins' oldest daughter. Chaos, wrapped in the most beautiful package I've ever laid eyes on.

Lengthy blonde hair lays in snow-dampened waves over her shoulders. Her sweater, dark blue and hugging every bit of her perfect frame. The hem hovering inches above her jeans, showcasing her insanely toned midriff. One accentuated by a glittering, diamond belly button ring. Her dark, slightly tattered jeans hugging the abundant curve of her hips down to her toned calves. The perfection finished off with short-cut black boots with silver buckles on the sides. Boots similar to the ones I'm wearing. After my first thorough sweep, I instantly go in for another hit of her. This one far more intoxicating as I explore her slightly heart-shaped face, rich doe eyes, and lengthy painted black lashes. Her features utterly perfect and accentuated by thick, highly glossed lips.

Fuck me.

Frozen where I stand and utterly mystified, when the rambling suddenly stops, I'm met with an equally arresting stare. It's when she cocks her hip, her eyes narrowing in scrutiny—even as they light with mischief as she rudely addresses me—that I bite my smile back. A grin I fight hard to keep at bay because it becomes obvious in those seconds that I've been set up. At the sight of her, not one bit of me is bothered by it. Not in the least. Because I already know I want that chaos and everything that comes with it.

CHAPTER ONE

Thatch

Present Day

"STOP IT PEYTON!" GRACIE SCREAMS AN OCTAVE ABOVE her normal ear-splitting volume as the woman formerly known as my wife fumes in front of me. Hair full of suds, her glaring left eye starts to involuntarily twitch. Not long ago, I'd be racking my brain for a clue as to why. Though my wife is vocal enough about her grievances, she sometimes keeps them bottled for long stints. That's when things tend to get scary.

Though I've never been a man of many words, less than a handful of years back, we found ourselves unable to speak to one another without offense or resentment setting in. Those run-ins followed by days of tense silence. Been there, done that, and since our blow-up that Christmas, I've started communicating a bit better, which had us getting somewhat back in sync—just like the good old days. So, as I gaze upon my gorgeous, simmering, soap-covered wife, I silently commend us both on our ability to communicate better. Even as I physically see her decision to verbally berate me.

"Love you," I shoot out preemptively just as she opens her mouth to deliver my ass to me. My sentiment has her pausing a millisecond, her eyes losing a smidge of their *terrorize him* sheen. A small win.

"Repeat after me, Thatchalamewl," she draws out one of my more ridiculous pet names. At the arrival of it, I take it as a sign my strategy wasn't completely ignored. Though, I used to find this name far more endearing when it wasn't the equivalent of *middle name* serious. Ah, these little games we play.

The trash bag I'm holding grows heavier in my hand as I tense due to the sudden silence upstairs. Too quiet. Something's afoot. If I had to guess the culprit—Peyton. His accomplice—our baby girl, Gracie. Though far from a baby now. So far, that I shield my eyes from her wardrobe choices—daily—to try to keep the memory alive.

It's the growing confrontation in my wife's rich brown eyes that has me flitting my focus back to her as I soak in her state. I see it the second her demeanor shifts to *middle name* serious. The tiny lines around her mouth deepening with her frown. Disappointment. Words of said emotion forming on her tongue as a handful of suds from her head slide down her slender neck and disappear into her robe.

"I, Thatch," she drones on as I debate on Smart Pop and softcore porn in our newly finished basement after everyone is lights out. . . *or* a quick, stress-relieving tug in a hot shower. As selfish as the thought of sex may be in this moment, I've been unsuccessfully attempting to shift from our cozy pajama setup—me bottoms, her tops, and TV reruns—to the action arena starring the two of us sans the flannel sometime before the morning whistle blows. And by whistle, I mean the symphony of our children's mixed screams.

Lately, I miss touching her intimately and that touch being welcome.

I miss her sounds, her skin, her moans, and connection. Her full attention. In some form other than "honey do, did you, will you?" and "why did you, do you?" It's been a long time since I've been in the "do that, so good, do it again" area.

One I'm getting desperate to get back to. As far as typical men think in the number of sexual thoughts a day, I feel like I'm below par in the depravity department. But the last time we got truly intimate, the leaves hadn't fully turned. There wasn't a hint of snow on the ground. Now that our driveway is salted and the foliage is dusted white, I can feel myself coiling up due to pent-up frustration.

"I, Thatch," I mumble in feeble attempt to get somewhere between the two territories at some point in the next week.

"Do solemnly swear," she prompts, her command sounding like the growl of a small dog. Like a terrier or maybe a Jack Russell. I've always wanted a Jack Russell, but they're known to be a hyper breed, and we're all stocked up on hy—

"*Thatch*," Serena snaps, bringing me back.

"Do solemnly swear," I continue, as sweat starts to bead at my temple—not from fear but because I can feel her slipping further away. Marriage has its phases, and after two decades and counting with Serena, I know this truth all too well. I live it and very intentionally endure it because the hard-earned sweet spots are so fucking worth it. Tonight, that shift seems to be getting further out of reach, and I know there are two distinct reasons why. Two eerily quiet reasons upstairs. Too quiet.

"To never again bother my wife while she's bathing," Serena finishes, her hair still dripping rapidly where she stands in our kitchen. Which is ironic since it was she, herself, who interrupted the rest of *her own bath* to bitch me out. They say it's always the ones you love most that you take aggravation with life out on, right? Well, from what I can tell at this moment, my wife loves me more than anyone in the history of fucking ever. Which would be flattering if affection truly played a factor in any part of this bullshit.

No, this, what's happening right here, is part of the buildup that started just after Thanksgiving. The animosity rolling off her in thanks to the stressful weeks leading up to the main event. The pressure cooker state of mind that all spouses experience during the period coined *the holidays*. *Days* my ass. I prefer to think of them as hell on earth—*weeks*. Weeks in which peace is anywhere but on planet Earth for any ringed man equipped with a cock. The proof evident in the task list I get bombarded with annually that no male, even in his prime, can undertake successfully. A list I swear is meant to purposely set up this cock wielding, peaceless man for failure. Hellacious weeks in which the tiny woman in front of me—who I would and often do walk through hellfire for—evolves into my own personal terrorist. That is, until the blinking lights disappear, the scent of pine goes back to its designated cleaner bottle, and the last shred of tinsel is sucked up by our Dyson.

Maybe I shouldn't discriminate and include the single but attached guys. It's been a while for me, but I bet they're just as battered down during this time by their would-be wives. I bet a few of those ringless guys are reconsidering the diamond they bought right now due to the state of their significant others. Though in truth, it's not their fault, it's the pressure—

"Thatch!" Serena summons, knowing how squirrel my thoughts get when I'm knee-deep in my wife's disappointment.

"Jesus, baby, okay. Get it over with."

"To never again bother my wife while she's bathing," she repeats, as the image of the first time I laid eyes on her shutters in. The vision having helped greatly in recent weeks. A reminder of the girl I first laid eyes on and fell for as quickly as the snow surrounded her in those life-changing seconds. Surprising myself when I stuck. Even all these years later.

"Unless someone is bleeding or nuclear war breaks out," she continues as the trash bag grows heavier in my hands.

"Unless . . ." I quirk a brow with my suspense-filled pause. "You know what," I shake my head. "I'm calling bullshit, babe. I think we should turn this into a negotiation."

"Now's not the time," Serena dismisses.

"Actually, it's the perfect time. When do I get a dad moment? When *do I* get bath time?"

See? Communication.

"You get time," she counters unconvincingly.

"Yeah?" I lift my chin. "*When?*"

"When you . . . go out with the guys."

"October fifth, *last year*," I clap back. She frowns as I straighten my spine, knowing I've got her somewhere in the vicinity of where I want her.

"Fine," she sighs, giving up easily—too easily—as the suds in her hair start to sink into her scalp. "We could both use a private moment. Peyton turns eighteen in thirteen and a half years," she delivers like a sentence. "I guess we can get our time then."

"Jesus, it's that long?" I ask, to which she nods, her eyes lowering. Seeing her surrender so quickly starts an uneasy gnawing inside my chest. Serena rarely, if ever, backs down.

"Babe," I retract, tossing the bullshit aside. "I'm sorry, I really tried to wait until you—"

"No, it's," she shakes her head in frustration. "It's okay, God, never mind. You work so hard, Thatch. You don't deserve this. I'm sorry, I love you."

Alarm bells start going off as I study her closely. Dark circles lay like stains under her eyes. She's paler than usual, and from the way her robe is cinched . . . thinner? The most gutting part is that her return stare is lacking all signs of life. Our typical borderline playful tit-for-tat I was up for, but this? Something's most definitely wrong.

"Go, I'll take—" A tell-tale thud sounds upstairs, and both of us instantly snap to, heads tilting, ears perking. The long, loaded silence that follows has us both hauling ass up the stairs. Heart thumping wildly in my chest, I make it to the door a split second after Serena and stop behind her at the threshold. The blood in my ears roars as I take note of our boy child just as he grips the rope . . . hanging from his bedroom ceiling fan.

"Daddy, look!" Peyton orders before sailing through the air as Serena and I simultaneously sound nuclear warnings, a stunted second too late. Peyton instantly drops from the rope, landing in an impressive dismount on his mattress. Stunned silence passes as I make the decision to go parent in lieu of awed spectator—especially after seeing the state of his ceiling fan, which now hangs by nothing but wires.

"Son," I sigh as Serena uncharacteristically ambles into Peyton's room before calmly perching herself on the edge of his bed. Staring up at the fan, I mentally try to work out how in the hell our four-and-a-half-year-old kid managed to secure a rope to his—"Gracie!" I shout, summoning our twelve-year-old nightmare into the circus tent.

"I'm on the phone!" She barks from her room.

"Good thing it's not attached to a wall," I holler back.

"What!?" She counters in evident confusion.

Feeling aged by the fact she probably has never seen a rotary phone, let alone a beige, wall-mounted classic, I clip out my order. "End your call and get in here, now!"

The overexaggerated stomping of feet fills the hall as Serena stares through our son, looking utterly clueless as to who he is.

"What, Dad, what?" Gracie snaps.

A second after I glance toward Gracie, I'm palming my eyes, an entire body flinch following as I toss words blindly in her direction. "Put some damned clothes on, Jesus . . . never mind. Want to tell me how your brother manipulated you into hanging a damned rope from his ceiling fan?"

"I thought it would hold," she offers. Glancing in a safe direction, I watch as Serena scrutinizes her cuticles, which gives me pause. The sight of her like watching a firework fuse fizz out just as it's supposed to go off.

"Thought it would . . . hold," I repeat. "He's four, Gracie. *Four.*"

"One, two, tharee, four," Peyton sounds before waiting for the applause that isn't coming. Clearly slighted, he continues his count as Gracie sounds up again.

"I can't watch him all the time," she huffs.

"I asked you for ten minutes so I could take out the trash. Ten minutes. Could you maybe not have set him up for irreparable brain damage during that time?"

I brave a glance in her direction as Serena sits idly by as if this conversation is nothing out of the norm. Staring at her for long seconds, I realize it isn't. In fact, this is the exact type of situation we've been dealing with *hourly* for months, hell, more likely *years* now on end.

"I told him it wasn't a good idea," Gracie defends.

"Ah, so, you weren't able to reason with a four-year-old? Noted. Next time we can talk about a more reasonable argument you can have with someone whose most recent accomplishment was not smearing poop on the potty."

"I didn't smear poop, Daddy," Peyton defends.

"I'm aware, Son." I look down to my wife, who's completely checked out. "Serena, want to weigh in here?"

"I'm not here," Serena relays on exhale. "I'm in the Florida Keys, having a sippy cup full of champagne delivered by a cabana boy."

"You can't say that anymore, Mom," Gracie snaps. "It's *hospitality worker*."

"Thanks for clearing that up, Gracie." I cross my arms. "Tell me, while you're so busy correcting us on proper verbiage for those in the service industry, did you maybe once think that helping your brother turn his twelve-foot room into a jungle gym might not be the right move?"

"Mom, I need twenty dollars," Gracie counters as Serena's face draws up and her chest starts to heave. I glare at the side of her head, knowing she's doing a lot more than tipping the cabana boy in her alternate reality. She's been reading a lot of books lately. Come to think of it, that's all she's done in recent months. From the covers, most of them starring half-naked hockey players. Only once have I benefited, and it backfired. I can still feel the sting of grapefruit juice in a place where no man should ever experience grapefruit juice. From then on, our room has been a no-fly zone consisting of *Frasier* reruns.

"Serena," I snap, jarring her out of oiling her fantasy man down.

"I give up," she utters, and in her posture, I see every single word she just spoke as truth as her hair starts to harden from the residual shampoo. "I can't handle any more of this, Thatch."

"Yeah, that's not going to do tonight," I counter. "Babe, we made these together," I point between them, "and must deal with them together. There's no holiday in parenting."

"Sign me up," she says, as if it was an offer, while rising from the bed, tilting her head up at the ceiling fan as if it's nothing out of the norm. Just next to her stands our smiling son, his eyes on it as well, his expression morphing into one of . . . gloating? It's then I flit my focus to our tween-aged daughter, who's composing a text, utterly unaffected.

Serena turns back to me, her eyes vacant, depleted, utterly void of life. It's then that the image of her standing in the doorway of her parent's house resurfaces. The side-by-side mental comparison jarring. Next to the shell that was once my wife stands a gorgeous nineteen-year-old, the setting sun glinting off her hair as she shouts out to her parents from the open door.

Now, seeing both the girl and woman side by side, I realize what's so painful about the two of them. The utter loss of confidence in her posture. As well as the life in her eyes. A sudden surge of protectiveness thrums through me at the idea that I've somehow let this happen. That I've missed something vital.

"Baby, go," I immediately coax, palming her back and ushering her toward the door and away from the two threats. "Finish your bath. I've got this."

With a nod, she wordlessly drifts down the hall, her shoulders slumped as I snatch Gracie's phone and usher her inside Peyton's room before snapping the door shut.

"What in the hell?" I ask between the two of them.

"Dad, I was—" Gracie's protest is cut short by my glare before I share it between both our children. "No, not just tonight. What has gotten into you two? You went from somewhat mannered and reasonable to utterly out of control."

"I not out of control," Peyton shouts. "I was just playing!"

"Peyton O'Neal, yelling at your father after you wreck your room is absolutely not okay." I scrutinize the two of them and see my words have zero effect. None. "This, whatever this is, is over," I spout. "In the last two weeks, I've had to patch drywall, twice," I stare down at Peyton before shifting to Gracie, "and pick you up from school three times for gossiping in class, over the teacher, and being an all-around jerk."

"Jerk," Peyton points at Gracie.

"Pot, kettle," I counter. "You get sad faces every single day, Peyton. Every single day!"

"I'm trying, Daddy!" Peyton hollers, taking Gracie's lead.

"No, you're not. You're not even trying to do your chores. You're both being the worst version of yourselves when you know better. Neither of you are doing anything to make us proud. Your mother . . ." I stare in the direction she left, or rather fled. "Can't you see how sad she is?"

Both talk over me in shit excuse, neither hearing a word I've said.

"Hush!" I boom, and the room instantly goes silent as Peyton's eyes widen. The daddy tone I haven't used in far too long coming into play as I nod toward Gracie. "I'm at my wit's end, Gracie. You don't care about what's going on in this family, and I get it. I was young too—"

"A hundred years ago," Gracie spouts snidely.

"A hundred years ago," Peyton parrots as the blood vessels in my body tighten to the point I think my head might pop off. It's then I feel the snap, the hold I've been gripping tightly onto since I carved the turkey dissolving in my hands. As I free fall, resignation sets in, and my mouth starts to move of its own volition.

"You two don't appreciate anything. Not what we do for you on the daily, not the rules for this house or outside of it. You don't do anything at all that we ask of you. You're spoiled, disrespectful, ungrateful, and just plain defiant. So, guess what? Starting now, Rudolph is crossing some things off your lists," I declare as both their defiant smiles drop. Rudolph, because despite our best attempts, even at four and a half years old, Peyton still considers Santa his nemesis. "Which means, Gracie, you aren't getting that Mac."

"What!?" she shouts.

"An octave higher, and I won't even think to stop Rudolph from delivering the ridiculous amount of makeup."

"Dad!" Gracie immediately disobeys.

"Now the makeup is gone, too," I cross my arms, feeling lighter with every blow I deliver.

She palms her mouth as if it will actually silence her as I turn to Peyton. "You can forget about your Rail Ride tickets. Gone. That fan will cost a few hundred dollars to replace."

"Daddy, no!" Peyton's face twists, and I flinch inside as his eyes threaten to well with tears.

"I love you both more than life, but that woman . . ." I point in the direction Serena fled. "I don't recognize her anymore. And do you know why?" I wait a good minute until their collective whines quiet. "Because she spends ninety percent of her time taking care of you and begging you to take care of yourselves and each other."

It's then a notion strikes me, and without thinking it through, I start speaking it. "As of right now, you're both about to learn the hard way that no one is coming to save you from yourselves."

"What's that mean?" Gracie asks, a hint of fear in her voice, but not enough.

"That means we leave for Grammy and Gramp's in two days. If I get one more call to pick you up from school," I declare to Gracie before I flit my gaze to Peyton, "or I trip over one more toy or have to patch more drywall, you *get nothing*, and I mean *nothing* for Christmas."

"Daddy, Rudolph won't come?" Peyton asks, aghast, everything in his expression as if he should have a hand to his chest.

Gracie immediately opens her mouth, eyes glinting with the damage she intends to do. "God, Peyton. Don't you know? Rudolph isn't—"

"Finish that sentence," I warn, "and I swear to God, you will hate your life more than you're showing me you do, Gracie O'Neal. You know what? I'm taking off Christmas list items six and ten just *for thinking* of doing that to your brother."

"You can't do that!" Gracie screeches.

"I just did. You're going to learn to speak, not scream, even if I have to strip you of everything. Do you hear me? You've been screaming for three damned years, you're done."

"Daddy, no Rail Ride?" Peyton questions again, lips trembling.

I take a knee in front of my son and command his eyes. "Peyton, did you know you shouldn't swing from your ceiling fan?"

"Yes," he answers instantly, and I find myself missing the days when 'mep' was his standard answer. Where his innocence and youth could stifle some of my disappointment in his behavior. But he does know better. Both do, which only reinforces my decision.

"Why did you?" I prompt.

"I dunno."

"Did you know it was wrong and you would get hurt or in trouble?" I continue.

"Yes." Another instant reply that has me sinking in my skin.

"And you did it anyway?" I barely get the words out because it's obvious there's so little remorse in him.

"Yes."

"That's why, Peyton. *That's why*," I sigh.

I turn to my oldest and shake my head. "And you. You want to be a grown-up and not have your parents looking over your shoulder? Well then, you have to grow up. I can't trust you with your brother for *ten* damned minutes. So, guess what? Like your mom, I'm done, too. I'm done giving you what you want other than a lack of a parent."

"Dad, I need twenty dollars for the Friendsmas basket swap."

She didn't hear a word. Not one. "Guess you'll be the only friend who doesn't have one."

"That's not fair!" She shouts.

"Scream one more time, Gracie, and the whole list disappears, the whole damned thing."

"I'm sorry," she retorts, barely above a whisper.

"Ah, so you are capable of talking," I say. Opening the door to free myself, I pull the plug on Peyton's TV with my order. "Bed, *now*."

"I have to brush my teeth," he protests.

"Why? You don't do it anyway. You mess around in there and paint the walls with the paste. Bed. Now."

Peyton marches toward his twin and barricades himself under the covers. "Fine, stupid Daddy."

"You just lost your Mega Legos."

"Daddy!" He shouts, pulling the covers down *to glare* at me. Who would have thought the cutest kid to ever exist would be such a shit. I do. That's who. In fact, that's all I think when I look at him now. No more lingering on the baby who stole my beating heart the first time he looked up at me, but a kid who thinks I'm no one to regard for any reason. Just someone to boss around and take orders. Can a four-year-old have so much power over any human? Am I that much of a chump? Why am I so hurt? Am I thinking reasonably? Do I need therapy? Do I even fucking care right now? Serena's forlorn expression flits through my mind, and I instantly make her my priority. This war I'm declaring for her. Any version of her but the absent woman who fled this room.

"Daddy, you're not being nice," Peyton states.

"Pot kettle," I snap. "You're not acting anything like the son I taught to know better, so why should I be?"

"I don't know what kettle is, but you're not the daddy I want, too."

"That's either, Son. Not the daddy I want, either, and want to go for number two on your list?"

"I dunno what number two is," he snorts.

"The number of days you better learn how not to backtalk your daddy. But," I improvise on a whim. "I think I'll put you both on probation until Christmas."

"What's that?" Peyton asks.

"Your future after prints and handcuffs if you don't find some

act right," I sigh, ushering Gracie out and turning off the light before closing the door.

"What's act right?" Peyton inquires through the closed door as
I stand just outside of it, gripping Gracie's forearm to stop her from
stomping away.

"Your baby brother screams at me instead of talking to me and
orders me around like I'm an employee." No reaction. None. "Wonder
where he learned that behavior?" I drawl out, and her mask of in-
difference doesn't shift as she eyes the phone in my hand. "He could
have really hurt himself," I try to reason with her, even as she bristles
with contempt. "Jesus, kid, do you even care?"

"I was watching him," she offers. But it's so clear she doesn't.

"No, you weren't, and I was taking out the trash for you while
your mom was in the bath because it's *your chore*. I was covering for
you, but you don't appreciate that, so you can get down there and
do *it now*."

"If I do, can I have my phone back?"

"No, and don't ask me when," I add. She opens her mouth, but
something in my expression has her clamping it shut. "I'm done,
Gracie. If I thought your mom and I had done a horrible job con-
veying what human decency is, then I would be a lot less pissed, but
we have. Daily. For years, and you know better. I'm fed up."

"Whatever."

"You just lost your Visa Gift card, want to go for your damned
Bum Bum cream?"

"Daddy, please no," she whines.

"Then I suggest you shut your mouth and get to the trash."

"Dad," her voice wobbles, and I shake my head adamantly.

"It's over. I won't be manipulated by your tears, your pleas, by
anything, Gracie. By absolutely anything you try, so you might want
to think long and hard about any moves you make in the coming
days. And if your brother so much as has a hair out of place or in
any way harms himself before Christmas Eve, I swear on all I am,
you get nothing for Christmas. Not even coal."

"What?" She utters in confusion.

"God, I *am* old. Go," I order.

Minutes later, after securing the house and setting the alarm, I'm stopped at our bedroom door by the sight of my wife. Her hair now soap-hardened, she sits on the edge of the bed in an utter stupor.

"Baby," I coax as she turns to me with watery eyes. "Take a deep breath."

"Why? What happened now?"

Stepping inside our bedroom, I shut the door and lean against it. "It's time."

"Time for what?"

"It's time to admit what no parent wants to admit," I cross my arms.

"What?"

I shoot her a pointed look, and she reads it effortlessly and nods. At least we've still got silent communication.

"We've failed, haven't we? We're failing," she sighs, a thin tear trailing down her cheek. I stalk over and whisk it away with my thumb before firmly shaking my head.

"I don't think you fail at parenting," I tell her honestly. "Not if you try every day. Not if you give it all you have, and Serena, we have. We do, every day we try so hard, so hard that it's *all we do.* No life other than that, and that's no life for us at all. I know parenting means sacrifice, but enough is enough."

I pull her shaking hand from her lap and press a kiss to it before noticing the bite mark on her arm. I lift my eyes in question.

"Peyton bit me when I asked him to pick up his toys earlier. Just walked over and bit me like a dog. And hard, like he wanted to hurt me, Thatch."

"Jesus Christ," I stare at the dents in my wife's arm as the resignation becomes a stronghold. "It's time to admit what no parent is supposed to think or admit out loud."

"No, Thatch," she tries to pull her hand away, "we can't."

"The fuck we can't. And once we do, what I want to do about it is going to make you just as uncomfortable, but first things first. We *have to say it*. We've voiced it before, and for the most part, we were joking, but it's not fucking funny anymore, is it?"

A pregnant pause before she shakes her head.

"Say it," I order as her eyes spill over. The sight of her tears solidifying every threat I made upstairs to the tiny terrorists torturing my wife.

"Our kids are assholes," she releases on a breath.

"Yeah, baby, they are. Total assholes, and we're not fucking going out like this."

CHAPTER TWO

Serena

T HATCH KNEELS IN FRONT OF ME AS EXHAUSTION KEEPS ME weighted to the bed. I can feel the sticky suds drying on my skin but can't summon an ounce of energy to remedy it.

"All I looked forward to today was my bath," I admit. "Because it meant the war was over. It meant fighting to get the kids herded into the SUV and home without six demanded stops was over. Battling and begging them to tidy their rooms and for Gracie to do her homework was finished. Keeping them tame enough for me to make their dinner was the very last feat. The entire day, I daydreamed about the fizz of the bath bomb and the heat of the water. Of twenty or even ten minutes of uninterrupted time alone. I would have settled for five. But as it seems, not in this life." I shake my head.

"I fucking hate this," he whispers.

"Did we spoil them that much?" I ask.

"No, I hate this defeated look," he murmurs, staring up at me. "Decades together, and I've never seen you back down from a fight. Not this easily. I hate it, and I can't believe I'm saying it," he shoots me a boyish grin, "but I want my fighter back."

Thatch grabs my hand, drawing my ring finger up and pressing a kiss to it. A ring he got for me three Christmases ago—when we were at our worst. That year, we couldn't get along to save our lives. It was what I like to call the resentment year. We were bitter and stressed. Since then, we've been far more vocal and honest, and it's greatly improved our relationship. But now, and daily, it's as if we're just trying to survive being parents.

Sex is scarce lately—the intimacy has all but vanished, and as he gazes up at me, I wonder what he sees. My vision blurs with memories of just the two of us over the years. Staring down at my gorgeous husband, I take notes of my biggest draws to him—his thick blond, bordering curly, strawberry-kissed hair and gorgeous green eyes. The fine lines surrounding them only making him more appealing. He's aged beautifully, and he's sexier than ever.

Jesus, when is the last time I really looked at my husband? Truly saw Thatch past the haze of our chaotic lives? I can't remember. Staring at him now, I decide he's still the most beautiful guy I've ever laid eyes on. Before I met him, I never thought a redhead would be my type, but the second we locked eyes, I had one. Even with the laundry list of unattractive shit he does daily, getting lost in his deep jade stare still does things to me. Attraction I thought I'd lost years ago, but remains, coming and going with the marriage tide. But as Thatch stares up at me earnestly, for the first time in far too long, he captures my attention fully.

"This is not what we signed up for," he whispers softly.

"I don't think anyone signs up for this, at least this version of it. *Did* we spoil them, Thatch?"

"Yes," he answers instantly. "But we've been in this shit situation for *years* now. Since the business took off and we started bringing real money in." Oddly enough, it was my ring that started it. Thatch took a side job to cover the cost after cooking our books that month to surprise me. That venture had him taking on more independent jobs for extra cash. When the housing spike only increased—both in and surrounding Nashville—the demand had Thatch breaking completely free of being a middleman. Since, he's become one of the most wanted contractors in Tennessee. While it was a terrifying gamble at first, within months, he started bringing in stupid money. So, naturally, we wanted to give the kids everything their hearts desired—Thatch especially.

"We got caught up in the excitement of having the money," he voices, "and gave them everything they asked for. Now, they expect everything. *Nothing* is special, earned, or deserved because they get everything on a whim. And Jesus, Gracie is one more flippant comment away from a narcissist," he relays gravely. "She's self-centered, ungrateful, disrespectful, rude, demanding, and manipulative. She's on the verge of thirteen, baby. We have to stop this, *now*."

"She is so manipulative," I agree, "and she's not even nice about it."

"As much as I loathe using them as examples, I knew better than to bite my mother. I knew if I pulled anything like that, an ass-whooping was coming. Hell, if I so much as spoke to her crossly."

"Me too, but they've changed the rules," Serena whispers. "No ass-whoopings."

"I get it, but how in the fuck do you reason with kids who give no shits?"

"You can't. I've tried. I try so hard. Gracie—"

"I love her, but I don't like her," he says with a wince. "I don't like my kid, Serena. She's a nightmare to be around, and Peyton is picking up all her nasty behaviors with surprises of his own. He's becoming a dick."

"Thatch," I widen my eyes. "You don't mean that."

"Right now, I absolutely do. We can't pussyfoot around this, babe. They're out of control."

"I know Gracie gets some of her bad habits from me," I admit. "I'm at fault for some of this."

"Not that way, not that way, hell no," he disagrees, and I take some comfort in his adamant refusal. "There's a difference between being sassy, confident, opinionated, and being horrific. You're not the latter. And I'm no saint," he continues, "Peyton called the lady at the deli a cunt the other day, and you hate that word, so who's the real MVP?" He points to himself. "But screw blaming ourselves for *all of it*, I refuse to. We've had dozens of talks with each of them about right and wrong and beyond. Enough that they understand what's morally sound. They used to address me as Sir. Used their manners. Said thank you. Where the hell did that go? They have no respect because we're not backing anything up or putting our feet down. If we don't start right now, nothing changes."

"Then after Christmas," I suggest, and he whips his head back and forth.

"This is the perfect time. At this point, they have no other incentive to do better other than to behave before Christmas."

"Thatch, we can't take their Christmas away."

"Baby, even Peyton knows our threats are empty."

"So, what do we do?" I ask.

"Exactly what you said," he delivers, "we're quitting."

"Yeah, right," I roll my eyes, "be reasonable."

"I am," he states, his tone unwavering. "It's time they realize how good they have it."

"We can't quit being their parents. That's . . . crazy, not to mention illegal."

Standing, he grips my hand and leads me into the bathroom. Turning on the shower, he tests the water and turns back to me.

"So we'll take a holiday. Did you know Peyton put hot sauce on my eggs this morning when I was on a conference call? Knowing how it affects me? I didn't realize it until four bites in." He shakes his head. "I was in the shitter for *two hours* this morning."

I press my lips together, and he gives me a hard stare.

"Laugh it up, but what's he going to do when he's ten, slash my tires? Cut my brake lines?"

"I wouldn't put it past him," I say, and we share a sad smile.

"I miss you," he whispers.

"I miss you, too," I whisper back. "I swear, Thatch. I feel like I haven't seen you in weeks."

"Same," he shoots me a pensive look.

"What?"

He shakes his head.

"Tell me," I insist.

"Sometimes, I miss the old us. Ride or die, no fucks given, make out on a whim—Thatch and Serena," he says, startling me with his candor. He sees the surprise in my eyes and keeps going. "I know we grow up, change, and evolve. It's par for the course, but we used to really have fun."

He grips the back of my neck and presses his forehead to mine. "We're in this thing for life. Who says it has to be all responsibility with absolutely no time for *us*? *They*. But they *who*? Experts? Well, they say those that *can't do*, teach, so maybe those experts don't have fucking kids. This is our life. Our family," he declares with a slightly mad sparkle lighting his green eyes. "Fuck date night once every two months—which we haven't done in *three*—and why?"

He presses in. "Serena, say it . . . fine, I will. It's because we don't want to subject other people to them. Not even Whitney and Eli. That's telling enough."

"Where's the truth serum, Thatch? You're never this vocal about your feelings unless we're fighting or—"

"It's in your face, your eyes, it's everywhere on you, baby," he relays mournfully.

"I look that bad?"

"No . . . that *sad*. So, I say we do things differently. We've spent so much of our time trying to set a good example, living for those kids, I don't even know who *I am* anymore. I know forty fucking Wiggles songs," he pulls back and rolls his eyes, "but I can't remember the last time I rocked out to a damn song I wanted to listen to."

"That's being a parent," I point out. "You're a good dad, Thatch. Please know that."

"And you're an incredible mother, Serena. So let's stop beating ourselves up that the little shits we made don't recognize it. *At all*. Come on, let's talk more in the shower."

"I'm not in the mood," I mumble, hating that I have nothing left for him. "I'm really so tired."

"This isn't about sex," he utters, his tone defensive.

"I didn't mean it *that way*. You're right, I'm just . . . sad. I don't want to have sad sex."

"I get it, I'm . . . fuck," he glances over at me. "I don't even know what I am," he utters, tugging off his O'Neal's Contracting long-sleeve T-shirt. One we designed together when our business started to really take off. Pride fills me as I soak him in while he undoes his buckle. A sudden shift has me wanting to steal more moments like this with him. Even if it's doing the unthinkable by blaspheming our kids.

"You want to quit?" The sparkle in his eyes increases. "Well then, let's fucking quit. Let's force them to realize how frustrated we are. To understand we're living for them and what we sacrifice daily. I propose we do it in a way that's going to *stick*."

"How?"

"By driving our point home in a very unadult but effective way," he declares, disrobing me, his eyes rolling appreciatively down my naked body. And thank God for that—even if the last thing I want to do right now is have sex. It's when he pushes his boxers down, his cock half-mast, that I sweep him appreciatively. Baby steps into his forties, and his build is incredible. Credit to his job, he spends his days lifting, hauling, hammering, and nailing, and it's evident in his physique he cuts no corners. I continue to feast on his efforts as we both step under the twin rain shower heads he installed last year—a perk of being a contractor's wife—and start to suds up.

"But if we're going to do it, we need to really do it," he says as he turns his back, palming the newly installed penny tile. It's then I zero in on one of my top three favorite parts of Thatcher O'Neal—his perfect bubble ass. An ass I often sink my teeth into out of adoration in play and for sexual sport. "We're going to go rogue," he states, pulling me to him under the steaming water and tilting my head up to help rinse the soap from my hair.

"Meaning?"

"Toss every bit of bullshit that's not working—the books, the online advice, and the judgmental rants of backseat driving parents. These are our kids, and it's time for something different. How extreme we go is up to them. Let's truly let *them decide.* Their behavior will make the decision. Not one parent has probably ever used the naughty list as a true incentive. So, let's be the fucking first."

"Won't that make us the assholes?" I argue.

"Yes, but it's a lesson they won't forget. This is serious. Our four-year-old is biting, cursing, and driving his pre-K teacher nuts. Gracie is learning to be an egomaniacal asshole. They have no remorse to the point I'm terrified we're raising twin sociopaths. So, this is not just for us. It's for them. They can't continue like this and survive in this world. Even if we cave last minute, I say we scare them shitless until we do. Perfect we might not be, but we're going to make them, at the least, appreciate the parents they do have. But you have to trust me, and you have to be *all in.*"

"Thatch, you're the nicer, less aggressive parent. I trust you wholly. If you think we should go *there,* then I'm worried. So yeah. I'm with you."

"No backing down," he states, his voice filled with a rare determination. "I mean it, babe. If we undermine one another, in no way will this work."

"I swear," I say, running my hands down his muscled shoulders. "So, when do we start?" He bends eye level, a sexy smirk twisting his thick lips as he leans in, the twinkle in his eyes a bit seductive.

"*Right now.*"

CHAPTER THREE

Thatch

"OH MY *DAWD!*" PEYTON ERUPTS FROM THE LIVING ROOM as I stir awake. A dozen scenarios play out in my head as I scramble to sit, then stand, fear thrumming through me as I do my best to come to. It's the explosion of words from upstairs that has my shoulders easing.

"Oh my God, I'm so late! . . . Mom, why didn't you wake me up?!"

Climbing back into bed, I palm Serena's stomach and pull her to me, her shoulders shaking with silent laughter. I press my lips to what skin is available at the neck of her plaid pajama top, or rather, mine. While we both got a little worked up last night in scheming up a way to get our sanity back, sadly, we both dozed after the adrenaline wore off. Suckling on her skin, I pop my mouth off and whisper a "good morning." When she cranes her neck to look back at me, I'm met with a welcome . . . smile.

"Hello smile, it's been a minute."

"Yeah, but I kind of feel bad already," she says *through* her grin.

"No, you don't," I chuckle as she nestles a little into me.

"I needed that sleep so badly," she admits.

"Me too," I say, glancing at the clock. Eight-thirty. Our first Christmas miracle.

"Daddy!" Peyton summons again, this time more in demand, which I ignore in lieu of memorizing my wife's newly reborn smile.

"When we decide to be parents again, we have got to teach that kid to better use his G's," I drawl, running my fingers along Serena's thigh. Her brow lifts in a clear sign of no-go as I bring them beneath the hem of her shirt to her stomach.

"I think he knows we think it's cute when he mispronounces it and uses it to manipulate us," Serena surmises. "I can't believe I just said that out loud."

"I'm glad you did, damn . . . I think you're right. Ready for this?" She nods. "Ready."

"Good," I rake my lip, and her eyes follow. She told me she thought it was sexy once, and I do it often as a natural tick. Probably too often, which has had it losing its potency over the years. This morning, it seems to be working, which fuels my second decision. One I made before I drifted off last night, which is to woo and seduce my wife. To try to give her the version of me I'm sure she misses at times. The attentive version of me that showered her with affection without words. Words always being hard to come forth with for me. Something engrained early by my parents. Even so, I managed it other ways by putting her needs first. Now being the perfect time, seeing as how I've freed some up by ignoring the child screaming my name in summons. Just as Serena is feigning deaf to Gracie's shrieks. It's when the shouting threatens to go nuclear that Serena sighs and begins to pull away. Mentally blocking the havoc happening a room over, I keep her idle.

"Hold steady, baby," I console before attempting to distract her. "Do you know what I've been thinking about? A lot lately?"

"What?" she hesitantly settles back into place, her eyes on mine.

"The night we met. An ingrained image of nineteen-year-old you filling your parent's doorway. The second you burst through the front door, you started talking so fast, but I couldn't register a single word. Not one. You were wearing a dark blue sweater that showed your midriff, a solid white scarf, and jeans that clung to you. And fuck, baby," I murmur, running my finger down her cheek, "I thought I was going to die right there."

Her lips part because as many times as I could have, fucking should have, I've never told her this. Not in this much detail. Not once in our decades together. It's always been something I've held close to my chest. But maybe the appreciation should start here, between us. An example to set. Though the hoisted boom box-wielding—lovesick fool with a witty, breath-stealing diatribe—guy I'll never be. Voicing sentiments like these is rare, few and *years* between.

Though now, and in gauging the look in her eyes, it seems I've saved this story all these years later, for this exact moment. A time where our kids collectively screech outside our bedroom door like the sky is falling while we batten down the hatches.

"When I saw you, I thought," I pull her flusher to me, where I'm propped on my side. "Whatever she says after tonight, I want to hear it. Even though you were straight bitching, all I could see was how beautiful you were compared to the pictures I'd been walking past for months. Of how they didn't do you justice."

"Jesus for Christ, Daddy!" Peyton bellows, as my inclination to go to him builds, trying not to laugh at his misuse of the phrase because he treats it like a campaign slogan.

"I thought," I continue, adamant about attending to the doe-eyed beauty I'm holding, "I *want her*, and everything that comes with her. Even the attitude, especially the attitude. I. Want. That. Girl." What I don't mention is the sinking feeling just after those initial seconds. That I wasn't worthy of her and never would be.

"Dad?! Mom?? Where is breakfast? I am so late! And I still need twenty dollars!"

Eyes locked, Serena palms my jaw, her eyes misted due to my sentiment. "You never talk to me like this. Not really."

"I know, but I should, and I want to. I—" I falter briefly, "—you know it's never been easy for me to put a voice to how I feel."

"Thatch, you *show* me every day—"

"Twenty-two years together," I interject. "You deserve the words," I run my finger over the bite mark on her arm. "You deserve better from everyone in this damned house."

"Thatch," she draws out, shock clear in her expression as I condemn myself for letting her go so fucking long without words she does deserve. Words that, no matter how close we get, have always been so hard for me to articulate.

"I want to kiss you right now," she says, cupping my neck lovingly, "but my *breath reeks.*"

"Who gives a fuck," I utter a second before I crush her mouth. An instant later, our bedroom door pops open before the handle is smashed into the drywall. I wince at the probability of some damage now behind our door. Hard and now pissed, I snap my attention toward my son, who is standing in nothing but his underwear, his eyes wide as saucers.

"Daddy!" Peyton demands. "Mommy! I have been calling you to come!"

"Well, we were busy," I clap back in irritation. When Serena goes to move, I keep her where she is, dragging my knuckles along her stomach. It feels wrong touching her this way with my son so close. A little forbidden in a sense, but the goosebumps that form in my wake on her skin are telling. Knowing I'm getting too close to a full salute, I reluctantly drag my touch over her smooth skin one last time before I pull them away to draw a line in the sand.

"Son, you will *knock* before you come in this room from here on out. This isn't the first time I've said this."

"I know, Daddy, but—"

"If you know, then do it. Shut the door right now, knock, and ask permission to come in, and if you slam it open again, you will spend today learning how to patch dry wall. *Now,*" I order.

"But I'm already in here," Peyton whines, "and—"

"Peyton, now," I command.

"Oh, my Dawd, Daddy, I'm trying to tell you someone stolded our Christmas tree!"

"What did I just say?" I hold my ground and feel Serena tense next to me in wait.

"But Daddy!" Peyton cries, a meltdown brewing in his voice as I dig in.

"Go out that door, knock, wait until we answer, and tell you it's okay to come in."

Peyton drags the door behind him, yelling through the gap as he closes it. "Someone stolded our tree!"

Ignoring every word, I gaze down at Serena before dipping and stealing another morning breath kiss. A beat later, another knock sounds outside the door, a split second before it pops back open.

"Peyton," I bark after ending our kiss abruptly. My eyes still on my wife as her chest heaves as she stares up at me like I'm a different man. Resignation sets in again at the look of her. For her, I'll find more words. For her, I'll fight our two screaming hellions back into some sort of bearable submission.

"What?" He feigns ignorance.

Shit. Maybe he gets it from me.

"Did we ask you who it was?"

"You know it's me, Daddy. I told you!"

Walking over, I push his tiny chest so that he's clear of the threshold and snap the door closed in his face before locking it. Serena's breath catches audibly behind me as I hold my palm in the air beside me in a gesture of holding steady. As fucking ridiculous as it is, we're declaring war today. So today, I fear, might be the hardest. We've failed at disciplining our children enough that they refuse to obey the smallest of orders, which is the most dangerous part of all of this. It's the added image of Peyton in the Lowe's parking lot last week that keeps me firmly behind the door.

"Daddy, someone stolded our tree!"

Biting my tongue as Serena lets out a nervous laugh, I cross my arms until a knock sounds.

"Daddy?"

Silence.

Knock. Knock.

"Daddy?"

"Yes?"

"Can I come in to tell you someone stolded our tree!"

Serena's muffled laughter sounds before she utters, "we're going to hell, Thatch."

I grin over my shoulder. "Yeah, well, we're taking them with us."

She shakes her head and drops it back to her pillow, clearly amused, as I unlock and open the door.

"Now that you have knocked and I have answered, you can come in and talk to us."

"Daddy," he gazes at my irritated junk, "why is your pee-pee jumping?"

Wincing, I hear Serena's muffled laughter. "Because I have to go to the bathroom, and I haven't had a chance due to you screaming. State your issue, Son."

"I told you five times already, stupid Daddy, gah!"

I push Peyton's chest gently back out of the door and shut it in his face, locking it a second time.

"I knocked!" He belts through the wood.

"Go tell some other stupid Daddy five times."

"Thatch," Serena draws, and I shoot her a warning look over my shoulder.

"How do you want me to tell you?!" Peyton shouts in exasperation before calling for backup. "Mommy!"

"Nope," I cross my arms on the other side. "She's not going to help you."

"Mom," Gracie joins in outside the door. "Where is breakfast? You didn't wake me up, and I have five minutes! And why did you take the tree—"

"Gracie, we're talking to Peyton. Quiet," I snap.

"Gah, I just said that I don't have time!"

"And now, you've lost item fourteen."

"Dad, that's almost all of it!" She shouts.

"Did you just yell?" I counter as the bathroom sink runs behind me and turn to see Serena smiling around her electronic toothbrush. She's so digging this, and sadly, so am I. Turning back toward the door, I bark out my command. "Wait your turn, Gracie."

"Hurry up, Peyton," she snaps.

Knock. Knock.

"Daddy," Peyton whispers. "Someone stolded our Christmas tree, and all the decord is gone." A small thud sounds, and I bite my laugh away because I know he's now got his face plastered to the wood. "Please, Daddy, I need you to come see."

Opening the door, I stare down at my frazzled children, and a sick satisfaction thrums through me. Maybe I am going to hell.

"Better, Peyton. It's a shame it's gone. I guess Rudolph knows you get sad faces from Mrs. May every single day."

Peyton's eyes widen. "He knows?"

"Oh, my God," Gracie says, poking her head into my bedroom.

"No one gave you permission to enter, Gracie," I say, tugging her arm and ushering her into the living room, where not a trace of Christmas décor remains. A pang of guilt hits before I catch my twelve-year-old's vicious side-eye. Jesus.

"I wonder if he took the tree in Triple Falls, too," I respond to her cutting glare.

"Oh my dawd!" Peyton exclaims. "We have to call Grammy right now. Daddy, call her!"

"Nope, she's sleeping," I say as both follow me into the kitchen.

"Mom," Gracie starts the minute Serena clears our bedroom threshold. "Why didn't you wake me up? I'm late."

"You have an alarm," Serena replies instantly. "That's what it's for."

"But you always wake me up."

"Not anymore," Serena says, flashing me a heated look, which temporarily stuns me before I shoot her one right back. Is this turning us both on? Are we evil? Are our apples not falling far from the tree?

"Mommy, look, the tree and your dectorations is all gone!" Peyton exclaims as Serena lines up next to me, a fellow soldier armed up.

"Huh, wonder where they went?" Serena asks, feigning ignorance about the situation.

"Did you know that I knew I was going to fall in love with your mother the minute I saw her?" I tell both kids, giving Serena more honesty. "I knew I had to make her mine."

"Gross," Gracie spouts, "I don't want to hear *that*. Dad, Gemma is going to be here any minute, and I'm not ready. I need twenty bucks to buy a Friendsmas basket. No, I really need forty bucks. I think we're doing more this year."

"Sorry," I shrug. "Fresh out of cash, and you don't deserve it."

"It's okay," she ignores me entirely. "Mom can give it to me."

"You didn't take out the trash," Serena says. "So, no allowance this week."

"No, no," Gracie counters quickly, manipulation in full effect with her next practiced technique. "This isn't for me, this is Friendsmas, remember? Allowance isn't included."

"Guess you should have saved it," I utter.

"All parents give for Friendsmas," Gracie says, cocking her hip.

"Yeah, I really don't care," I counter as Gracie's mouth drops. "Do you, Serena?"

"No," she says matter of fact, "I don't think I do."

"I wouldn't say love at first sight," I continue, "but I knew something real had just happened, was happening. It was right before Christmas, twenty-two years ago *this month*," I declare to both our kids as we hold our gaze.

"Dinner was good, but later that night was better," she replies.

"We didn't even kiss, but it felt like we did, didn't it?"

Serena nods, keeping my gaze a second longer.

"I don't care," Gracie retorts, "I'm talking to you about Friendsmas."

"And I'm talking about your mother and the fact we've been

together a long time. Because that's all that matters *to me* right now," I say, taking Serena's hand and pushing past our kids to escort her to the kitchen. "Cereal, babe?"

"Sounds good," she says as I pour us each a bowl and table the milk. As we begin to eat, I feel both our children's expectant gazes on us.

"Daddddy," Peyton drawls. "You didn't pour *my cereal*."

Gracie starts to frantically brush her hair, and I glance over to see her calculating eyes flitting between the two of us.

"Daddy," Peyton says softly because apparently whispering is behaving now. "I need cereal."

"Oh, my bad. Here, buddy," I say, pushing the box his way.

Peyton laughs nervously, and Serena's eyes implore mine as I issue my silent order.

Hold the line, baby.

"I can't pour the milk! It's too heavy!"

"Oh, well, that's too bad," I say, taking another bite. "You get the Emerson's billed, baby? They're leaving for Hawaii—"

"Done and dusted," Serena says as Peyton struggles to pour his milk.

"You're not going to help me, Mom*may*!" He pushes out, the *may* at the end, only used when he's flustered, or a command he's issued isn't followed to his finite specifications. How did we let it go this fucking far? Feeling Serena's inner turmoil from going against her maternal instinct, I grip her hand over the table. "She's busy, Peyton. Do it yourself."

"I can't."

"Well, you managed to swing from a ceiling fan with some help," I shoot Gracie a pointed look, "so I'm sure you can figure it out."

"Mean Daddy!"

"That's right," I snap, "Mean stupid daddy is here to stay," I taunt as he fists his hands at his sides. "Until you start to behave and use your manners."

Grabbing the box, Peyton struggles to pour his cereal as Gracie continues to stare at us, waiting for us to give. A long minute later, the click of her loafers sounds on the hardwoods as she pours Peyton's milk.

"Okay," Gracie starts to try to reason with us. "I'm sorry about the fan, but he wouldn't shut up. You don't have to do all this. I know you're mad, Daddy. I'm sorry. But Friendsmas is important. If I don't get Gemma a basket, she won't get one."

"That's too bad," I state as Gracie slams the milk on the table.

"Please, I'll be so embarrassed," she pleas as a car horn sounds.

I look over to my daughter, who is seething mad, her face reddening, and shake my head. "Like how embarrassed I was when you humiliated me in checkout at Target last week?"

Serena looks between us in confusion as Gracie gawks. "Dad, I didn't mean to—"

"Yes, you did," I state, taking another mouthful as my wife sounds up in support.

"My parents watched us like hawks all night," she says, tightening her hold on my hand. I hadn't told her that my daughter had humiliated me and utterly degraded me during checkout last week. Just as Serena hadn't told me that Peyton had bitten her. Pathetically, and seemingly before last night, I think we were too embarrassed to admit these things to each other. Which only adds more ammo to our growing pile. A silent understanding passes between us as I nod.

"We were probably so obvious," I utter.

"I loved your name," Serena chimes in. "Is that weird?"

"Only because I still hate it," I shake my head.

"Can I *please* have the money?" Gracie asks, panic clear in her voice.

Serena and I continue our banter. "You looked so beautiful that night."

"It was jeans and a sweater," she drawls.

"One that showed your navel," I wink. "And your belly button ring."

"Er my gawd," Gracie sighs. "Fine, please, I'm sorry, okay? I'll take out the trash and do extra chores when I get home. I'll even watch Peyton."

Another honk sounds.

"It was your name and the red in your hair. I never saw myself with a redhead. But I've never seen hair like yours before or since."

"I have hair like Daddy's," Peyton says, feeling ignored. ". . . Daddy, pour me more milk," he orders when neither one of us acknowledges him.

"I don't take orders, Son."

"What?"

"You have to ask politely," Gracie states. "And Rudolph didn't come last night, Peyton. *Daddy* took the tree down," she spills in contempt.

"Bye bye Bum Bum cream," I spit dryly as Peyton gapes at me.

"Great, so I get nothing for Christmas," Gracie scoffs.

"That's up to you. And for a smart girl, you sure are acting pretty stupid."

"You can't say that to me," she gasps.

"I just did, daughter dearest."

"All right, fine, Daddy, fine. I get it. I know you got mad last night when Mom got so upset, and I'm sorry. Peyton is, too, but you didn't have to take down our tree and take our presents back. We can be sorry, can't we, Peyton?"

"Yeah, Daddy, we can be sorry," Peyton echoes promptly, nodding. "*Really* sorry."

"Uh huh," I say, taking another bite. "I've got to run, babe. I've got to get that check from the Rasors to cover payroll."

Serena nods as I stand. "Love you."

"Love you," she answers as I turn to ready myself and do a one-eighty, stalking over to my wife and taking her mouth in a borderline inappropriate kiss. When I pull away, she stares up at me, slightly stunned.

"We made out for weeks," I murmur, "kissed and talked for hours and *hours.*"

"I wouldn't exactly call it talking," Serena shakes her head as if dazed.

Have I really been so silent all these years?

"More like bickering," I say.

"Because you were infuriating," her weighted gaze follows me when I scoop up my bowl to rinse it.

"I didn't want you to know—"

"*Anything*," my wife counters.

Gracie stares between us as we ping-pong back and forth, seeming just as bewildered by our affection and banter before she speaks up. "Okay, the joke is over. I need the money," she panics. "We're going shopping after school."

"Tough shit," I state.

"Tough shit," Peyton parrots, knowing better.

"No Playdoh set," I tell Peyton.

"Jesus for Christ, Daddy!" Peyton shouts in scold.

"Gracie, go to school," Serena jumps in, standing as Peyton doles her his order.

"No, Mommy, you eat *with me*."

"No, I think I'll get ready," Serena delivers before walking out of the kitchen. Peyton gawks at her.

"But I don't want to eat *all alone!*"

"You don't need me to eat with you. You don't like it when I talk to you. You bite me."

"I was just playing," he calls after her.

"I don't like playing with biters," Serena tosses over her shoulder before shutting our bedroom door.

"I sorry, Mommy! I won't today," Peyton yells to the closed door as Gracie stares after her. It's then I feel genuine unease start to roll off my daughter—the gravity of what's happening as she scrutinizes me. It's then that I finally give her my attention while delivering the raw truth.

"You think I haven't been onto you? You think I'm clueless? I'm not, Gracie. Never have been. I just hoped the manipulative side of you was a phase. A warring hormones type of moment in time. Something that would eventually fall away as you aged and grew out of it, but you know what? You're just not nice. At all. I'm surprised you *have* friends."

Gracie gasps as the horn sounds again.

"So you're really not going to give me the money?"

"Case in point," I shake my head. "You don't care about anything that matters."

"I care about my friends getting a basket."

"So you can get yours," I state. "Go to school, Gracie, because if you miss your ride, I'm locking you out of this house."

"Mommy!" Peyton barks in order.

"Enough," I bark back. "You bit your mom. You can eat alone."

"You're going to be mean to a baby?" Gracie jabs, and it lands, but I manage to counter.

"Nice try. You going to let a baby swing from a rope?"

Thirty seconds later, Gracie slams the front door so hard the walls rattle. It's then I deduct present nineteen and text her as much. Then I remember her phone is in the safe. Guess she'll find out on Christmas.

"Why is she so mad?" Peyton asks.

"Because she knows her parents aren't going to put up with her being bad anymore." I narrow my eyes on him.

"What?" he asks, chewing slowly.

"I think you'll get the idea really soon, my boy."

I walk out, leaving Peyton at the table, stopping behind the wall just out of sight as he finishes his breakfast alone. Heart aching as he mumbles to himself, I resign myself to the fact that this is for the better—for the long run. To set a new standard. Truth is, we have failed as disciplinarians. When things got significantly better for us financially, we went overboard. Maybe we got too busy maintaining the new business that we started to give in to them. But there's no excuse for their behavior. None justifiable enough to have me rethinking this. Especially with Gracie's reaction.

Day one, Thatch. Day one.

It's not the image of Serena the first time I saw her that sticks out in my mind anymore as I eventually join Peyton and wash out my bowl. It's the image of her this morning. The feel of her against my fingertips. The smile that greeted me. For the first time in years, I feel present. I feel like I'm actually living my life. And though this sting is uncomfortable from the stunt I just pulled, taking action feels right.

I want that smile back. The one that says her whole life is in front of her. And more importantly, a smile that says my wife has the life she wants.

CHAPTER FOUR

Thatch

"WHO ARE YOU?" SERENA RATTLES OFF BETWEEN *perfectly plump, glossy lips.*

"Thatch, Serena," Ruby introduces while stalking toward her daughter. "Is that any way to treat a guest of this house?" She scolds before pulling Serena in for a hug. "We told you about the young man who answered the want ad your father placed to help build the deck."

"No, you didn't," Serena counters, her eyes on mine.

"That's because you only hear what you want to," Ruby mutters as Serena gives her a half-assed return hug, her eyes still zeroed in on me.

"Young man?" She mimics, clearly guestimating my age. This I consider a win because she's doing it to satisfy her own curiosity.

Play it cool, O'Neal.

Shoving my hands into my jeans, I nod toward the open door where snow is still filtering in. "Aren't you cold?"

Ruby grins, taking the scarf dangling in Serena's idle hand before Serena snaps to, turning abruptly and closing the door behind her. As Ruby hangs her scarf on a nearby coat rack, Serena zeroes in on me. Tossing her shoulders back, she stalks toward me, openly sizing me up

*before stopping just next to me fireside. Palming the air to warm her
hands, she fixes her gaze on the flames as she speaks.* "So, if the deck is
done, why are you here now?"

"Jesus, kid, you're an asshole," *Ruby says through a sigh.* I can't help
my grin at her point-blank delivery. It's one of the things I love most about
Ruby, and it seems her eldest daughter is no less subtle. "I'm sure your
father and I have taught you that the art of conversation doesn't start
or need to include an insult." *Ruby turns to me.* "Sorry, Thatch. Try to
hold your own while I finish dinner. I'll send Allen in to bail you out if
I can find him." *Ruby gifts me a departing wink before she disappears.*

"Just asking a question," *Serena shrugs before turning toward the
fire I still have my back to. Up close, she is fire, and I take notes as the
flames lick along her profile. The first is that her lips are overly glossed.*

"You get a lot of compliments on your lips?" *I ask.*

Said lips simper with a smile. "Maybe, why?"

"It's obvious," *I mutter, and she frowns before she takes offense,
eyes narrowing.*

"Ah, so, my mom ducks out, and your true colors shine through. Not
the nice boy she said you were. Figures."

"Thought you said she didn't tell you about me? And it's just a
question because from where I'm standing, you could signal and land a
plane with the amount of high gloss you have going on there." *I imitate
her flippant shrug.* "Was wondering where Whitney picked up the habit."

"Uh huh, well, I guess mystery solved. Nice to meet you, Thatch,"
she shoots me a withering stare, and I widen my eyes in amusement.

"There are those well-embedded manners. A real pleasure, Serena,"
I smirk as she glares back at me, full of piss and vinegar as she stalks off.

"Mom," *she glances back at me just as I flick my gaze up from her
ass,* "where's Brenden and Whitney?"

Wedged into a tiny desk in Mrs. May's classroom, I shoot my son
a withering look as he shrinks beneath it. A freshly delivered paper
full of sad faces, his report for today, further stoking my agenda.

"So again," she relays, unable to fully disguise her scolding. "I ask that you give him a stern talking to about the language, the biting, and interrupting naps."

Much to my dismay, it's not Gracie's school I got the call from today. No, this summons for today's parenting lesson came thanks to my son.

"And what do you suggest I say?" I ask, knowing the clock is ticking out on picking up that check. It's size enough to safely cover my employees' Christmas bonuses as well as cushion our commercial account for any unexpected expenses over the holidays. A check I was prevented from collecting due to an urgent call regarding my son from Pre-K because Serena is at her OBGYN appointment."

"Pardon?"

I shift my focus from the toy-littered classroom to the fresh-faced twenty-something subtly calling me out. "I asked what you would say, Mrs. May."

"Ms. It's *Ms.* May."

"Ah, I see. Ms. May, my question remains the same."

"Well, you tell him to use his words, of course, but not profanity. Never to bite. And to take his naps when the teacher says so without disturbing the other children."

"I see."

"You don't agree? She asks, furrowing her brows.

"I pay twenty-six thousand dollars a year for my child to learn his A, B, C's and 1, 2, 3's at this institution. For his teacher to help shape his mind and assist in molding him and correcting his behavior."

"You don't pay me," she counters, her tone testy.

"True, and vice versa. I don't believe you sign my checks, either."

Her expression hardens. "What is your point, Mr. O'Neal?"

"The accusation in your voice. It's just as unappreciated as my insinuation you aren't doing your job, either." I glance up at her daffodil-handed clock as precious seconds tick by. "This is the fourth time you've called me here in two months. Do you not think during the ride home each time that I haven't spoken those exact words to my son? Words you've given me?"

"Well, no," she frowns, "I'm sure you have."

"Do you know what a lick is, Ms. May?"

"A lick, like a lollipop?"

"Just the opposite, a lick, is what you got for bad behavior when I was in school, which is slang for spanking. Some teachers got creative. In fact, I had a teacher by the name of Mr. Duncan who drilled holes into his two-foot wooden paddle for added suction and used duct tape around the handle to make sure he had a good grip," I widen my eyes as hers bulge. "So when we misbehaved in junior high and high school, we were called outside and got what's known as 'licks.' Fun part is, this would take place during class, and we had to count them aloud while everyone outside the door listened."

"Wow, that's—"

"Seems pretty brutal, right? Can't say I was a fan. Can't spank a kid now because it's now being viewed by some as corporal punishment," I tick off, "which I'm not even arguing about. Last I heard, time out has been deemed ineffective. So now, we're encouraged to reason, promote word usage, and discuss feelings. Fine. I'll take your advice *and theirs* on this. You're the experts. I'm sure you have a degree in child development, right?"

She nods.

"I've read a half dozen parenting books over the years, but a scholar I'm not. So, we can continue this tango, and you can tell me exactly what to say and how to say it, but here's the thing—*I have Ms. May.* I've had this very talk with my kid repeatedly. Yet, here we are, chatting about his behavior *again.* So, unless you have any new material that *works,* I'll be passing on any more of these conversations. Because Peyton is the one who needs discipline, *not me.* So please start *disciplining him* as you see fit *in your time with him* and not *me.*"

"Mr. O'Neal—" she starts.

"I don't know what to do," I admit, moving to get out of the desk, which is making my knees ache because of its height, only to find myself lodged—*fucking perfect*.

"See, I wake up on time," I begin to struggle to dislodge myself from the tiny human's chair, twisting my hips furiously, "brush my teeth, go to work," I grit out with the struggle as she gapes at me. "I do my chores and my absolute best to correct the behavior of my children on *my time*." Neck heating, I frantically start to twist my body as my aggravation builds that this is the only fucking seat she offered. "I'm polite enough to strangers, say please and thank you, and team play as best I can." I grip the desktop and begin to twist it along with my hips to no avail, my grunts filling the room as I continue my rant. "I even pay . . . my t-taxes on time. . ." I sputter breathlessly while thumping the metal legs furiously against the hardwood. "So." *Thump.* "If." *Thump. Thump. Thump.* "You want to kick my kid out . . . *Thump. Thump. Thump. Thump.* "For being an *asshole*, you have that luxury."

"Daddy!" Peyton admonishes. "You can't say a bad word to Ms. May!"

"See there!" I shout like a crazed lunatic, standing abruptly, the desk coming with me. "Right, there! He *does* know *better!*"

Her jaw hangs as I jerk at the desktop one last time, and the metal finally frees me just enough to rip it from my body before I slam it back on the floor with a defiant *thwack*. "He. Knows. Better," I finish with a flustered flourish. Turning, I see Peyton standing stock still, his own eyes bulging. "Get your coat, Son. *This instant*. We're leaving right now."

Peyton immediately shoots over to the wall of colorful built-ins adorned with hooks before grabbing his jacket.

"Mr. O'Neal," Ms. May coaxes softly as if trying to reason with another four-year-old. "Please know I wasn't trying to insinuate you aren't a good parent."

"It's fine, I," I hang my head. "Sad thing is, my child is showcasing that truth on his own," I run my hand through my hair as I level with her once more. "Look, I have an insanely healthy respect for the fact that you went to school to learn how to educate my child and others. Also, for the fact that in these dangerous times, you put yourself at risk daily to do so, and I'm sorry I got cross with you, but here's the thing . . . my kid isn't going to shape up with a stern talking to. Not at this point in time, but I'm working on it. That's the best I can offer you today. That, and I'm sorry for his behavior *and mine.* Peyton, let's go."

At the door, I turn back to Peyton's teacher, who stares after us, looking a little bit lost and slightly traumatized.

"His mother and I really are doing the best we can," I offer once more, and she nods, a touch of pity in her return stare. "Merry Christmas, Ms. May," I grumble, feeling every bit the jackass I look like.

"Merry Christmas, Mr. O'Neal," she offers just as feebly before I palm Peyton's back to guide him out.

"Mewery Christmas," Peyton echoes in parting before I guide him down the hall and out of the school.

Silent minutes in the truck follow until Peyton finally starts to brave a conversation. That's the thing about kids. They can sense a parent's mood and the seriousness of all situations. Only blind to it when they're truly at play. But they know. The truth of that irks me as he speaks up.

"Am I in *big trouble,* Daddy?"

I bite my tongue, absolutely refusing to entertain this shit again because I meant every word I said. We've had these useless talks. One too many times.

"Daddy, I asked you a question!" Peyton shouts as I ease to a stop and lock eyes with my son. As the seconds tick by, he laughs nervously, and I keep my expression grim. Normally, this is where I would chime in and put him at ease because I hated that feeling when I was a kid. The tense seconds before my father's explosions always got my nerves so frazzled I was a jittering fucking mess. Something I wanted to spare my own children from, but mine seem to be utterly lacking any healthy amount of fear as of late. The image that's been haunting me nonstop for days slams into me as I stare at him. The cold sweat the memory induces covering me as I rattle from within. It's then I know it's not just their behavior that has me taking these measures. It's more. Much more, and it's *my fear* that's part of the catalyst.

"Daddy, why are you not talking to me?" Peyton asks, his eyes dimming slightly as he tries to figure me out. Ignoring the sting in my chest, I keep at our stare off until the light turns green.

"Wiggles," he demands, dismissing me and what just transpired. Programmed, I immediately thumb the station button on the steering wheel to obey and stop myself. I don't take orders anymore.

Grinning, I flip through the stations until I hit classic rock, specifically a song I'm all too familiar with. In hearing the opening, I'm granted a nostalgia kick and take it as a sign I'm on the right path. Cranking it up to deafening, I ignore my son's roaring protest the whole ride to pick up the check. Exhausted from the day already, the second we hit the garage, my cell rings, and I frown when I read the caller ID.

"Hello?"

"Daddy, you didn't play Wiggles!" Peyton shouts as I exit the truck and slam the door on his berating.

"Is this Thatcher O'Neal?"

"Yes, how can I help you?" I ask, stepping back and opening Peyton's door to see he's already unbuckled himself, arms raised for me to get him down as he continues to air his grievances.

"Sir, this is security at Tree Hill Mall," the man says as my stomach drops. I pause, hoisting Peyton, whose shoes hang in the air between the garage floor and the cab of my F150.

"Daddy, let me down!" Peyton orders.

I cut my eyes toward my son, and he quiets enough to let me catch the ass end of what's being relayed over the line. "—caught your daughter shoplifting at Victoria's Secret and have detained her here at the mall."

"She . . . was stealing?"

"Yes, Sir."

Feeling kicked, I stand utterly stunned while mixed emotions start to war for dominance as crimson threatens my vision.

"I'll be there in twenty minutes," I manage to reply, utterly gutted as I re-load Peyton into his seat, shutting the door on his newly barked order as blood starts to whoosh in my ears. Idle in the garage, I lean back against my truck for long seconds while absorbing the latest blow. I've had moments as a parent that have leveled me over the years. Downright debilitating moments. One of which I had last week—the worst one to date. This one coming a close second. After calming myself enough to get behind the wheel, I bend, pressing my forehead to it as I give myself a few more needed seconds. I don't want to drive this upset with Peyton behind me.

"Daddy . . . why did you buckle me? Are you crying?"

"Peyton," I rasp out hoarsely. "I need you to be quiet right now."

Ignoring his backtalk, I restart my truck, and just as we start to pull out, Serena pulls into the driveway. Pressing the brakes, dread fills me at what I'm about to have to relay to her. While at the same time thankful for the sight of her. For the reminder that we're in this together as we both roll down our windows.

"Hey," she greets before reading my expression. "What's wrong?"

"Mommy! Mommy, come get me!" Peyton shouts.

"I saw I missed a call," she sighs. "Ms. May?"

I nod, and she winces as Peyton roars behind me.

"Want me to get him?" Serena asks.

"Yes, but we don't take orders anymore, and it might do him some good to see his sister in handcuffs."

Serena's eyes bulge. "What?"

"Yeah, our tween has decided to make her shoplifting debut at Victoria's Secret," I manage to push out.

This is karma, Thatch. Pure and simple. This is also the chaos that comes with the girl.

"No, Thatch," Serena's eyes search me frantically with concern. "Oh, my God."

You wanted the girl. You got the girl. You got the life you asked for. You made a promise.

"Baby, look at me," I coax as she exits her SUV and Peyton screams for her in a way that neither of us can hear one another. I grip my wheel, knuckles whitening as I resist the urge to lash out, knowing the easier thing to do would be to pass him off to her. But I'm done with easy, if that even fucking exists. God knows that everything, when it comes to them lately, seems so damned hard-won.

"Quiet, Son," she snaps at him. "Your daddy and I are talking."

"But Mommy—"

"Peyton," she uses in her sharpest tone, "one more word, and you're in big trouble." Turning back, her eyes soften on me. "What did Ms. May say?"

"The usual, but I told her we're working on it. Left the game plan out. How did it go at the OB?"

She bites her lip, and I tense at her hesitation before she speaks. "I-it's okay, I got a boob smash."

"Ouch, want me to kiss and make them better?"

She ignores my blatant attempt to keep things light. "Thatch, are you okay?"

"No," I admit honestly. "Not. At. All."

"What are we going to—"

"What we're doing," I cut her short. "I've got to go get her."

"Okay," her eyes shine with concern for me.

"I'll deal, just . . . give me a shot of those lips," I demand. "Give me a reason to come back." She grins at the arrival of the same line I used when we were kids. Stepping up on my running board, she leans in through the window and kisses me chastely.

"Nope," I pop the P, and she shakes her head.

"Thatch, you're acting a little crazy."

"I'm going a little fucking crazy," I admit, keeping my voice low enough so Peyton can't hear me curse. Though I curse a lot, I try to muffle myself as often as possible—even though they know better.

"Want to come with me to no fucks given land? I hear the weather is nice there."

"Already packed my bags," she promises. "Before we go, did you deposit the check?"

I tense, eyeing the clock. Due to my aggravation with Peyton and, just after, reminiscing because of the song, I'd steered home to Serena, failing to run the one fucking errand that mattered today.

"Jesus," I glance at my dash clock, "twelve minutes."

"Give it to me, babe. I can make it to the bank in five."

When I hand it over, she steps down.

"Nope, get back here," I insist.

"What?" she searches the cab for something obvious, "is there another?"

"It's a matter of incentive," I drawl.

"Thatch, we don't have time."

"I think that is what got us into this mess," I murmur. "We're going to make that time, steal it if we have to, and babe, I need it," I declare a breath before she steps back up on my running board and lays one on me. I deepen it briefly before releasing her. As she steps down, I'm rewarded with the same dazed expression I got this morning.

"Good enough?" She taunts, catching on.

"You can do better," I shrug. "Don't race there, okay? We've probably got enough in our account to cover it."

"Just go on, *Handy Man*, I've got this."

"See you in a bit, *Brat*," I wink as the use of our ancient nicknames melts some of the ice threatening to form around my heart.

In a matter of seconds, she shoots away in her SUV as I follow her out of our neighborhood and click my signal in the opposite direction . . . to go bail out my twelve-year-old daughter.

CHAPTER FIVE

Serena

J ACK AND DIANE BLARES THROUGH DADDY'S ANCIENT RADIO
speaker from the open window of the hut-sized shed as I approach.
Thatch had been quiet at dinner, only looking at me once the whole
time we ate. He'd been polite to my parents and spoken to them with
ease. It was easy to recognize he felt comfortable around them. But he
still had a slightly on-edge air about him, too. As if he was ready to leave
on a moment's notice or be asked to.

Opening the squeaky door, I catch sight of Thatch pulling the level
from Daddy's toolbox as if it's his own. As he places it atop a piece of
wood he's measuring, I take in his long-sleeved thermal, worn jeans and
boots, which are almost exactly like mine. When I first saw him, I was
blindsided. With his insane build, the view I currently have of his back
side is no less mouthwatering. His muscular frame straining the material of his shirt and tapering down to his trim waist. His ass fills out his
jeans to the point his shirt is hitched up a bit because of it. His thighs
are just as impressive, bulging the denim, as are his calves. From what
I can see, he's all muscle. His strawberry blond hair is a beautiful blend.
It's on the redder side, but not obnoxiously so, and wavy. To the point it

looks as if it would be curly but seems to be purposely cut exactly where it might start to.

"Looking for something?" he sounds up, his voice deep, gravelly before his jade-green eyes bolt to mine over his shoulder. Instantly stunned by the feeling of his full attention, he rolls his eyes down me briefly before shifting his focus back to the workbench.

"Thought my dad would be out here."

"He's picking up Whitney and Brenden from the movies. He announced it right after dinner," he glances back again, brow quirked, "remember?"

"Oh . . . yeah," I say, my neck heating a little as I swallow.

"So?" He stands to his height as I again try to guess his age. He's got to be in his twenties. I just can't place where. He seems too mature to be in his early twenties, but looks it.

"You were quiet at dinner," I tell him, stepping inside and leaning against my stacked palms on the wall of the shed behind me.

"Yeah, well, you talked enough for both of us," he quips, his insult delivered with a grin as he keeps his eyes on the two-by-four he's measuring. "Off carbs, still debating on accounting or a business degree. Are over winter already. Not a fan of the dorm roommate because she's a slob. And you will 'just die if Wretched Gretchen comes to visit this Christmas . . . oh, and you're positive Whitney stole your favorite jeans. Did I miss anything?"

"Whatever," I roll my eyes, moving to step back out of the shed.

"You could just come out and ask me," he says, turning his back against Dad's workbench. The full view of him is too much to absorb in one pass. My eyes bounce from his muscled pecs to his bulging biceps, which I decide comes second to the rugged cut of his jaw and stunning jade eyes. His lips are a little mismatched in size. His top lip slightly smaller than his overly full bottom lip. One he rakes now as I follow the movement.

"Ask you what?"

"My age, Serena. You've been hinting around to it all night."

"Have not," I lie. During dinner, neither of my asshole parents were helpful at all on that front. Both knowing what I was subtly getting at, and neither giving me a clue. But something about tonight had me thinking that they invited Thatch over specifically to meet me. Especially with Whitney and Brenden at the movies. Too coincidental. Surprisingly, I'm not grossed out by it, not at all with the man standing in front of me. By the time I come out of my thoughts, he's already turned back to the workbench, measuring again.

How long did I space out?

Obvious much, Serena?

Growing uncomfortable with his effect on me, I simmer where I stand while trying to gain my bearings. I've gone back and forth with a decent share of hot guys, but there's something about this guy that's both appealing and irking me.

"Instead of standing there, you could make yourself useful."

Shaking my head, I step back in. "You so sound like my dad."

"We've been spending a lot of time together since we finished the deck," he offers.

"Don't have any friends your own age?" I ask, closing the space.

My reply is a glimpse of perfect white teeth. "And what age would that be?"

I shrug. "No longer curious."

"Uh huh. The handful I considered my friends back when are earning a degree. So, I guess you could say they left me behind."

He's college-age. Good enough. "And you didn't go, why?"

"That's personal, isn't it? Hold this," he states, screwing some metal into the wood as he runs a pencil down it before jotting some measurements.

"So, you're into construction?" I ask.

"You ask a lot of questions."

"Just making conversation," I state as he steps up to where I am, so close I can feel his body heat and catch his scent. Which is light but heavenly. Thankful when he bends, missing my shiver, I watch his blond lashes flit along his cheekbones as he examines the wood.

"What are you making?"

"*Just tinkering around,*" he states.

"*Now you really sound like my dad.*"

"*I can think of worse men to bear a resemblance to.*"

"*Such as?*"

He stands to his full height, which I guess is about six . . . two? Tall enough to have me looking up at him as he zeroes in on me. The connection of eyes doing what it did to me when I caught sight of him in our living room the first time. My nerves fire as heat settles low in my belly.

"*Worse men,*" *I watch his lips as he speaks.*

"*Okay, so,*" *I mumble,* "*you're not much of a conversationalist.*"

"*You getting that?*" *He inches a little closer before making his request.* "*Excuse me.*"

My neck heats as he brushes just past me to continue his . . . tinkering.

"*So, classic rock, huh?*" *I wrinkle my nose.*

His chuckle sends another shiver through me and it takes him agonizing seconds to answer.

"*Allen's radio, so Allen's station. Love this song, though.*" *He smirks.* "*What do you have loaded on your MP3 player—Pink?*"

"*Yes. Amongst other things,*" *I lean down and gaze along the opposite side of the wood.* "*If you're looking for a pristine piece, hate to break it to you, but this one is warped.*"

He frowns. "*The hell it is.*"

"*No, look,*" *I say as he walks over, practically encasing me as I run my finger along the slight bend.* "*See?*"

"*Fuck . . . look at that,*" *he whispers, and I turn to see him staring directly at me. My scalp prickles as I drink him in up close. So close, we're practically sharing breath.*

"*Looks like I have to start over,*" *he says, dropping his eyes as mine drop to his lips.*

"*Then you know what you're making,*" *I conclude. He glances back at me before we both slowly rise to stand as I start to rattle due to the insane energy bouncing between us. Damn, this guy is hot. No . . . hot is not a good enough description for what he is. Thatch is . . . beautiful.*

The connection continues to thrum as he bends slightly, eyes lit as his lips twitch with amusement. Which is all I seem to be a source of for him.

"Ask me," he states.

"How old are you?"

"Old enough," he quips.

"Lame," I utter as he rakes his lower lip.

"To you, I probably am," he states, brushing past me. "And I've overstayed my welcome. Take care, Serena."

"It's only nine-thirty," I call after him, glancing at the ancient hammer clock hanging over the workbench. A present Mom got Daddy years ago.

"Yeah, it's past your bedtime, isn't it?" he states.

"You do know I'm in my first year of college, right?"

"Fresh in," he counters.

"I'm nineteen, thank you very much. Come on, hang out a little longer. I have nothing better to do."

"In that case, I'll pass," he scoffs.

"I didn't mean it like that."

"Well, you said it like that, so I guess you'll have to entertain yourself."

"No problems there," I quip, producing the dime bag I secured earlier from my pocket. "So, if you want to join, be my guest."

Both his brows rise as I wiggle the bag. "That'll be a hell no."

"Why? Afraid my parents won't like you?"

"Yep, and I like them a lot more than you."

"I'm hurt," I palm my chest, "really, that's going to keep me up tonight . . . say, at around one thirty. I'll be in here pondering why I'm so unlikable."

"Jesus, you really are a fucking brat."

"There must be something you like because my eyes are up here," I state. "You cracked on my lips, but you keep staring at them."

"It's the glare," he spouts, "like a space station. Tell me, did you gloss after dinner?"

"As all girls should, and it's your loss." I tuck the bag away. "And if you're worried about Allen and Ruby judging you, they used to smoke, and often. In fact, I busted Mom with a joint a few years ago."

He shakes his head, flashing me the smile that hits me just so. "You."

I grin. "Me what?"

He walks out of the shed as I call after him.

"So, you coming, or what, Handy Man?"

"I guess we'll see, Brat."

Gracie walks in from the garage, eyes downcast, and Peyton follows, neither greeting me as I finish whipping the mashed potatoes. I trail both their paths as Gracie heads for the stairs, and Peyton stalks into the living room before kicking his soccer ball. A ball that smacks into our newly installed blinds. Thatch walks in, his expression just as grim as he cuts his eyes between our kids before flicking them to me. "Hey, baby."

"Hey, Handy Man."

His jade gaze softens substantially as he snatches a carrot from the cutting board. "Smells good in here."

"Roast," I tell him.

He lifts his palms with a shit-eating grin. "I know better than to ask."

I can't help my smile. Thanks to Eli, who told him years ago never to ask me what's for dinner again, it's been a running joke between us.

"Well, it's the same dinner we had on the night we met," I tell him. "Brown sugar carrots and all."

He grins. "You remember what we ate?"

"I remember the whole day, *every year*. I just thought pressuring you to acknowledge the day we met anniversary, and a wedding day anniversary is a bit much. How did it go?"

"She tried to steal perfume and got busted by one of those stickers on the bottom. *Amateur*."

His expression dims considerably as I palm his jaw. "It's not your fault, baby," I console. "It's not, believe me." The pain in his eyes is so evident, along with the knowledge that this latest blow has hit him hard.

"Probably why I haven't spoken a word to her," he glances over to where Gracie's paused at the stairs, watching our interaction. When neither of us says a word, she slowly starts the trek up, and not long after, we hear her door close.

"Did she try to talk to you?" I ask, studying my husband as Peyton continually kicks the ball—destructively—at our expensive shutters before turning to glance in our direction.

"Don't react," Thatch says.

"I'm not. I see it," I say, resuming my chopping.

"And yeah, she tried for about five seconds. I heard her bullshit excuse until I turned up the radio."

"You didn't," I shake my head, biting my smile.

"Oh yeah, I did. Because what productive conversation could we have? So, me and John Mellencamp chilled on the way home. For the *second* time today."

"You remember the details too?"

He nods. "Of course."

"I can't believe you remember so much," I rasp out, still shocked by his recollection this morning of what I wore. Thatch has delivered enough real sentiment over the years to hold me, but never quite like he has in the last twenty-four hours. Twenty-two years together, and other than during sex, he's never this vocal or intimate. PDA, always, but even that has waned over our decades as a couple. I pray it lasts as he gazes back at me and speaks as if he's reading my thoughts.

"It's not at all hard to remember the night that changed my life," he relays thoughtfully, "so, yeah, I played our song again on the ride home. *Fuck* the Wiggles," he chuckles, even as his jade eyes sting with disappointment. Itching to comfort him, I'm taken away when Peyton again kicks the ball. This time, his aim has a lamp toppling over. A very expensive lamp. I cringe inside, having spent weeks looking for the right one for the hall.

Having spent even more endless hours setting up the dream house we moved into not even a year ago. One we dreamed of, saved for, and imagined our whole adult lives. A home that is being treated like it's nothing. Like all our hard work was for nothing as our kids continually trash it. Tearing up the walls and spilling on the floors and furniture. And now, ripping out ceiling fans and breaking décor we could never have afforded a few short years ago. My heart breaks that they care so little about the home we broke our back to provide them. Peyton's behavior is a little more understandable, but the fact Gracie doesn't so much as try to stop him from the destruction is painful. I cringe as our shutters are battered a third time, biting my tongue as Thatch stiffens next to me.

Wincing as the ball pings again, I look away to keep myself from lashing out. "Jesus, Thatch, aren't we here, present as much as we can be every day? I work *from home.*"

He slides his arm around my waist and nuzzles me as he speaks. "If you need to hear it again," he places a hot kiss on my neck, "I'll say it, Mrs. O'Neal. You're an amazing, highly attentive mother. That's why the presents they know nothing about are so specific and special because you know them so well. Things I would never have thought of giving them. You gift as well as your mother in that sense. So yes, we're present for them, Serena. You more than me, but as much as we can be."

"Don't be offended, but I can't wait to get to Triple Falls," I admit. "I need it."

"Me too, babe," he says on an exhausted exhale. "We could both use a little gravity," he adds, a firm believer in our family motto. Grammy P's words keeping us all tethered.

"Just remember when times get hard, when your problems are blinding you, that you're on a floating planet in the middle of a vast galaxy filled with the unexplainable, and the only thing holding you to it is an invisible force you can't see."

The momentary piece I find in her words shatters with the next thwack of Peyton's soccer ball before as I blow out a breath of frustration. "Maybe we shouldn't go with the way they're acting."

"Leave that to me," he assures. "I'll make sure everyone is clear on what's going on."

"You know they won't listen."

"Your mom has been subtly warning us for years. It's Eli and Whitney we'll have to reign in. But once they spend an hour with the latest version of these two, I don't think it will take much convincing. Trust me, okay?"

"I am, I do," I whisper as he kisses my neck again, his tongue included in the mix, sending goose bumps in their wake. This level of intimacy still a little jarring while at the same time a welcome balm to the sting. A comfort amongst the chaos.

"Me and you, baby," he murmurs in solace before pulling away and flashing me a boyish grin. "Hey, want to make out tonight? Pay homage?" He asks as I turn to him, my lips lifting at his expression.

"You're serious?"

"After they're down, you and me, and the firepit on the porch we never use. We'll bundle up, drink a little wine, smoke a little. Maybe play a little 311."

"I was reminiscing about our love shack before you walked in. I've been thinking about it all day, honestly. So, yeah, let's do it."

His haunted expression—one he's trying hard to shield—eases some as he seals our date with a promising kiss. As we pull away, Peyton kicks the ball right toward us. It bounces over the island, coming close to nailing me. Miraculously, Thatch manages to snatch it before calmly walking over to the knife block. Grabbing the butcher knife, he slams it into the plastic ball and pushes the air out until it deflates before dropping it ceremoniously in the trash.

"Daddy! That's my ball!"

"Not anymore, Son," Thatch states, "I'm going to shower, babe, then I'll set the table." He leaves me with a heated look before sauntering past Peyton and shutting our bedroom door.

Peyton and I stare after him, dazed for different reasons. For the long years we dated and after Gracie was born, I had to work hard to make Thatch a more active participant in the area of discipline and decision-making. He didn't trust himself and was far too passive at times. Which was extremely challenging because of his mission to give our kids a better environment than the one he grew up in. But it's apparent now that Daddy Thatch is in the house, and he's taking charge. Somehow our children have finally managed to snap the most level-headed parent they have into action—and I'm so fucking here for it. In fact, it's turning me the hell on.

Bring it on, Daddy Thatch.

Grinning after my husband, I glance over to my son as he turns to me, his lips parted due to his father's actions. "Mommy, did *you* *see* what Daddy did?"

I flit my gaze from Peyton to my favorite lamp, which is currently lying in questionable condition on our hardwoods. Simmering because of it, Peyton continues to fruitlessly badger me until finally taking my cue and following my line of sight.

"I didn't broked it," Peyton exclaims loudly as I wordlessly turn and put the squash casserole in the oven.

CHAPTER SIX

Thatch

"YOU CAME," SERENA SOUNDS SMUGLY, BARELY VISIBLE IN the small light filtering through the lone window—that is, until she flicks her lighter. "Were you worried about my self-esteem?"

"Petrified," I retort dryly, "and don't light that, I can hang for a minute, but I can't smoke that with you."

"You don't smoke weed?"

"No," I lie.

"Bullshit," she calls, studying my face over the small flame. "I could see you foaming at the mouth when I pulled out the bag."

"Embellish much? I was not."

"So, you were foaming at the mouth for me." She taunts as a statement.

"Your confidence issue is heartbreaking, Serena, truly. I hope you get the help you need."

"Do my parents know what an asshole you are?" She asks before sparking up anyway and exhaling the rest of her question. "Or do you pose for them?"

"Your parents don't interact with the asshole in me because they don't purposely provoke him and don't consider confrontation a personal sport," I say, pulling the joint from her fingers and easily holding it out of reach.

"Hey, that's mine."

"So why am I here then, Serena?" I chide, handing her back her joint before walking over to peer through the window facing the house. The deck Allen and I built sending a shot of pride through me, as well as the inkling that I shouldn't be here. Not alone with his daughter like this. I'm positive now that her parents set us up, but I'm pretty sure they wouldn't appreciate how the rest of this night is playing out. It's the static that kicked between us hours ago that had me coming back. That also had me pacing outside my truck parked a street over before I finally decided to do a fly-through.

For what, Thatch?

"You came for me," she declares with surety as I turn to see her watching me curiously.

"That's undecided," I tell her honestly.

"Well, that's mutual. I don't know if I like you, either. And who are you, anyway, Thatch?"

"I'm as certain of that as you are about yourself."

"Fair enough, so, what's the decision maker for you. Or," she pulls on her joint, holding the smoke briefly before exhaling, her question playful, "or better yet, what's your deal breaker?"

She smells so fucking good, like some sort of clean-scented bloom. A whiff of her earlier had my cock twitching in my jeans. The inch-close stare off had me wanting to snatch her and mark her skin, interested in knowing what her moan might sound like. It's a fact already she's a mouthy, highly opinionated fireball, but there's heart beneath her sass. Bored blind by her empty conversation at dinner, it was still obvious to me that she consists of more. Still water and all. Though, with Serena, it's like turbulent rapids of smoke and mirrors.

Then again, I hope she's as shallow as she depicts herself to be because that static between us is dangerous. Discovering there's something real inside her, worth knowing, will be even more so for me. I told Allen when we started on the deck that I was leaving Nashville, so I can't help but wonder if the reason for this setup is his attempt to keep me here. But, by way of his daughter?

No fucking way.

Firstly, Allen is crazy protective of his family. Though I'm certain I've earned his trust, he would never go to those lengths for me. The idea that he sees me as a fit for her has my chest tightening while, at the same time, a painful unease sinks into me. For the second time in minutes, I glance at the shed door, willing myself to bid her goodnight and walk through it.

"So, are you going to smoke or what?" She prompts, sensing my hesitation.

"Or what," I say, staring diligently at the house before waving her smoke away. "Why do it in here?" I ask. "Your dad is sure to smell it. Is this some shitty attempt at rebellion?"

"It would be pitiful, but despite what you've decided about me, I didn't give Ruby and Allen too much shit. Not even when I was in High School."

"You mean five minutes ago?"

"You're twenty," she delivers, "that doesn't earn you a lick of seniority."

I grin. "Who told you?"

"You just did. But you could pass for older."

"Why's that?" I ask as she continually offers the joint between our exchanges, and I wave each offer away.

"Your maturity," she delivers without hesitation. "Something tells me you don't get off on things the way other guys do."

"Maybe you're wrong."

"I don't think so, Thatcher," she drawls out, guessing my true name. Which I hate.

"Easy guess," I deadpan.

"Don't get me wrong, it's not like I don't know how to have a good time," she says, touching her finger to her tongue to rid it of some loose bud, "but Whitney's given them far more shit. I think she'll be the one doing keg stands in her future. If she hasn't already."

"Yeah," I chuckle, "I can see that. I like her."

"She's seventeen," she grumbles, pinching the rest of her joint between her fingers.

"I'm aware, and she's a cool kid. We get on well. I get on with Brenden, too."

"It's weird you know my family so well. Weird we haven't crossed paths until tonight either, with you being here so often."

"I think you know why I was here tonight."

"Did you know?" she asks, seeming bothered by the idea.

"No, or I would have passed, and they know it."

"Should I palm your face hard in offense?" She snaps. "Or is this your idea of fucking charm?"

"Oof, I meant no offense," I can't help but grin at her nasty little bite, "but I'm not in the habit of getting set up by a girl's parents."

"Wonder why they think you're a good fit for me anyway."

I stalk toward her, and she steps back, a smile quirking her lips as I back her against the wall of the shed. "You have some fucking mouth on you," I quip as she stares up at me, her eyes screaming for me to close the inches between us.

"You have no idea. But please don't go thinking I'll get docile and agreeable when a boy compliments my lips. Or anything else."

"I'm thinking I already know that about you."

"We seem to be thinking a lot about each other," she drawls.

"Don't flatter yourself, Serena. I'm also thinking you're ninety-nine percent pain in the ass, one percent sunshine."

"Not nice, I'm at least two percent sunshine."

I palm the wall next to her head and bend so we're as close as we were earlier. This time, she reaches up, palming the back of my neck and leaving it there. Her lips glistening as she stares up at me expectantly.

"You gloss those lips up for me?"

"I didn't wear it for you before I got home, so there's your answer."

"Liar," I call in bullshit, glancing back toward the window, trying *hard not to close my eyes as she runs her nails slightly but seductively along the back of my neck. Fuck, she's bold, and I'm already hard just thinking about parting those ridiculous lips with my tongue. Turning back to her, I gauge the curiosity in her eyes.* "Set up or not, I'm pretty sure they wouldn't appreciate this situation."

"Whatever," *she sighs on exhale, pulling her hand from my neck.* "Seriously, Thatch, you're that freaked out?"

"I'm not scared of your parents, Serena, but they've been good to me, and I don't want to shit on that."

"Shit on it how?"

"You know good and fucking well how. Don't play ignorant."

"I really don't," *she taunts innocently. In a flash, I grip the wrist holding the joint and press it against the wall behind her. Her eyes spark and ignite, spurring me on as a smirk upturns her perfect lips.*

"Yes, you fucking do."

"Tell me anyway, Handy Man."

"You like playing with fire, but there's all different kinds of fires. You strike me as a girl who's too fucking smart not to figure out what kind of flame she's messing with, and we both know I shouldn't be here." *I state, ill at ease at the idea I won't get invited back.*

While I'm a few hundred short of finally getting the fuck out of Nashville, the Collins' house is truly my only refuge. Though, my future consists of leaving everything and everyone here in the rearview. Only giving the people in my future a one-sentence summation of where I came from before burying my past six feet—the subject never to be broached again. All my memories and the city tainted by the people I share a name with.

"Did you go to school here?" *She asks.*

"For a while, yeah."

"What does that mean?"

"It means," *I deny the joint again when prompted.* "That at one time, I attended school here and then stopped."

"Jesus, you're a hard shell to crack."

"Not really. I'm just not a fan of your line of questioning."

In an instant she's practically pressed against me. "Well then, let's just be quiet."

"Whoa," I whisper, getting lost a little by the glazed look in her eyes. "You're beautiful, truly, but this isn't right."

"And it isn't that serious, Thatch. We're just having fun."

"Fun," I press my lips together as I crowd her a little more. "What do you take seriously?"

Her chest heaves as she stares up at me. "I don't know. School. My health, and anyone who fucks with my family."

"Finally, some conversation with substance," I say, snatching the joint from her fingers and stomping it out with my boot while keeping the space between us scarce. The feel of her inches away alone enough to catch some of the static. "Now you sound like Ruby and Allen's kid. That I'll stay for."

"What is your fascination with my parents?"

"You don't have any idea how good you have it, Serena."

"How good do I have it?"

"You're beautiful and intelligent, have the world at your fingertips, and an incredible family. As far as I can tell, you've got everything you need."

She frowns. "And you don't?"

"I have this thing I'm starting to love," I tell her honestly. "And this guy who's teaching me a lot about it."

"My dad," she concludes.

"Is it so hard to understand that I don't want to fuck that up? Because the truth is, there's not a lot of people around here that will take the time to teach me."

I dip lower, and in response, her eyes start lighting a path straight into me. Every cell in my body ignites for a second, third, hell fucking fourth time tonight as my brain continually wills me to walk away. I'm so fucking close to my exit. A matter of weeks. She'd be a complication, or maybe she's just the distraction I need to make it through.

No, fuck that. Allen deserves better, and so does she. I won't be that guy.

"Thatch," she murmurs, holding my gaze as I start to thrum, fucking ache for her. *"I can tell this is important to you, and I promise I hear you."*

"Ah, so she does listen," I whisper, *"she gets it."*

"I think I want to," she whispers back so sincerely that my pulse skips.

Fuck.

It's all I can do to keep from closing my eyes, the temptation becoming too much. Her voice is a raspy, soothing mix. Her tongue touched with the faintest hint of southern twang, which sets me alight as I reach up and run a lock of her silky blonde strands through my fingers. In that moment, I feel like I'm tainting her and drop it. With that sinking feeling, I decide to make good on my exit. It's the haze in her eyes that warns me away as I lean in, tempted just to brush my lips against hers. Just a little. But it's my good sense that wins out, that has me whispering one last fast "good night" *before I ease back and successfully will myself to the door.*

It's my foolish, ignorant fucking everything else that has me clipping a reply when she calls after me in summons.

"Same time tomorrow night?"

"Maybe."

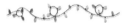

Pulling up to the cabin, I note the lights are already up, thankful for the addition of Eli to our family. Who, with Allen's blessing, relieved him of the annual staple gun task when he lit up the mountain as part of his proposal to Whitney. The sun sets steadily as they shine brightly, guiding us up the driveway and toward the A-frame cabin perched cliffside.

Built in the late seventies, the home is far from a relic and utterly idyllic. Its interior is no less perfect, with large floor-to-ceiling windows and a story-tall stone hearth that can host a fire big enough to warm the entirety of the house. Toss in Ruby's classic, no holds barred décor, and the cabin both looks *and feels* exactly like the type of place one would want to spend any holiday. Specifically, this one. Gazing at the house perched on the mountain cliff, I'm thankful coming here for Christmas has been a new tradition in recent years. Since the original owners, Grammy P and Grandpa Joe passed away, Ruby is determined to keep their memory alive. We all are. I forever remain thankful that I was lucky enough to know them and grieve their loss along with the rest of the family.

Putting my truck in park, I glance over to Serena, who's wearing her typical hoodie and leggings. Her hair tied in her usual messy bun as she stares on at the setting. But it's her neck, or rather the fresh but faint mark just beneath her ear, that keeps my attention.

"I love you," I whisper over the cabin.

She whips her head toward me, her eyes shining with sentiment, her lips parting. "I love you too, babe."

Leaning over, I give her a brief kiss, ignoring Gracie's gag and Peyton's order to stop kissing his mommy. Serena surprises me by pulling my neck to bring our lips back flush and extending it to spite them before leaning over, her whisper just for me.

"Ride or die, no fucks given, make out on a whim, Thatch and Serena in the house."

"My fucking girl," I give her a half-grin and mentally roll up my sleeves. "Let's do this."

She nods. "I'll grab our suitcases."

Hopping out, I open the SUV door as Peyton unbuckles himself, and Gracie jumps out, stretching her legs. Grabbing Serena and my suitcases from the bed of my truck, I call after Gracie as she starts to climb the double set of short stairs that lead to the front door. "Gracie, you forgot to get your suitcase."

Gracie stops just short of the second flight and turns back to me. "What?"

"Your suitcase. I'm assuming you'll want the full wardrobe you packed, the makeup, and your toothbrush."

"Yeah, so bring it up," she demands.

"Yeah, I think I'll pass." I look down to Peyton. "You too."

"Daddy, I can't carry my suitcase! It's too heaby!"

"Hmm, sounds like your problem," I walk past Serena—whose

own eyes are widening slightly—and cut any words she might have with the swift jerk of my chin. Serena nods and follows me up the stairs, elevating her voice.

"Thatch, do you need help? I'm happy to carry mine." Serena offers to set an example. Winging it, we've decided to make the rules up as we go.

"No, baby, I'm good, but thank you for asking."

"Dad, you can't leave us out here. We can't bring our own suitcases up!"

Stopping, I put Serena's case down and palm the storm door. "I believe your mother told you to pack one case and only what you need."

"I need my toys!" Peyton barks. "I didn't pack them all."

"Well, your mother packed for you, and you threw it all out and packed your toys."

"I need them!"

"Then I guess you can carry them in. *One by one.*"

"I need my clothes, too!" Gracie protests.

"Then bring them in," I retort dryly. "I'm not your bellman."

"This is bullshit!" Gracie spews as I push through the front door and inch back slightly to see them both standing at the foot of the porch, waiting for a reaction.

"Gracie, need I say it?"

"I'm sure I lost another present," she scoffs, "I don't care."

"Well, good, then I won't care either. And when you bring your cases up, grab all of the trash you tossed on the floor of my truck. You can trash your rooms all you want, but that space is mine. Clean it up, or you can find your own ride home."

"You want us to bring our own suitcases up those icy stairs *and* clean your truck?"

"Mep," I spit, seeing the salt on the clear steps as Serena bristles next to me.

"This bullshit!" Peyton parrots.

"Oof, that's like four presents left for Rudolph to bring. It's going to be a short Christmas," I declare to Serena before walking into the house. Pulling my wife and our suitcases in, I slam the door in Gracie's screaming face. Turning, I'm met by the knowing smirk of my mother-in-law, who stands just next to the garland-smothered, heavily lit staircase. Her greeting one I'm all too happy to hear.

"I was wondering when the great reckoning was coming," she sighs.

Serena opens her mouth to speak, but I step forward. "It's here, Ruby, and honestly, if it gets to be too much, we'll take them home."

"No, no," she says, walking over to embrace me. "I'm with you, Thatch." She turns to Serena. "I'm with both of you. This has been a while coming."

Serena lets out a sigh of relief and walks straight into her mother's open arms.

"We've screwed up, Mom. I don't know where we went so wrong."

"No, baby, you would have screwed up if you let it go on any longer. It's going to be one hell of a week, but your father and I are behind you. I promise."

"They're going to ruin Christmas," Serena whispers mournfully.

"Oh, honey, we won't let them. I've got a few tricks of my own," Ruby assures.

"Thank you," Serena whispers as I kiss my mother-in-law on the cheek, as she consoles my wife, while reading my expression.

"Gravity," Ruby whispers, releasing Serena.

"Gravity," I utter back before pulling her to me.

CHAPTER SEVEN

Thatch

"**E**LEVEN DAYS," JOSHUA WARNS OVER THE LINE. "*I'M NOT fucking around, Thatch.*"

"I understand," I state as I glance over to Ruby, who's putting Allen through his paces. The last few minutes spent making him rotate the tree from every imaginable angle, where she scrutinizes its placement from feet away.

Their difference in size is almost laughable as she orders her husband around like he doesn't dwarf her. Ruby can't be more than five foot one or two, at most. Though her presence alone has her towering over Allen, who is covertly glaring at the side of her head between twists of the monstrous tree. His patience visibly thinning as he rotates it 'a little further right' while glancing over at me, a 'help me' in his expression. I manage to shoot him a reassuring grin as Joshua runs through his laundry list of threats. Standing in the kitchen, I twist the coiled cord of their landline phone around my pointer, the blood quickly building as it goes purple. The tightening feel of it matching the state of my insides as I'm berated on the phone while watching the Ruby-Allen show.

"I heard you," I state emphatically, glancing down at my other *fingers.* Most of which are cut or calloused. All worked close to the bone to keep the asshole on the phone satiated enough to keep his distance. In those seconds, I envy Ruby and Allen—their dynamic, their life, their current dilemma, and daily problems. All of which I would trade in a nanosecond in exchange for my own.

"You better have," Joshua snaps. "I've bought you enough time."

"I'll be there, okay? I'm working on it. Everything's the same. Nothing's changed. I'll let you know if it does," I state, watching Allen turn the tree for a fifth time.

"Let me make this clear, you don't want me coming to you," he threatens.

"We're crystal, and you won't have to," I assure before he hangs up. Fucking dick.

Resisting the urge to close my eyes, Allen shoots me another pleading look as I decide to try and help him as best I can.

"Right there, Allen. From where I'm standing, it's perfect. No gaps."

Ruby looks over to me and steps back a little further before giving Allen a decisive nod. "It'll do," she says, "thanks, Thatch."

"No problem," I say, as Allen grumbles about me not being the one to 'drag the fucking thing in.' A second later, Allen warily eyes the boundless boxes of Christmas décor currently filling their living room. As if on cue, Brenden stalks in from the front door, eyes zeroing in on the enormous spruce pine as he speaks up.

"It's crooked, tilted a little too far right, Mom," he reports as Allen shoots him a death glare.

"Oh?" Ruby tilts her head in response as Allen runs a finger across his throat for his grinning teenage son. Brenden, the second born of the three Collins siblings, is no less outspoken than his sisters. In fact, I have a suspicion his sisters' collective candor has made him a bit more of a daredevil. Evidence of that is in the satisfied look in his eyes with the further aggravated state of his father. I can't help chuckling as he gives me a knowing salute, which I lift my chin to before he stalks toward his bedroom.

Still rattled by my call with Joshua to engage in any more

conversation, I slip out the back door. Not missing Allen's "oh God, now what?" before he and Ruby begin to comically bicker. Nervous energy flitting through me, I stalk back to the woodworking station I set up on the deck before I decided to brave the call. A call that never fails to set my nerves alight. Joshua's typical, needless, and over-the-top antics only adding to my stress.

Asshole.

But as usual, I'm at his mercy, and I have no fucking choice but to play my part. Resuming where I left off, I position the wood against the table saw. I started fucking around with woodworking after Allen and I finished the deck. My latest obsession is perfecting bevel and chamfer cuts to attempt to create more ornate, intricate edging. Not long after I start, I become blissfully lost in the workings of my hands. Only pulled from concentration when I somehow feel her approaching before her boots sound on the deck.

"You stood me up, Handy Man."

"Had something come up," I offer, keeping my eyes lowered. "Didn't have your number."

"Then give me your cell phone. I'll put it in," Serena offers.

"Don't have one of those at the moment."

"You don't have a phone?"

"Not today," I counter with edge, embarrassment threatening as I keep my eyes lowered.

"Okay, jeez, vague much?"

"Vague always," I turn to take her in and immediately regret it. Her gorgeous locks are swept back in a sleek ponytail, which I immediately picture wrapping into my fist. Her latest form-fitting, cropped sweater is bright white. The deep scoop neck giving a peek of mouth-watering cleavage. Today, she's dressed to hurt me. My suspicion only confirmed when her pouty lips lift in satisfaction at my thorough once-over. No doubt a ploy to make me regret no-showing last night. Her tactic working because, at present, I can't rip my fucking eyes away.

It's then I realize there's my attraction for women, and then there's my attraction for Serena Collins—which are not one and the same. That

*truth hammered home as bated seconds pass because no matter how hard
I try, I can't stop picturing what I shouldn't be. Especially the stretch of
her mouth around my cock, or the look of us connecting as I sink into her.
As of now, I can't stop imagining the part of her lips while driving into
her for the first time. Of making it hurt so she never forgets it—or me.
Of making it so fucking good after, she'll summon the replay for weeks
or months. Lost in the sight of her, I imagine what her palm-sized tits
would look like with my marks covering them.*

Allen's daughter, asshole!

*"It's too bad I only have one joint left," she drops just as intention-
ally. Translation—last chance, Thatch.*

*"A real shame," I counter, flicking my eyes up to her smirking mouth
and purposeful lack of gloss. Battling the urge to act on the dozen fanta-
sies forming in my mind, it's only when she greets Allen that I fully snap
out of my stupor. Faking a pencil line on the wood I'm working with, I
keep my eyes averted as his boots sound on the deck.*

*"Hey, Daddy," Serena greets him, her tone saccharin. "It looks re-
ally good out here."*

*In a call of bullshit, I catch her inquisitive gaze and accompany-
ing smirk just as she quirks a brow in an unspoken question of 'tonight?'
When I give her the faint dip of my chin, she flashes me a soul-snatching
smile. Satisfied, she pulls Allen in for a hug.*

*"You two really did the damned thing out here," she says, seemingly
sincere with her compliment. "I mean it. This deck is beautiful."*

*Pride swelling, I flit my own gaze to the pattern of the weathering
wood that Allen and I carefully planned out before hammering each
board in. Allen thanks her as his own eyes trail appreciatively along the
massive deck. Our careful planning making the wood more like a natural extension of the house. The addition only amplifies the view past
the neighborhood to the distant rolling hills beyond. Though it took us
months to finish because of my inexperience, Allen patiently and pains-
takingly schooled me every step of the way.*

*I wasn't bullshitting Serena when I told her Allen had taught me
a lot about carpentry. In doing so, he introduced me to a lot more than*

a way to distract myself and help me get through my personal shit. He also gave me a glimpse of a possible light at the end of a very long tunnel. An avenue I intend on pursuing as far as I can.

But first things first, and that's my imminent exit. Though, it's the girl dressed in dark jeans and a bright white sweater who has me becoming less anxious to hasten it—the reason I intentionally didn't venture to the shed last night. Ironically, and now, the very reason I decide not to miss my closing window with her tonight.

I'll have earned my freedom in a week or two, which should only relieve me. But gaining that freedom now means leaving Ruby, Allen, Serena, and the rest of the Collins family behind. A family who has taken me in and shielded me from the shit show that is my life. The idea of them filling my rearview has me sinking in my skin as her eyes weigh heavy on my profile. Allen greets me warmly before he checks my work, full of encouragement. Unable to help myself, I trail the girl who just sent my chest pumping and catch the sweet upturn of her sinful lips as she walks through the back door of the house. Our eyes holding briefly through the glass as she pulls it closed.

It's during that short exchange that every fiber of my being lights with the same message it did the first time I laid eyes on her.

Fuck.

"I want to pick first!" Peyton demands as Ruby emerges from the kitchen with Frosty's hat. One we use for the annual mystery Rudolph drawing. A tradition in which we all pick one name out of the hat to buy a gift for twenty bucks or less. The rules remaining unchanged since the Collins kids began marrying and multiplying. The tradition is an effort to have every adult open at least one gift while keeping the budget reasonable so the bulk of each family's Christmas fund is spent on the kids. The catch being that each gift is meant to let the person you're buying for know how well you know them. Ruby, a veteran in mysterious and highly subliminal gift-giving, is now only matched in skill by my newest brother-in-law, Eli.

Even so, I've fared well enough in mystery Rudolph over the years, having known and been a part of this family for a little over half my life. It's that thought that has my lips curving up after reliving that call with Joshua. My current problems now similar to those I was envying during that time. As shit as things have been lately, at least I have that silver lining.

"What's that grin about?" Eli asks, nudging me where we sit side by side at the breakfast table.

Turning, I meet the ice-blue eyes of Whitney's husband, who, short years ago, appeared as the ghost of Whitney's Christmas past after a seventeen-year hiatus. Formerly college sweethearts, Eli broke Whitney's heart suddenly after eight months of serious dating. Long years later, and through the most serendipitous of circumstances, Eli got a job working with Brenden. Shortly after, he took his shot, accompanying Brenden for Christmas here at the cabin to deliver a belated apology before managing to win Whitney back. It was the same year that Serena and I had hit our communication stalemate, which turned out to be a blessing. Brenden and his wife, Erin, had their own issues during that time. That year, Brenden's blind ambitions had him moving his family from Nashville to Charlotte to kickstart his company—Networth Inc. Their resolution being sorted when Brenden moved her back. But only *after* finding out that Christmas that she was miserable and hiding it to support his business venture.

It was a good Christmas for all of us. One I hope we can mirror this year, at least in the resolution sense.

"It's a miracle Thatch smiles at all, having married this one," Brenden chimes as he saunters in, his youngest son, Jameson, on his hip. Brenden's older two, Wyatt and Conner, trail behind, as does Erin, who greets us all with a warm smile and ready hugs. Though all of us reside in Nashville, Brenden and his crew pulled into Triple Falls especially late last night, leaving only Eli and Whitney awake to greet them.

"Hey man," I say, getting up to give Brenden a bro hug just as he runs his fingers down my wife's scalp and forehead before giving her pig nose. The table collectively laughs as Serena swats his hand away before standing to embrace him.

"You're such an asshat," Serena greets, hugging him fiercely. While Whitney is my wife's other person, she has a heavily concealed soft spot for her overly sarcastic, highly self-involved little brother.

Conversation explodes as the mixed greetings begin, and I can't help my chuckle when Allen takes out his hearing aids, AKA his 'ears' to avoid the commotion. My amusement is cut short as my narc of a son calls him out for it an instant later.

"Grammy, Gramps took out his ears!" Peyton exclaims.

Allen gives Peyton the stink eye as he defends his actions. "It's really loud in here, so I wonder why?"

Peyton stares back at him cluelessly as Ruby scolds him. "No one likes a tattle, Grandson."

"But Grammy," Peyton protests, "you always tell him to put in his ears!"

"That's right. *I tell Gramps*," she points to herself. "Not you. Children have no place telling adults what to do."

Get him, Grammy!

"Well, I tell my Daddy *all the time* what to do, and he does it, right, Daddy?" Peyton counters, stealing my grin while making me his bitch with that delivery. Neck heating, I duck under the stares of every adult surrounding us before I remember myself, glowering at Peyton as I voice my reply.

"Did I turn the radio to Wiggles yesterday when you ordered me to?"

"No," Peyton replies instantly, but with contempt.

"Did I get your suitcase?"

"No."

"Did I read to you last night when you ordered me to?"

"No, and that was not nice!"

The heads surrounding us whip back and forth as I finish. "So, yeah, Daddy doesn't do what you say anymore because you're not nice."

Inquisitive eyes bounce between me and Serena before she nervously speaks up. "Soooo, Thatch and I need an emergency meeting with *all adults* before we leave to shop for mystery Rudolph."

Gracie immediately snaps to, eyes darting furiously between Serena and me, which I consider a win.

"We just got here," Brenden groans. "There's already a fire?"

"Don't worry, bro. I said *adults*," Serena drawls out dryly, "so you can color with the rest of the booger pickers."

"Awesome. Tell me, how was the flight here, sis?" Brenden counters.

Serena frowns. "You know we drove."

"Ah, so you finally gave the broom a much-needed break. Probably lost some frequent flyer points, but you must have, what, at least two *million* miles on it by now?"

"Walked right into that one," Whitney chuckles as Serena, who's already in motion, flips the top of the ketchup bottle in her hands before unloading it on Brenden's freshly plated eggs. No visible trace of yellow left by the time she tables it.

Brenden immediately shovels a forkful into his mouth, speaking around it. "Doc says I need to eat more vegetables." He shoots Serena a wink. "Thanks for looking out, big sis."

"Eat poo and keel over, brother," Serena delivers sweetly before pulling Erin into a hug. "I love you. *Only you.*"

"Not me too?" Conner asks, Brenden's oldest. Though our niece is mostly as soft-spoken as her mother, she's become more participatory in sarcastic ping-ponging the last year or two, which is the Collins' official love language.

Serena snatches Conner into a hug next. "Definitely you too, and you," she says, embracing Wyatt, Brenden's middle child. Wyatt, who speaks as often as Brenden and Erin's youngest son, Jameson, who's *half* his age and still in diapers. Not only is Wyatt politely mute, but he's forever dressed like he stepped out of a baby GQ closet and seems to prefer it. I see it the second Serena joins me in juxtaposing our kids—who are closest in age—just as Peyton voices his distaste for his mother's generous affection.

"The hell? Mommy, you didn't hug *me* good morning!"

Erin's jaw drops as Peyton spills some ketchup-covered eggs on his 'Stealing Hearts, Blasting Farts' tee before rubbing the stain in further with his smothered fingers.

"Because you bit me," Serena states.

"That was a long time ago!" Peyton defends.

"Peyton," Whitney admonishes. "You *bit* Mommy?"

"Yes," he states without an ounce of remorse. "It was a long time ago, Auntie Whit." I can practically see the batting of lashes in his tone.

"Days," Serena says. "Days ago."

Peyton's eyes bug as he scolds her. "No one likes a tattle, Mo-*may!*"

"The . . . fuck?" Eli utters softly, confusion riddling his expression as he looks to me for an explanation, and I whisper my update.

"Yes, your favorite nephew is now displaying sociopathic tendencies. And that's just the tip of the iceberg. Buckle up, brother," I utter in warning.

"Really?" Eli asks, watching closely as Peyton shovels more eggs into his mouth. The year Eli appeared, the family fell for him as fast as Whitney did, but my son was the first on the bandwagon. Peyton and Eli have bonded closely and heavily since. So much so that I can feel genuine paternal concern now as Eli observes him.

After the last of the greetings are exchanged, I flit my focus to Whitney who is all smiles this morning. Still newlyweds, both Eli and Whitney are a mere step into their forties and have no kids of their own. The circumstances behind it are part life's shitty hand, and I suspect now purposeful in not exploring other options as they both live for family gatherings, Whitney especially. It's obvious as she beams at the overly full table and catches my eye.

"What in the hell is up, *stranger?*" She confronts me instantly. Over the years—and from the start—Whitney and I bonded quickly, having become best friends over time. To the point we sometimes hang out, and often Christmas shop together. Those get-togethers have been scarce in the last year. Though I assumed her new husband would take some of the heat off the fact I've been more absent, I can see the hurt in her eyes now.

"I know, I know, I'm sorry," I can feel Serena tuning in next to me. "We've been swamped."

"No . . ." Whitney ping pongs her focus between Serena and I, "something's definitely up, but I'm guessing we'll find out at the meeting?"

I nod, already dreading the conversation as Ruby rounds the table with Frosty's hat.

"Grammy, I *said* I wanted to pick first!" Peyton booms over the noise of the entire table before all goes quiet, and Serena and I are accosted by the first lingering look of judgment.

"Well, since you're being naughty about it," Ruby steps in, saving us, "you get to pick *last*."

"Grammy! That's not nice!" Peyton screeches as I wince. "Why is everyone not being nice to me?"

"Because you're misbehaving, Peyton, and you know it," Ruby relays evenly. A heartbeat later, my son is slamming his fist on the table, his fork in hand to amplify the noise. The instant Wyatt starts to join in, a mere word and stern look from Brenden stops it. Serena and I watch as Wyatt obediently forks a bit of his eggs, chewing like an adult before dabbing his mouth with his napkin. His sweater and starched undershirt sparkling as he politely asks his mother for more juice. Envy takes a stronghold as Serena and I hold our gaze, and I mouth my Christmas wish, "I want that."

Nodding, she blows out a loaded breath as all adult eyes start to curiously trail back to us. The mystery of the conversation we've asked for already unraveled as our son continually shows his ass.

Not twenty minutes later, every one of those adults' jaw is hanging slack as we list our grievances and why we're taking the steps we are.

"So, as of now, you two are Bebe's kid-sing it?" Whitney states without hesitation. Her use of movie terms as verbs never ceasing to amaze me.

"What is Bebe's kids?" Serena asks.

"It's a movie," Whitney says in short explanation, her voice full of concern.

"It's every parent's worst nightmare, is what it is," Brenden states. "What is wrong with them? Gracie told Conner to shut up just before they left the table. No one tells Conner to shut up . . . like ever. Little witch."

"Watch it," Ruby warns Brenden before he lifts his palms in feigned innocence.

"I'm just saying, I see it. They weren't like this last year."

"Serena and Thatch almost stayed home," Ruby states. "I don't think any of us wants that."

"Speak for yourself," Brenden jokes a second before his face twists in pain. "Oof, baby, shit, do you sharpen that elbow at night?" Erin lifts the elbow she just dislodged from his ribs in threat. "Of course, I don't mean that," Brenden continues. "Well, sans Serena."

"You know, you joke, brother," Serena counters, her tone watery, "but you act a lot like me. Say the same type of shit, and call it *confidence*," Serena defends. "The difference is my delivery. And I get it, I'm the *bitchy one*, and it's a running joke in this family, but this shit is not funny. I'm your sister, and I'm hurting right now, and I'm asking you for fucking help."

"Babe," I hedge softly, and Serena looks over to me, contempt for her brother shining clear in her eyes, as well as guilt. Most of it is her belief that Gracie's behavior is her fault. She gives me a nod to take the floor, her emotions already running high. Which in her defense, I understand because Brenden's kids are models for behavior, which only makes us both feel worse.

"Let's put that shit away for a second, okay, brother?" I tell Brenden.

Brenden frowns at Serena as his discomfort sets in. He's not the guy for emotional conversations. Unless the conversation is with or about Erin, his inclination is to forever run away from talks of this sort. Which has gotten him in trouble in the past. But it's just part of who he is. Even so, he reads the room and thankfully steps up. "Sorry, sis."

"Yeah," Serena says dismissively, waving him away.

"No, I mean it, Serena, I'm sorry," Brenden insists, and Serena reads the sincerity in his expression and nods.

"Me too, bro, I'm just stressed, and Bebe's kids don't have shit on ours lately."

"We're in trouble here," I interject. "Peyton is terrorizing his teacher and classmates in *pre-K*. He's biting and mimicking Gracie's worst behaviors. Days ago, he was swinging from his damned ceiling fan because Gracie helped string it up to keep him occupied while she talked Tik Tok bullshit or whatever fascinates tween girls these days."

"Jesus," Eli whispers, his eyes darting between us. "He could have—"

"That's why the destruction of our brand-new house is the least of our concerns," Serena tosses in as Whitney inches toward her sister. "It's gotten to the point we can't go a single day without some incident. And these incidents are supposed to be the *once-a-year* type of incidents."

"The latest?" I continue. "Gracie got picked up for shoplifting after we cut off her allowance." Whitney's eyes immediately snap to mine, Ruby and Allen's attention growing just as heavy on my profile while I swallow the sting of that admission.

"Thatch," Whitney summons, brown eyes earnest when I glance over, "that is *not* on you."

"I know, or in a way I do," I say unconvincingly. "Then again, isn't it?"

A short silence lingers, and it's damning as hell. Even so, Whitney steps forward, intent on consoling me. "Thatch, it was a decision *Gracie made*," she says in my defense. "And we're with you," she glances toward Eli, who looks pained.

THE SLEIGHT BEFORE CHRISTMAS | 81

"That," I say, pointing at him. "I know how close you are to Peyton, brother, but this shit is serious. He—" I swallow, still unable to talk about the image haunting me. "They're disobeying us to the point it's getting dangerous. Really fucking dangerous," I relay in a grave tone. "So, either we leave here within the hour, and we understand because this is your holiday too—"

"My ass," Allen finally speaks, looking equally disturbed. "We do this together," he insists adamantly.

"Or we stay," I finish, "but fair warning, this is likely not going to be fun."

"We'll be fine," Whitney says. "Just tell us what to do."

"Follow our lead," I say, looking at each of them pointedly. "That's all we ask. We're not asking you to watch them or step in. In fact, we're asking you don't."

"Can they do the activities?" Whitney inquires.

"As long as they behave," Serena answers. "The minute they don't, they're out."

"We're in," Erin says. "Whatever you need," she continues, looking toward Brenden, who, to his credit, looks equally bothered.

"Got it," Brenden says as Ruby glowers at him. "Got it . . . Mom, jeez, you don't have to give me the demon mom look. I *can* be serious," he defends. "I do have children of my own." All of us—including his own wife—give him dead stares as he ducks beneath them and spouts off. "I'm quickly becoming offended."

I roll my eyes. "Follow our lead, and if you guys don't mind, let's try to keep cursing to a minimum. I know I'm the worst, but let's just try. Do not undermine us. We'll call for backup if we need it."

"We trust you," Ruby states, the concern in her voice evident as she keeps my gaze.

"With the actions we've decided to take, it might be hard to watch," I warn them all.

"Yeah, well, desperate times," Ruby says in support, "and I have a few old tricks up my own sleeve, my boy. If you need them."

"I'm counting on it," I wink at her. "You have permission to get 'em, Grammy."

"Is this why we haven't taken them in months?" Whitney asks. I swallow as Serena's eyes water.

"Oh, sis, you could have told us," Whitney consoles.

"We're embarrassed," I admit aloud, gripping Serena's hand.

"Nothing to be ashamed of, do you hear me?" Ruby admonishes. "I've been there, as have many other parents. Brenden's kids are freaks of nature in that respect," she offers, and Erin smiles, taking zero offense.

"I'm the perfect father," Brenden says before narrowly missing Erin's killing blow.

"Any questions?" Serena asks.

Brenden holds his hand up, and Ruby snaps it back down with words alone. "I've hidden it so well this year, my baby boy, that your lips won't be tasting that damned nog until I say it's time."

"Shit," he utters. "Fine, but if we're going to deal with Operation Crack Bebe's kids, I'm going to need something to take the edge off."

"You touch my eggnog before I say the word, and I'm going to take something off you, son. I'm not bullshitting."

"You know, you could make a double batch, so this conversation is moot—" he shrinks under Ruby's glare. "Fine," he grumbles. "I won't touch it . . . today. No promises about tomorrow."

"Gravity," Ruby says, ending their back and forth and unifying us with a single word. "Understood?"

All of us nod, and as everyone starts to file out of the bedroom, Allen palms my shoulder, holding me behind. "Tell me you know this is not your fault."

I turn back to him and close the door, seeing his concern etched everywhere. "I'm trying not to blame myself. Serena is too, but ultimately, we are responsible."

"You are and aren't. As parents, we get to demonstrate and teach them the difference in what one decision looks like and warn them about others. I know how terrified you were when Serena got pregnant with Gracie, but you were a born father, Thatcher. And since have been a natural. A better father than me, if I'm honest."

"I can't see that."

"You're more attentive. Which I regret. You *are* a good father, Thatch."

"Thank you, and I promise, I'm trying not to take it too much to heart, but Jesus, it stings. Truth be told, I haven't been so attentive since the business took off."

"Hey, it's sometimes hard to know how to balance if you don't know where to. Just trust your instincts. But know that sometimes life has a way of giving us a taste of what we fear most to let us know just how little we need to fear it. There's no real control, Thatch. I think that's the scariest part of parenting. If I would have known how terrifying being a father was, and not just because the newborn's head wobbles like it's about to fall off," he chuckles, "but every single day, Jesus, I can't say I wouldn't have done it, but my worst fear is—"

"I got a glimpse of it, Allen," I relay, the image popping in again, "and I promise you I'm only more fucking terrified."

"Want to talk about it?" He offers.

"I can't, truly, I can't. But when I can, I will."

He nods.

"Thatch, Gracie doesn't know any other life than the one you've provided and the way you taught her. If there's a bad example for her behavior, you didn't set it. Tell me you believe me."

"I appreciate what you're saying, I do, but my ears are fucking ringing. You're screaming at me, Dad."

"Oops," he says an octave lower, and we share a grin just as Ruby bursts back into the room, holding out his 'ears.'

CHAPTER EIGHT

Serena

"YOU'RE NOT GOING TO SMOKE TONIGHT EITHER?" I ASK Thatch after he denies the joint I offer, crossing his arms as he leans against Dad's workbench. His eyes continually roll over me in assessment as if he's debating something.

"What's your issue, pusher? Is this your dealbreaker?"

"Of course not," I frown. "I can get you a beer or something."

"I don't have to have a buzz to hang with you," he states with an edge.

"Geesh, a bit testy tonight, are we?"

"Sorry," he utters, "I'm not trying to be a dick."

"Well, you could try and talk to me."

"I am talking to you."

"You know what I mean," I cut through the bullshit. "Why are you so on edge? Even when you chill here, it's like something's going on just underneath."

"That's called being human," he mutters, "we all have shit going on."

"Fine," I sigh, sliding down to the floor and crossing my boots. Taking another hit, I glance up to see the same quizzical stare as I take him in.

He's dressed similarly. Long-sleeved thermal—this one deep blue—tattered jeans and boots. Tonight, his hair is a little more tousled, as if he's been running his hand through it all day.

"What?" I ask after a few bated seconds. He shifts so he's standing next to me before sliding down the wall, mimicking my stance before tapping his boot against mine.

"Okay, hit me," he states, and I hold out the joint.

"No, Serena," he waves the smoke away as if he's allergic, "with your questions."

"Why is Allen Collins your best friend?"

"Because, in a way, he saved my life."

"How?"

"By giving me a job. I needed the money."

"Your parents—"

"Are not in the picture," he dismisses.

"What do you do for fun?"

"Don't know anymore," he says, lifting a leg and resting his forearm on it. "It's been a while since I attempted fun."

"You're right, you're too boring for me," I joke, nudging him.

"I'm not the one meeting a bore in a miniature shed every night. I'm working my ass off. What's your excuse for your naked social calendar?"

"I'll sound like an asshole if I tell you," I say.

"Oh, it's then you'll sound like one?" He chuckles and I glare over at him.

"Sorry, tell me."

"Forget it."

"Don't be a brat," he nudges me. "Tell me."

"I don't know. I guess you could say my senior year sucked because I was already over it before it even started. I was mentally done with high school and even skipped my last prom because I went the year before. I couldn't wait to graduate and get to college. I think my aversion to pretty much everything about it annoyed my friends to the point they stopped inviting me out, and I kind of didn't give a shit? If I'm honest, I was relieved."

"So, a loner?"

"I mean, I guess you could put it like that. Guys in my school weren't worth the effort, either. I've been bored for a long time. You're turn," I say, and he nods. "So, did you come for me tonight?"

"Maybe," he muses before lifting his hand to push the bulk of my ponytail behind my shoulder. The touch gentle and surprising.

"Are you being weird because there's a girl?"

"Weird how?"

"Like," I shrug, "won't do anything?"

"Do what exactly?" He taunts, and I deadpan.

"If there was a girl, I wouldn't be here dodging twenty questions," he chuckles, and I decide I love the sound even if it seems to be at my constant expense. We stare off for a few silent seconds as that same pull draws me and intensifies. Unsure if he feels it, his jade eyes seem to deepen as the question comes to mind, and I take it as a good sign. So far, and in mere days, Thatch has had my head spinning, my heart thundering, and my attention constantly drifting back to him, and I'm not sure I like it. I've already made too much effort, and hate how desperate I'm starting to look. I swore to myself I wouldn't try so hard tonight, but the way he stares, it can't be one-sided.

"I really am just trying to get to know you," I blow out a breath of frustration.

"What would satisfy you?" He asks, his eyes trailing down my face, to my sweater and jeans, and back up.

"Uh, how about the fucking truth?" I say before hitting the joint again.

"Man, that mouth," he whispers before his eyes drop to it. "Why are you so hellbent?"

"On?"

"On everything," he chuckles again. "Such an intense girl."

"I'm just opinionated," I state without apology, "and not a fan of bullshit. Like my mom. And you seem to be full of it."

"Not like your mom," he corrects. "And I'm just private."

"More like secretive to the point of infuriating, and maybe I'm a little mouthier," I admit with a shrug.

"Little bit," he lifts his fingers, presenting an inch before expanding them space wide.

"You like it," I wrinkle my nose, and he rakes his lip with his teeth.

"Do I? What else do I like?" he asks.

"Right now, my sweater," I smirk. "The view," I add. "My lips."

"Hmm," he utters.

"You like me," I nudge him.

"Wouldn't go that far."

"Seems like you won't go at all," I sigh. "You have yet to lay a hand on me, Thatch. Any plans to?"

"No," he clips instantly.

"Well, that's a shame," I drawl. "I was wondering what kissing you would feel like." I toss the joint. "I'll stop now."

"I said hand," he whispers, lifting his finger and carefully tracing the seam of my lips, which part at his gentle touch. His delivery so soft and deliberate in contrast to his irritation as he speaks. "Why are you making this so damned hard?"

"Because you like that too," I whisper against the pad of his pointer. "Thatch," I utter as his chest starts to rise and fall. "T-they set us up. I don't see the harm in a kiss."

"Yeah, well, I fucking do," he grinds out, even as he continuously sweeps his calloused finger across my lips. "Jesus, I do."

"Why?" I croak, his effect on me evident as he crooks his finger and slowly whispers it down my cheek. Sitting side by side, facing one another, our gazes hold in a heavy stare that has my skin tingling and my pulse pounding. He continues to stroke me with a lone finger, sweeping it to trace my chin before gliding it down my throat.

Outlining the shape of my oval necklace, he dips even further, tracing the scoop of my sweater. My breaths draw heavier and heavier as he teases me relentlessly with just a finger. Body alight, my lips part to take more needed breath as his eyes drop to trace the pad of his finger when it dips again. Robbing me of air altogether when he runs it over the swell of each of my breasts. In seconds, I'm a puddle of want as my body starts to pulse with need. The beat lowering between my thighs as he runs his finger back and forth over the skin of my chest. Back and forth, the hypnotic sweep pulling me under.

"Thatch," I whisper urgently, and his eyes close at the sound, his finger pausing briefly before he slowly reopens them. Inside them resides a fiery jade stare that reeks of something far more dangerous than any exchange before. A warning in his gaze that has my heart thundering with surety of my suspicion before he speaks it aloud.

"I'm trying . . . really trying to be a gentleman with you. Something I can admit I've never been before."

Done with the game, wanting to unleash what he's trying so hard to tame, I swiftly straddle him. Palming his shoulders, I slowly start to rock my hips, adjusting myself to grant my pulsing clit the friction it needs from the rock-hard bulge beneath me as I speak. "Well, don't start on my account."

"There you go, playing with fucking fire," he scolds, stopping my movement.

"Now, where were you?" I say, gripping his finger and pulling it back to the last place he touched, the skin still tingling in his wake.

"Serena," he objects as I dip and lick along his bottom lip before pulling back.

"All glossed up now, Thatch, just for yo—"

Palming the back of my neck, he cuts my words short with the hard press of his mouth against mine. The contact is like a shot to the chest as he swipes his tongue across the seam of my lips. An instant later, he's delivering his tongue before it easily finds and tangles with mine in a flawless dance. Our collective moans mingle as the kiss quickly turns. In those first seconds, I lose myself. My panties flood as I begin to move across the bulge beneath me. Moaning into his mouth, I tighten my thighs around him as I get lost in the sensation.

"Serena—"

His kiss is perfect. The pressure, the way he's running his tongue *along mine. The feel of his hair between my fingers, the muscle at my fingertips.*

"Serena—"

His clean scent—a mix of soap and freshly cut wood. It's utterly addicting.

As addicting as his groan, which vibrates on my tongue and in my throat as I capture and suck his. Gently grinding on his hardened cock, he jerks his mouth away again, eyes shut tightly, as he grips my hips hard to stop me.

"That's why," *he states, his voice coated in lust.* "That's fucking why, Serena."

"Why what?"

His eyes slowly open, his stare searing while lighting me up. Probing and demanding as he whispers my words back to me. "Just fun, right?"

My chest pumps heavily with the lingering feel of his kisses. It's then I realize he's utterly a mess—his hair picked through, his lips swollen. How long were we kissing? Wait . . . "What did you just say to me?" *I ask, hearing the hint of rejection in my voice.*

"I didn't mean it the way it came out," *he backtracks.*

"No, I think you did," *I say, pulling back to glare down at him.*

"Maybe I did, but not in the way you're taking it," *he blows out a breath that hits my tingling skin.* "I'm not good with words, Serena. With any of this."

"I agree. You're far from smooth, Thatcher," *I move to get off his lap, and he stops me, squeezing both my hips in prompt. As if we already have our own unspoken language, I know exactly what he's asking even as he remains mute.*

"I mean, we can fuck around, and this can be just fun," *I offer,* "but I'm not really cool with verbalizing it to the point that it feels cheap."

"You're going back to school in a few weeks, right?"

"Three, yeah, so?"

"Okay, so fun . . . 'till then?" *he asks, his question seeming . . . gentle? It's his eager return stare and matching tone that has me relaxing slightly.*

"I mean, sure. It's not like I'm looking for a husband, Thatch," *I relay truthfully.* He nods easily, though his eyes convey something other than relief at my confession. Palming my neck again, which sends heat straight to my core, he pulls me flush to him, his whisper a balm to the sting he just caused. "I didn't mean to fuck it up."

In apology, he takes my lips again, fusing it into me before he deepens it. Not a minute later, he pulls back and shakes his head.

"Fuck, you feel so f-d-damned g-good," he utters, his tone a little dreamlike as I chuckle at his delivery. He grimaces before glowering at me. "You're an asshole, Collins."

"I don't disagree."

"So much sass from that mouth," he utters, one side of his own mouth lifting. "Which I definitely like more when you're not talking."

"Then kiss me quiet, Handy Man."

"Nah," he strokes my lower lip. "I better go," he gently lifts me from his lap like I weigh nothing before standing. He adjusts his clothes as I glance up at the clock, gaping when I read the hour. Because hours is how long we've been kissing. Body tingling, it's then I realize I'm equally a mess, my clothes rumpled, my panties soaked, nipples sore from being hard for so long. I'm physically aching for relief as my body buzzes, alight—for him.

"Wow, I—" Turning when I feel his absence, I see he's already lingering in the door of the shed, watching me carefully. The look in his gorgeous green eyes stuns me speechless before he drops them and disappears out the door. But I don't call after him in question or wonder if he's coming back tomorrow—or rather, tonight—because his kiss and that look said it all.

Day one, and mere *hours in,* Peyton screams before dropping dead in the center of my mother's kitchen, which was formerly Grammy P's. Two generations of women who would not put up with this shit and didn't. Both of which would have probably already figured out a way to stop it as I fail them while watching my son flail his arms and legs as every adult in proximity recoils in utter horror.

Thankful we're not in the grocery store like last time—but no less mortified due to the number of eyes watching his latest melt-down—I continue whipping the fresh cream for the chocolate icebox cake as Peyton's screams increase. His audience having everything to do with the strength of his performance, I shoo Conner out of the kitchen to spare her as the glass door in the den slides open before Thatch appears with an armful of wood. I search his face helplessly as he glances down at Peyton, his sigh visible before he gives me a reassuring wink.

Eli at his back, his own arms full, he too stares down at Peyton as they pass. When both men have dropped their wood haul at the hearth, Thatch stops Eli from approaching by palming his chest and adamantly shaking his head. Feeling the urgency to make it stop by everyone surrounding us, I decide to continue to take my cues from Thatch, who steps over our flailing son, straddling him between his legs.

"Use *your words*, son," Thatch bellows, and I know it's out of contempt for judgment of all adults within range. Even if they don't understand his reasoning for it, I do. Thatch looks up to me just after, solidifying that it was more for me and that we're on the same page before he takes a knee, repeating his request to Peyton as instructed by *They*. The experts, the teachers, the ones who dole out what the disciplinary rules are.

"Peyton, please use your words," Thatch gently coaxes, "and tell Daddy why you're upset."

"Or pop his ass," my dad utters, shaking his head in both pity and irritation.

"Daddy, no," Whitney gently scolds. "Times are different. They're doing what they were taught."

"And we were taught to use our words," Thatch answers as if unaffected before addressing his son. "Peyton, *use your words*."

Peyton's screams increase as my husband makes one last at-tempt, our son's wails like thousands of nails dragging across my skin. I can feel Whitney's stare on me as I do my best not to react. Resisting my urgency to stop the noise and give in. Anything to make it stop.

"Peyton O'Neal, I need you to use your words," Thatch says more sternly, but to no avail. I continue whisking rather than acting on the urge to pack my family up and take them home, if only to stop the humiliation.

Gracie chooses that moment to pop her head in from the living room and add her unhelpful two cents. "Oh my God, Peyton, shut up!"

"That's not what we were told to do," Thatch states, again for everyone within range in an attempt to make them understand—in hopes they'll see why we're in this stalemate with our kids. While I know their opinion shouldn't matter, I can't help the flush of embarrassment that covers me as I look over to my daughter.

"Say another word, Gracie," I manage to warn through Peyton's piercing noise, "and *we are* going home. Want to test me?"

Gracie stalks off as my mom speaks up.

"This is because I didn't let him lick a beater," she tells Thatch grimly through Peyton's cries. Just after, Wyatt runs in, looking for a limbless child, one who is bleeding or some other emergency that warrants the meltdown happening in the kitchen. His eyes widen when he sees his older cousin flailing like a fish with no visible wounds.

"Peyton, please, son, use your words," Thatch orders one last time as Brenden enters the room, fish-mouthed, his expression just as baffled. Briefly, Thatch drops his own head before lifting his eyes to every single onlooker, his words echoing through the kitchen. "Are we clear?"

Ruby, Whitney, Erin, Allen, and Brenden all nod before Thatch shifts his gaze to an utterly mortified Eli, whose expression has morphed into one of heartbreak.

The two brothers share a strained look before Eli dips his chin. Not a second later, Thatch scoops Peyton up and carries him out of the kitchen. His cries echo up the staircase, just as piercing until they die out with Thatch's retreat. My guess is that he took him all the way up to the attic, now deemed Whitney and Eli's Raggedy Ann and Andy Room.

"Holy fuck," my sister whispers mutely for me, her complexion paling rapidly. "You've been dealing with *this* for *how long?*"

"I don't know anymore," I whisper back, releasing a tear that rolls down my cheek. "I don't even know, Whitney."

"Jesus, Serena, I'm so sorry," jerking the mixing bowl out of my hands, she pulls me into her for a hug. "Yeah, no, this has to stop. I see it."

I pull back and kiss her cheek. "Thank you for getting it."

"Girl," she stares back in the direction Thatch fled. "We're at Defcon 1, and so I say it's time for a juice box. We're upping juice box night to tonight," she announces. "This is an emergency."

"'Tonight is your night, bro,'" Erin chimes in, letting us know she's down by sounding our motto. One Whitney and I stole from an old movie, "Twins," and use to announce when we're ready to behave badly. Our new tradition of girl's night—pre-Christmas edition, started years back and has turned into an annual bitch fest. One in which we drink far too much and have no-holds-barred convos. Just after Mom and I set the cake, Whitney pulls out her keys and nudges me. "Get your boots on, sis. We're about to stock up."

"You too," Ruby says to Brenden and Eli, who are still camped nearby at the kitchen table for moral support. "I want both your boots on the ground for Thatch tonight. After the clock strikes ten, you guys have to take over, but your father and I have got them all until then, understood?"

Unsurprisingly, Brenden speaks up first. "Mom-*may*," he says in perfect imitation of Peyton, "are you telling your baby boy to get a buzz tonight? Because if so, you could—"

"Ask me about the damned nog one more time, son, and I'll rip your winkie right off your body."

Brenden opens his mouth, and Mom digs her heels in, pulling the rare tone she uses to scare us even though we're all in our forties.

"I gave you life, and I'll take it away." Brenden swallows. "Take care of your brother, jackass. *Your needs* don't matter tonight."

Brenden has the good sense to remain quiet, though I know there are at least a dozen comebacks on the tip of his tongue. Eli grins at Brenden before turning to me. "I'll come with you two and get man night supplies."

"Tequila. It makes me ha*ppy*!" Brenden clips immediately in demand. "And don't be cheap, bro. We all know you're wealthy!" He belts before running from the kitchen, narrowly missing my mother's swinging wooden spoon.

Hours later, I'm sipping on a delicious fruity concoction Whitney threw together. One I'm almost positive includes every rum imaginable—dark, light, and lights fucking out. Aside from Mom's annual nog, Whitney is responsible for providing the rest of the Collins' Christmas booze supply for the week. No slacker now because as soon as she hears the sputtering of my crazy straw, she pops my lid, refilling my cup with her ready pitcher.

"I love you, bro," I tell her, giggling as the warm buzz starts to filter through me, the three of us huddled on the porch just outside the den.

"Okay, who wants to start?!" I ask between them, all too eager to give a confession I've been holding far too long. "Erin!" I exclaim, and she jumps as a hiccup escapes me. "How are things on the home front?"

"Awesome, actually, but Serena, why are you yelling?" she giggles, probably due to her own buzz. My little sister does not fuck around and is not at all stingy with her pour.

"I think my son blew my ears out," I tell her just as loudly, opening and closing my jaw to pop my ears before leaning in. "Huddle in bitches, I have news," I utter under my breath before I crank up the volume again. "I mean, I like my nail polish, but what do you think, Erin?"

"It's nice!" She shouts back as both of them stare at me like I'm growing a third ta ta. Wrapped in matching blankets, snow flurries

begin to dance between us, joining the party as Whitney scrutinizes me before speaking up.

"What the hell is happening right now? Are you cracking, sis?"
Erin stares on at me, equally as confused.

"You idiots," I hiss low. "Don't you remember how to play anything off? I told you to huddle in," I pop my head up, scanning the
windows before leaning in. "You're already blowing it, so *huddle in*."

They both lean in as I bulge my eyes. "The walls have ears."

"Ohhhh," Erin says, nodding.

"So you know what she's saying?" Whitney asks.

"Not really, no. Not at all," Erin says with a giggle as I palm my
face and lean further in.

"I think we're still safe for now, but Erin," I whisper, giving her
the come-hither finger.

"What?" she whispers, the rum buzz clear in her eyes.

"Get up and pretend you're adjusting your blanket around
you, but as you do, *very subtly* peek through the window to see if
the den is *empty*."

Erin immediately stands to follow my order and Whitney
grips her arm, narrowing her eyes on me as if I'm setting her up.
"What are you up to, sister?"

"Let her look, damn it. It's for the greater good," I say, tongu-
ing the crazy, twisty elf straw Whitney picked up while we were
out shopping for mixers.

"The den's all clear, why?" Erin asks, shivering as she rejoins us.

"I keep forgetting to tell you. It's like I get amnesia when
we leave this cabin. And Eli went shopping with us earlier, so I
couldn't, but . . ." I lean in, and they do, too. "You guys ever wonder *how* the guys *knew* not to ask us about asking what's for dinner? We know Eli told Thatch, but did you ever once question how
Eli knew in the first place to tell him? To tell Brenden? Because I
can promise you that's *one bitch* I kept to *myself* and only shared
with you because I choose my battles. And I can remember exactly

when we had that convo and it was *here*, on this deck, during our first girl's night," I pin Whitney, "Christmas twenty-*twenty-one*."

Both Erin and Whitney pause before their jaws drop, and I nod.

"That's right," I point to my sister, "the same year in which your husband joined the fam. And I think he's been spying on us *every year* since."

"Bullshit," Whitney defends before pausing and sinking into the idea.

"Yes honey, your husband's a dirty little eavesdropper. And he did it last year too because I got that present I told Thatch I really wanted when we got *home*."

"So, what's that prove? Make it make sense," Whitney defends.

"Because I set Mr. *Potato Ears* up," I state. "Thatch said, 'Amazon shipped it late,' but I knew better because I didn't want the exact teapot I saw on McGee and Co. website until *that night*—"

"I love McGee and—" Erin starts.

"Me too, but stay on point, sister. We have a snitch in our midst, and we all know in this family, snitches get *stitches*," I tell her. "Payback is in order, and we need to hurry up with a game plan before your husband cracks that window. I raise my hand and we all silently listen. "Erin, do one more check before battle."

"Battle?" Whitney gulps.

"All clear, and it does seem a little harsh," Erin states. "I mean, nothing but good has come out of it, right?"

"Horse shit, girl's night is *sacred*. It's not like we're crashing their ball sack pack party right now."

"Ball sack pack?" Whitney giggles.

"I just came up with it. What do you think?" I look between them, and they nod. "Anyhoo, we can't let them fuck with girl's night. And don't forget, we've shared plenty of girls-*only* shit out here too, probably stuff they've used *against* us."

"That fucker," Whitney giggles, lifting her sparkling finger. "I love him so much."

"Yes, *newlywed*, we know. Give it a few more years, and you'll have a healthy distaste for him like a real wife," I jest.

"No way," she says in denial as Erin and I give one another knowing grins.

"Hear that, Erin? Whit thinks they'll be different," I roll my eyes, my straw getting further away from my mouth with every sip as I perk my ears, and they tilt their heads, listening too.

"Still clear," Erin reports, now on a mission.

"Remember what else we talked about that night?" Whitney asks as we all still, racking our alcohol-soaked brains.

"Vaguely, but," Erin palms Whitney's arm as if she's just been doused by ice water. "The backward hat trick! Oh. Em. Gee, Brenden does it all the damned time now! It's why I got *pregnant* with Jameson," she fumes. "Your husband got me pregnant!" Erin booms at Whitney, who immediately bursts into laughter. "You know what I mean," Erin corrects before shaking her head, "that summamma bitch."

"Erin!" Whitney and I sound before gaping at her in shock. Reason is, that our sweet sister-in-law, who married into this family, is a borderline saint—especially after marrying our idiot brother.

"Twenty-*six* hours of labor and the epidural wore off," Erin justifies in one sentence.

"Oh yeah," I bob my head, "payback is in high order."

"Off with his head," Erin says mercilessly.

"I do love him, but I'm kinda living for this," Whitney laughs maniacally, rubbing her mitten-covered hands together. "So, what do you have in mind?"

"A tactic that always works called divide and conquer," I waggle my brows. "Something tells me we don't have much time, so follow my lead."

Too afraid to spook them by having Erin look, and knowing the clock is ticking, we all remain quiet for a few long minutes, racing one another on finishing our sippy cups. Just as Whitney releases her straw to call bullshit, we hear a tell-tale squeak, followed by a slide. The three of us lift our lips in matching Grinch smiles before we burst into Oscar-worthy chatter. It's Whitney, though, who goes straight for the gold when her comment cuts through the air, landing hardest.

"I think Eli is afraid to ask for a finger in the ass."

CHAPTER NINE

Thatch

"I THINK ELI IS AFRAID TO ASK FOR A FINGER IN THE ASS," Whitney booms so loud in announcement that I duck for cover as Brenden immediately dry heaves. Eli's eyes bulge out of his head before he shakes it like he just took a punch to the throat and is scrambling for recovery.

"Why do you think that?" Erin asks, concern in her voice as if it's everyday conversation, just as Eli furiously swats at us while Brenden and me chuckle like hyenas.

"Shut the fuck up," Eli whisper-yells. "I didn't tell you guys this year to get myself busted in *minute one*. And she's full of shit, I've never talked about anal—"

"I have a vibrating butt plug," Whitney interjects, cutting off his objection. "He drank tequila tonight. It makes him crazy. So, I'm going to lube him up and use it on him."

"The. Fuck. She. Is," Eli shakes his head adamantly, even as the tequila buzz crazes his icy eyes in a pretty damned distinguishable way.

"Do guys . . . really like that?" Erin asks. "I mean . . . really?"

"Millions of gay men can't be wrong," Whitney says.

"Side's," *hiccup*, "that's where their G-spot is," my wife slurs. "I'll give Thatch a pinky now and then. A little wiggle here and there, and he fucking blows."

Brenden full-on gurgle gags as Eli palms his mouth to stifle his laugh, and I whisper a pointed "fuck you" to each of them. Mortified of what's coming next, yet intrigued at their openness—especially Erin's surprising curiosity—I take my spot next to Brenden and tune in.

"Well, I'm determined to find out," Whitney states as Eli pales and shakes his head, his ramblings coming out scattered due to his terror.

"I have n-no idea where's she ge-etting dis," he swears, his words barely audible as he white-knuckles his beer. "I've never even broached the subject," he points straight up into the air as if in a great debate, "or shoved my ass anywhere *near her* in suggestion during sex."

"Hockey books," I deliver point blank, palming his shoulder. "Look for hockey books on her Kindle. And whatever you do," I look between them, "do not let them fuck you with a grapefruit. No matter *what* they say."

Both of their eyes bulge as I give what explanation I can.

"It's a very *short story* with a very, very *painful* fucking ending. That's all you need to truly know. Bros don't let bros grapefruit. That's love I'm giving you."

I hold out my beer, and they tentatively tap their heads to it. Though I've stuck to brew, the two of them started strong with back-to-back tequila shots before starting on their own beers. Both of them taking full advantage of bro night—a first for us since the girls started their tradition.

"Anal play isn't that out there," my wife states. "Tell Eli not to be a prude."

Brenden shakes his head, his expression looking queasy. "These are my *sisters*. I can't un-hear this. I'm out." When he goes to stand,

Eli yanks him back down, pointing a finger very close to his face in warning.

"You wanted to come, so sit your ass down. You're not fucking this intel up for me."

"Let's talk size," Erin blurts, and Brenden immediately lifts, sealing the window closed before turning to us.

"We've heard enough," Brenden declares, "we need to respect their privacy."

"Convenient," Eli snaps. "It's cool, bro. We know you have some confidence issues in the winky department." Eli winks. "It's clear your wife loves you for *you*," he chides further as raucous laughter bellows outside the house.

"Will you two shut the hell up. We're missing it!" I say.

Brenden leans in, clearly affronted, as he issues his threat to us. "I will knock both of you off this damn cliff with my glorious fucking stiffy."

"Glorious?" I chuckle. "Whatever keeps you confident, bro," I jibe and pat him with a consoling hand. "Now man up," I snap. "Eli, go ahead and crack that bitch back open."

"I knew it was a bad idea to let you two in on this," he shakes his head.

"I'm good," Brenden says. "Good," he takes a long swig of beer.

"We *have* gotten some priceless advice *and* gift tips over the years," I relay to Brenden as the girls break into more laughter, "and we're thankful, aren't we, B?" I nod toward Eli, who scowls at us, trust broken.

"Yeah, yeah, go ahead, we'll be good," Brenden promises, crossing his heart with a finger while holding out an obvious pair of crossed fingers at the same time.

"I've been at this four Christmases running, and you two are not going to fuck this up for me," Eli instructs as he covertly lifts his hand, pinching the window just so and opening it while flashing a warning glare between us.

"—husband's got perfect girth," Whitney says of Eli's junk,

which has him perking with pride. "I mean *perfect*. He's blessed and shares it with me—*often*."

"Brag away, but *my man* has the perfect dick," my wife announces as I swell with pride. "If I could hand-pick a dick, I would order Thatch's every time," Serena boasts as my junk weeps with happiness. "God, I swear the first time I saw it, the angels sang."

"Yeah, this is getting weird. That's my best friend," Whitney says. "Like, I've known him since I was still in an A cup fighting for B. Let's move onto a safer topic."

"Thank Christ," Brenden says.

". . . but before we do," Whitney cuts back in, "how are your men on hang time? Like . . . is five minutes short to you—"

Eli immediately shuts the window, and Brenden and I share twin shit-eating grins.

"What's wrong, bro?" Brenden quips. "Not fun when you're on the wrong side of it?"

"It's been a stressful year, okay? *Once,*" Eli spouts, his scowl for his oblivious wife, "*maybe* twice this year I didn't go long game. She's fucking exaggerating," he excuses in exasperation. "Besides, it shouldn't matter how long if you get the job done *for her, right?*"

Brenden and I nod because it's the brotherly thing to do. Blowing out a breath, clear fear in his expression, he cracks the window again.

"—Brenden's balls are weird, y'all," Erin delivers, and Brenden's jaw immediately unhinges. "Like, I know balls aren't attractive to begin with, but his just look . . . *weird*. Like two little old men. Like little bald men with pointy noses."

Shoving my beer between my thighs, I palm my mouth with both hands to stifle my laughter as Brenden cups his junk in indignation.

"I don't go there," Erin continues, "you know, tend to them. Ever."

On his knees, a now seething Brenden maneuvers himself to blast his venom through the screen. "You sit on a throne of lies, my treacherous wife."

Just after he releases it, Eli tackles him to the carpet, and I dodge them both, leaping for and closing the window as pained grunts follow.

"Co-vert. . . *You*. . . *Stupid*. *Ass*," Eli grits out before Brenden takes the bait, and the two roll around on the floor, mostly ruining the integrity of the other's sweaters with a touch of chin slapping between.

"Get the hell off me, *minute man*," Brenden goes for the jugular as they begin a death roll for dominance, and Eli claps back.

"Fuck you and your *Voldemort balls*," Eli fires. It's as I watch them wrestle—mostly each other's sweaters—that my Spidey husband sense goes off.

"Fellas, stop. We're turning on each other, and I think this ploy was intentional." Acting on my hunch as they go at it, I slowly, so slowly, lift enough to peek out of the window and, at that exact moment, manage to catch Serena glancing in the direction of the window I'm peering through.

Bingo.

Sinking down and turning my back against the wall, I can't help the smile blooming on my face as my grown-ass brothers continue to exchange love taps and low blows.

"You smell delicious," Brenden says, pulling at Eli's V-neck, "too bad your one squirt *won't last*."

"Well, at least," Eli manages through a triple chin tap from Brenden, "I get my balls sucked!"

"That's my sister, you sick bastard!" Brenden quips before Eli hooks the side of his mouth with a finger. "Take it bwack."

"This is why I don't drink tequila," I state as Eli—AKA the sane fucking brother—practically backhands Brenden and laughs maniacally.

"We're so fucking busted," I conclude, allowing them to get whatever alcohol-driven testosterone is fueling them out of their collective systems. Sometimes I guess guys just need to have a sweater slash bitch slap fight. Thankful those years are behind me, I decide to let them in on it. "They set us up."

Eli's face reddens as Brenden pins him, giving him two consecutive love taps on the chin with his fingers.

"And you idiots took the bait," I state as they continue to wrestle on the floor, "like amateurs," I spout aloud to no avail. "You're *being played*, idiots," I finally clip out loud enough to break them up. Both of them stop suddenly and slowly turn their heads toward me. Now straddling Brenden, Eli lifts his head a second before Brenden gives him pig nose.

"How do you know?" Eli inquires, nostrils lifted. "Four years and my spy record is fucking spotless."

"I just know," I quip, taking a long drink of my beer. "You're busted, 007, or should we call you 005?"

"Unhand me, you heathen," Brenden states, unraveling Eli's fingers from the neck of his sweater before shoving Eli off. Eli lands on the hardwoods with an "oof" before popping back up.

"Women should rule the world," I chuckle as the two of them start to straighten themselves. "We've so been set up."

"Prove it," Eli says.

"Happy to. But you'll have to stop acting like cave dwellers and get over here." Both start to army crawl over, but in a last-minute move, Eli thumps Brenden's dick and scurries ahead. Brenden recovers with a curse, catching Eli's ankle at the last second and dragging him back. Eli's eyes bulge as Brenden starts pulling him in horror movie style along the hardwoods before I grip his hands and yank him free.

"Fucking stop!" I whisper-yell. "We've probably already missed all the best shit, along with everything else we're being set up for. We can resume the fucking WrestleMania reenactment *later*."

Brenden snaps to, his eyes earnest. "Promise?"

"Yes, now, shut the fuck up and listen." They both crawl over as I press my finger to my mouth and inch it open.

"Oh, oh! Let's do an impression of someone in the family and name them!" Whitney suggests as Serena immediately dives in, clearing her throat dramatically. "If it's not about me, I don't care!"

"Brenden!" Whitney squeals as Brenden glares at the window, muttering, "witches."

"I've got one," Erin says. "Murderfucker."

"Peyton," Whitney giggles, and I frown, palming my face. Parent of the year.

"Here's one," Whitney says, "AHHHHHHHHHHHHHH about everything."

"Gracie," all three say in unison as Brenden and Eli shoot me a sympathetic look.

"Sorry, sis," Whitney says. "Too soon?"

"Hell no, it's good to laugh about it. Better than crying," she says, and I find my smile at that. "Okay, not to bitch," Serena starts, as my smile disappears because I have a feeling this particular bitch is about me. "But if Thatch ever says '"here we go again,' when I come at him for something important, I'm going to *Lorena Bobbitt* his ass."

"Who is Lorena Bobbitt?" Erin asks.

A pregnant pause ensues outside as Eli, Brenden, and I physically shudder. The name alone is enough to have every male in population Earth recoiling as they did back in '93.

"Bless your sweet, saintly soul," Whitney says. "I don't know if you can handle such debauchery."

"I don't like this," Brenden utters.

"But in the decade and year of our lord of ninety-something," Whitney continues, making Eli and I grin, "let's just say our friend Lorena, in short definition, became the unspoken hero of many a woman because of what she's notoriously known for."

The three of us share wary glances as my best friend clears her throat. "You see, dear sister, one sunny summer day—"

"Was it sum-mer?" Serena asks through a hiccup.

"I don't know," Whitney says, "hush, you're messing with the vibe I'm setting."

"Fine, but I think you should at least know the weather for this story."

"Do you know it?" Whitney barks.

"No," hiccup, "but a dark, moonless night and lightning seems appropriate," Serena adds.

"Fine, sis, it was a dark stormy night, and *shut up*," Whitney quips, the only female alive allowed to shush Serena. "Where was I?"

"A dark stormy night, hiccup," Erin says with a giggle, just as amused by their back and forth.

"Yes, you see, our sister in spirit, Lorena of the Bobbitt, had just discovered her husband was *cheating*. And in sooo ..." she pauses for theatrical effect as Brenden, Eli, and I tense at what's coming. "... she bid her time and decided to get even ... and so one night—"

A pause.

"Jesus, Serena, on the *darkest and stormiest* night ever—"

"Thank you," Serena hiccups.

"She *chopped off his dick* with a *kitchen knife!*" Whitney booms as the three of us jump back.

"No!" Erin gasps.

"YESSSSSSS!" Serena and Whitney say in unison.

"But get this," Whitney continues, "she took his dick with her when she fled her house and threw it in a field!"

"NO!" Erin bursts before erupting into maniacal laughter.

In response, Brenden raises his arm, simultaneously pulling his sleeve up his forearm to reveal goosebumps spreading like wildfire across his skin. "I'm fucking officially scared," he says before fixing his glare on Eli.

"*Mep*," Whitney says, her fondness for Peyton's old substitution for yes and her nephew in her delivery. Even as she uses it to regale the worst imaginable story. "Lorena straight up took the biggest one for our team. Did both the crime and the time being the first to take the verbal threat we've all made at one point to our men *next level* ... making her my unspoken hero."

"I really loved being your brother," Eli imparts gravely. "But I can't sleep next to my new wife anymore."

I grin as Serena speaks up.

"Mine too. Did she even do jail time? I'm going to Google it," Serena states.

"Why?" Whitney prompts. "Want to see how much time you'll serve if you hack Thatch's winky?"

"I really loved you both," I speak up in my own farewell. "I mean it," I add before looking pointedly at Eli. "Thanks for this. You've ruined my marriage."

"We married lunatics," Brenden deduces, and we all nod in agreement.

"Turned out pretty well for the husband, John, I think that's his name," Whitney informs. "He went on to do pornos after he got it sewed back on."

We all grimace at the thought, our shared pain visceral.

"Eww, and that's kind of fascinating," Erin says. "Unspoken hero," she giggles. The sound eerie now that the good, close to saintly sister has gone bad.

"My wife can't hang out with your wives any longer," Brenden states emphatically. "I won't have it."

"Damn, can you imagine? It's the ultimate revenge," Serena boasts, a little too dreamily, as I shake my head in disappointment and reply to Brenden.

"I don't blame you, man. Not at all."

"Okay," Whitney says, "let's list what offenses we would all cut our husband's dicks off for."

The three of us are now plastered to the wall, and we lean in, cupping our mouths to make sure not a syllable is missed as we hold our collective breath.

"If Thatch ever says 'here we go again,'" Serena states. "I will seriously consider that jail time."

"Put that on my list, too," Erin pipes as Brenden and I share an eye roll.

"Here we go again?" Whitney asks.

"Oh, you poor, clueless little newlywed. Well, good on you. That doozy is probably around four to six years into the marriage time-line. You've got time," Serena reports. "Cherish it."

"They're onto us," I decide. "We're busted," I look over to Eli. "Game over, Welch. You get an A for effort, but you should know by now there's very little you'll get past a Collins girl. Especially for this long."

"You're sure?" Eli asks, closing the window.

"Mep," I state, a tug in my heart because I can hear Peyton saying it.

"Well, shit," Brenden says, "that was pretty anticlimactic."

"That's what your wife said," Eli and I quip at the exact same moment before sharing a fist bump.

"Hey," Brenden snaps suddenly, and Eli and I jerk back. "I've got something for you both," he digs into his pocket a second before gifting us twin birds. "Here you go, this one's for you, yep, Merry Christmas."

"Shit, it's been fifteen minutes," I say, my buzz kicking in, "we need to check on the kids," I look at Brenden. "Or someone does."

"That's not that long," Eli says as Brenden and I both turn to him.

"That's forty-five years in parenting," Brenden relays. "Go, you have as many as I do."

"Uh, buddy, recheck your finger count because I'm pretty sure you have more winning sperms than I do."

"Which is as many as you, plus one more," he counters.

"Astounding logic, jackass, and Erin has custody of the diapered one tonight," I report. "So that's two and two. We're even."

"I'll go," Eli offers, shaking his head as we both ignore him because he has no idea what he's offering, and we're trying to keep him alive.

"Rock, paper, scissors?" I ask Brenden. He nods, and three taps later, his paper is covering my rock as I look over to Eli.

"If I'm not back in ten minutes, Peyton did it." He grins as I palm his shoulder. "It was a good run, bro, but mark my words, either they know or they *suspect*. These girls are playing us for fools, so don't let your pride bust you."

"Come on, *Lie*," Brenden jokes of Peyton's old nickname for him. The use of my son's ancient verbiage motivating me to go see what he's up to.

"Let's go find Mommy's eggnog," Brenden states to his newest and most impressionable brother. Though buzzed, I know Eli can hold his own.

"I can smell it's close," Brenden flashes him a wolfish grin. "Our party doesn't have to be over."

"Give it up already, man," Eli says, trailing him into the kitchen. "You're never going to find it."

Their voices fade as I pry open the window just in time to hear Erin's report.

"Ah, they left, just saw them go into the kitchen," she says, as I curse the fact that I have to go check on the kids, knowing something juicy is afoot. Just before I close the window, I hear the only thing I need to.

"Y'all, I know this might be fucked up to say, but I'm lusting after my husband lately."

"Really?" Erin says.

"Oh, I've seen it," Whitney says. "Just like the old days when y'all first started dating. I felt that static, sis. Good on ya."

"I miss that," Erin says.

"Well, good news is, it comes and goes in waves, so you appreciate it more, and yeah," she sighs, "I'm totally jonesing for him lately, and he's making it hot."

Shutting the window with the intent of making it even better due to her praise tonight, I head up the stairs and am stopped just short of the large media room by my son's voice.

"No, we are not cweaning up the toys till I say."

"Why not?" Wyatt asks. "My daddy said to clean them up."

"Yeah," Conner says, "we were supposed to a long time ago."

"This is my cwub, so I say when we cwean. We're playing now."

Walking up to the door, I see Peyton hovering over Wyatt and Conner, who are staring back at him like the little devil he is. Conner—who is over twice his age—looks intimidated and swallows as my baby leans in.

"What's going on up here?" I ask, frowning when I see Gracie isn't in the room. "Where's Gracie?"

Conner opens her mouth to answer as I swear to God, my four-year-old son holds up a hand and silences her before fixing his narrowing eyes on me. "Uh, no, no," Peyton says, charging toward me to stop me from entering. "No, this is my cwub, and we don't have mean daddies in our cwub."

"Excuse me?" I ask, affronted as I attempt to straighten to my full height. I really shouldn't have drank that fifth beer.

"Yes, you are excusetd, *Thatcher*," Peyton draws out the enunciation, his full-on bully in effect as visions of red and blue sirens dance in my head. He pushes at my stomach, full-on kicking me out and shutting the door slowly as he does this, spewing his verdict. "No mean daddies allowded."

Utterly stupefied my son has taken the bully route and is straight up rejecting me, I immediately stoop to his level just as he slams the door in my face.

"I don't want to be in your stupid club," I snap through the door, now closed an inch from my nose.

"Good, Daddy, 'cause you aren't in it!" Peyton boasts. The fucker. Rejection stinging, I press my middle finger to the wood and enthusiastically flip my four-year-old son off as I spout my rebuttal.

"It's probably boring anyway!" I shout.

"We're having so much fun!" Peyton shouts back. "We have pizza!"

"You better not have put that on my credit card!"

"I don't know how to credit card! Grammy boughted it!"

"You don't deserve it! You can't even use your tenses correctly!" I throw myself into it, lifting a second bird toward the door as I continue to make obscene gestures at my oblivious son. I even toss a leg up in the mix and shoot a bird beneath it as he goes in for the kill.

"Go away, *Thatcher O'Neal*."

"Happy to Peyton smears poop on the potty seat!" I snap. "It's bedtime anyway for me!" Turning to stalk back downstairs, I'm met by the unhinged jaws of my brothers and immediately point back at the door. "Did you see that? He's a bully and the ringleader!"

Eli and Brenden—perched on opposite sides of the top of the stairs—begin to collapse into laughter as I push past them, shaking my head in aggravation. "Fuck you guys," I say, still stinging as I glance back, only once, and meet my son's glare through a crack in the door before he slams it closed. The little shit.

"Did you see that!?" I point out, as Brenden starts to usher me away, and I strain against him, "he's the ringleader!"

Brenden glances back just as Peyton screams through the door.

"Go away, Daddy! We don't want you!"

"It's okay, buddy," Brenden consoles with a palm on my shoulder, "you can be in our cwub," he mimics as they guide me down the stairs, "'cause *we found* our mommy's nog."

CHAPTER TEN

Serena

MOM SETS THE PLATTER DOWN ON THE TABLE, HER EYES drifting to Thatch, who has hardly looked up since she called him in from the deck, all but ordering him to join us for dinner. His kisses still fresh on my lips from only hours before, I rattle across from him as Brenden and Whitney go back and forth, forever annoying Dad.

"Thatcher, sweetie," Mom coaxes. "Want some ham?"

"Yes, ma'am," he states, taking the large serving fork from her before pulling a tiny slice onto his plate.

"Shit, kid, nonsense, eat," she orders, emptying half the platter on his plate before Thatch chuckles through telling her to stop. I look between them as Mom keeps her prodding focus on him. It's when Thatch finally lifts his eyes to hers that I see it. It's as plain as day—guilt.

He's riddled with it, and it's no mystery why. It's for being with me. Kissing me, touching me. Maybe I should leave him alone. He's made it clear since night one that we're not a good idea. Even as I think it, I sink back into the memory I've been playing on repeat all day. It was just after he delivered one of the most intense kisses of my life. A collection of thundering heartbeats passed as our snarky back and forth ceased to exist. Dazed by the kiss, we stared at one another, buzzing with the connection between us. Lips close to touching, he'd threaded his fingers through my hair, cupping the back of my head while tenderly running his thumb along my cheek. I'd leaned into his touch as his whisper hit me straight in the chest.

"Jesus, baby, I can't . . . fuck, I can't get enough of you."

It was that moment that flit through my mind the second my eyes cracked open this morning, and it's that exchange that has me mentally willing him to keep fighting whatever reservations he has about us. If only so that we can have more of those moments. But as of this one, here and now, he's refusing to even look at me.

He regrets it, has to, and yet his behavior isn't really all that different than it was the first night at the table. Maybe it's just the way I feel. Am I alone in this? I can't be. He was there in every sense of the word last night.

Or, is it just that easy for Thatch to play things off? To play me? He said he wasn't by any means a gentleman but was trying—for me.

From the way he talks, it's like he's ashamed of who he is, but he's only twenty. Too young to have done so much damage already. Right?

These questions play on a loop as they have all day, the answers buried in the locked jaw of the guy sitting across from me. One I'm now allowing to fuck with my head. Even so, I told him this didn't have to get complicated. That it could be just fun. So why does it feel like this? Why is he the one making it so hard?

If he's a player, big deal. That I could deal with. I have before . . . but what exactly is his true damage? He confessed he's not in a good place with his parents but seems okay with it. The bigger question is, why do I care so damned much? The answer rings clear in my mind just after.

He's all I've thought about since I walked through my door after driving back from college. Meeting him in that shed is the only thing I've had to look forward to since—besides being home. Maybe I'm being selfish by forcing him to push past his protests. I know I am, but the last three months have been some of the worst I've endured in the last year. My attraction to him has been a welcome distraction from it. Because of *that, I'm most likely reading into this too much. Am I making something out of so little because I need it?*

Gah, Serena, could you be more pathetic?

But even as I convince myself I'm alone in it and pushing too hard, I feel his kiss. I hear his whispers. I continue to feed on the memory of the look in his eyes that told me I'm anything but alone. I'm drowning in him already, in his mystery, but it's keeping me from thinking about what lies ahead. About the return trip to school. Of what's waiting, which is turning out to be a whole lot of fucking nothing.

Though now, and as he continues to speak the bare minimum while flat out ignoring me, his sweet words are starting to mean less and less. Especially when he excuses himself to chop wood the minute he cleans his plate. As he pushes his chair back, I search him, his face, his expression for any sign, absolutely anything. A subtle twist of lips, a smirk, something to show me I'm reading this wrong. It's when I'm left with nothing that I glare at his retreating back as he walks out the door, not hesitating a single second.

Knowing that going after him is stupid and pointless and that I'll probably be waiting in vain tonight, I continue to stare in the direction Thatch left as Whitney sounds up.

"What did the back door do to you, sis?" *She chides. Feeling a complete fool now and knowing I'm making it obvious, I fix my glare on her. Whitney lowers her eyes, her grin growing as Mom scolds her.*

"Leave her alone, Whitney."

"What?" *She feigns innocence.* "She stares at him all freaky like, that's probably why he ran."

"I like him," *Brenden states, utterly oblivious.* "He watches WrestleMania, too."

"Second daughter," *Dad barks as Whitney whips her face toward him.* "Shut your pie hole and Son . . .?"

"Yes, Daddy?" *Brenden asks, batting his lashes.*

"Shut up forever."

"That's just not nice, Father. Oh! Can we have pie for dessert, Mom?" *Brenden shifts, utterly unaffected. Feeling Mom's eyes on my profile as she answers, I resist the urge to glance at the door. Stomach roiling, I put my napkin on my plate, hating the indecision I'm feeling. Hating that I have never had to work so fucking hard to get a guy to talk to me in my life. In a way, Thatch is giving chase, and like a damned fool, I'm fucking following like I don't know better. But I do. So why am I?*

Let him go, Serena.

Deciding to do just that, I'm just about to excuse myself when Mom speaks up. "Sun is setting. It's going to be dark soon."

She relays this in a nonspecific, roundabout way as she stares out the window, but I know her comment is for me. Glancing over at her and eager for any sign of encouragement, she forks some mashed potatoes and refuses me. It's only when chatter resumes at the table that her eyes finally find and settle on mine. A wordless second later, I excuse myself. Wrapping my scarf around my neck, I slip out the back door.

Head spinning from far too much rum, I meander into our temporary bedroom after checking on the kids, who, thankfully, are out. The shower runs in the adjacent bathroom as I fight my leggings off and discard my hoodie on the floor. Overheated and slightly nauseous, I curse the fact that my buzz is wearing off so soon, and the imminent hangover is sure to be an epic asshole. Not long after, I'm piling pillows to situate them when a smooth voice—one I know all too well—filters through the air.

"Evenin', Brat."

Looking up from the bed to the bathroom, I find my husband dripping wet, a towel wrapped and tucked around his waist, eyes fixed on me in an unmistakable way.

"No, no, Sir, no, tonight is *not your night*, bro," I state, unable to help my smile as he drops his towel with an 'oops' pressing his fingers against his mouth like a sexy starlet would.

I'm already laughing through my protest as he wiggles his junk just a little in some sort of sexy drunken man dance. "Oh, Jesus, Thatch. I'm already spinning. Please don't even attempt it."

"Sup, baby?" he ignores my signals entirely, the glazed look in his eyes saying it all as he dips his gaze downward to his cock. I follow suit, still shaking my head in the negative. "See anything you like?"

"No, player, I do not. Tonight's not it, Thatch, so what are you doing? Oh, don't you fucking dar—" but it's too late. He's already got his meat stick in hand and has started the propeller on his fucking . . . helicopter.

"Who in the world of fucking stupid told you that was sexy?" I ask, rolling my eyes as my man starts to really work it, his propeller at full speed as he answers confidently.

"You did, wife of mine."

"The hell I did. Never in the history of *ever* have I told you that's sexy. Stop it this instant," I demand as he chuckles, working himself to the point he could get airborne as I sigh. "And we were on such a hot streak. You just ruined it."

"Yeah?" he teases, dropping it, "what's wrong, baby? Are the *angels not singing?*"

In an instant, I'm on my knees on the mattress and pointing at him accusingly. "I fucking knew it!"

"Yeah, well, I did too, minute one," he says, sauntering into the bedroom buck naked. "But," his eyes glitter down on me as he moves to stand at the edge of the bed. "I owe you one for making me look so damned good in front of the boys," he runs a finger down his cock suggestively, "*him* especially."

"It was *all for show!*" I refute as he pounces, tackling me beneath him on the bed before his expression dims.

"So the angels really didn't sing?" He pushes his bottom lip out in a pout.

"They might have sputtered a note or two," I grant as he moves to lay on his side and runs his finger playfully along the top of my panty line.

"So, you wouldn't pick my dick out in a police lineup?" he whispers, a perma-grin on his lips.

I can't help my own. "Exactly how drunk are you, Thatchalamewl?"

"A six-pack and three nogs in," he reports. "You?"

"Rum, far too much of it and too soon. I should have eaten more. This is going to hurt like a bitch. I took my Advil and drank a bottled water. Did you prep for battle, baby?"

He nods before grinning. "God, you're brilliant," he murmurs before kissing along my stomach. "Maniacal and evil, but brilliant."

"How do you know it was me?"

"I know my wife," he runs his palm along my skin. "That performance was all fueled by you, though, best-supporting actress definitely goes to Whitney for 'Lorena of the Bobbitt.'"

We both laugh as I pluck at his picked-through hair. "When did you *really know?*"

Bending, he begins licking along my navel, mumbling.

"What's that?" I ask, tugging his hair.

"No more information, it's bro code."

"Nope, our bond wins, always, and you know that." He continues his ministrations as I pull harder. "Thatttttch," I urge.

He kisses a pattern around my belly button before his grin wins out. "Fine, I knew when my soldiers got into a sweater fight."

I frown. "A what?"

"It was epic. They went feral, Eli has a dark side," he chuckles. "You know, it's pretty awesome being the veteran husband of us three," he declares dreamily as he traces the curve of my breast and dips to flick his tongue against it. The pull begins below, but I'm already feeling like shit and decide that . . . soon. Very soon.

"Baby, I'm seriously overheated and feeling gross, or I would totally pay homage to your beautiful penis."

He nods and continues kissing his way up to my lips, laying one on me before pulling away with his declaration. "Well, I'm holding out on you anyway."

"Really?" I can't help my grin. "Going to be stingy with the penis like you were when we started?"

"Oh yeah, I'm going to make you *beg for it*," he declares in a tone I haven't heard in years.

"Well, be that as it may, honey, you just helicoptered me. It will take *weeks* to erase that image."

"Challenge accepted," he drawls, his eyes glazed with his buzz. "Oh, and fair warning, the girls are *in for it* tonight. I warned them not to, but Brenden is possessed."

"Oh shit," I chuckle, "how *in for it?*"

"In for it, Whitney especially," he draws on my nipple—hard—before laying his head on my stomach and angling it to gaze up at me. "And when I feel better and can pinpoint which of the three of you is a real target, so are you, Serena O'Neal."

"Hmm."

"Ready yourself, woman," he warns, tracing a lazy circle around my responsive nipple. Ten minutes later, Thatch drools on my stomach as I grin down at him, having lulled him to sleep with the stroke of my fingers through his hair. Our position the same as it is most nights. Him lying on my chest as I absently rub his beautiful strands. Most nights, I'm distracted, the act more routine, but tonight I find myself soaking him in a little more. The strength of his nose, the cut of his jaw. His dark blond lashes. And though the eyes beneath his lids are currently dormant, over the years, I've been the recipient of thousands of looks, both good and bad. But since the night we truly decided on one another, Thatch never denied me his eyes and has never stopped looking back. Running my fingers through his featherlight, strawberry hair, I utter my whisper more for me than him. "I love you, Thatcher O'Neal."

CHAPTER ELEVEN

Thatch

S WINGING THE AXE, I BRING IT DOWN AGAINST THE WOOD and shatter it in two as I feel the weight of a gaze before propping another piece up to split.

"Hey," Serena drawls as she approaches. "You've been at it for a while," she thrusts a bottle of water in my peripheral as I sound my warning.

"Give me a little space." It comes out clipped and tense, and I see her posture draw up in offense as I manage to land another perfect cut. The wood falling in pieces along the side of the stump. It's taken me weeks to be able to do it, and like woodworking, I find satisfaction in it. I came out here in hopes the workout would help exhaust some of the thoughts circulating in my mind—particularly my thoughts about the girl standing feet away. Fat fucking chance of that with the way she's looking at me. After wordlessly positioning another piece, a water bottle lands at my boot, and I look up to see Serena now skewering me with her stare.

"You're welcome."

"Sorry," I say, picking up the offered water.

"Yeah, I'm getting that you are."

"I'm swinging an axe, Serena, which requires concentration."

"So you do regret it. Message received."

"You don't get it because there is no message."

"You've been nothing but hot and cold since the 'fun' started, so I'll skip the mind fuck, Thatch. Take care." She turns on her boots and starts to stalk back to the house.

"I'm not trying to be a dick," I call after her.

"Well, no effort necessary. You're succeeding without any."

"I don't regret it," I snap at her retreating back, "but I should."

"Why?" She stops and turns back to me. "Stop being subliminal and just fucking come out and say it already."

"It got more heated last night than it should have, and you know it."

"And? So what. It was consensual."

"We were in a fucking shed."

"Well, any time you want to ask me on a date, Thatch, I'm all ears."

"I can't date you."

"Like I said, message received."

"I didn't say I don't want to," I admit through an exhale.

"So then, ask me."

"I can't do that, either."

"Jesus, man, I'm cool with the brooding vibe and the vague answers, but it's clear you have something going on."

"Just the opposite, I have nothing going on." But you.

"There's something—"

"I don't want to tell you, in case that isn't obvious, and it fucking is, because I made it so!" I snap. "So stop asking me."

"Fine," she stalks up to me, her eyes drilling, demanding to see inside as I keep my shaking guard up, refusing to let her get as deep as she did last night. It felt too fucking good—and terrifying. Because it felt real and right. Which has fucked with me every second since making it the opposite of fun.

"Do you like me or not?" She demands.

I pause the axe. "Are you fucking joking?"

"You can want to fuck me and not like me. It's not unheard of."

Palming the top of the handle, I gaze over at her as the sun sinks between the naked trees behind her. Puffs of crisp air leave her as her eyes implore mine for any truth. Even in the dimming light, her vulnerability is everywhere—in her posture, expression, and gorgeous eyes as she allows me to glimpse it. The way she did so many times last night. Serena in the raw is the most beautiful thing I've ever laid eyes on. That being the most dangerous fucking part of all of this. I wasn't prepared for it, and I've never felt anything like that with a girl. With anyone. A draw so raw, so magnetic, it felt as if it was meant—fucking made for just us. Her question of liking her lingers in the air as I manage to find my voice through the shit the recollection of last night stirs.

"Do I like you? I've made that obvious, too."

"Then . . . I have no idea what to think," she goes to stalk off, and I reach out and grip her arm.

"This isn't a teen melodrama, so stop talking in absolutes, throwing tantrums, and trying to stalk off. You want to have a conversation? Then let's have it. I'm being honest and straight-up telling you I'm no good for you. What don't you get about that?"

"It's not that seriou—"

"I can still taste you, and all I've been thinking today is that I want to do it again. That's enough to fuck with my head. And you want that too." I step up to her, and she instantly lifts her eyes, her mouth, herself for access.

"So, if you keep pushing me, I'm going to take what you're offering—that I'm undeserving of—and without apology. I'm trying to be a better fucking man, Serena, but I'm nowhere near there yet."

Her eyes flare with intrigue. "Fine with me."

I shake my head in exasperation as she tilts hers.

"You can keep telling me you're no good for me, and I'm wondering why that's even an issue. We barely know each other."

"Exactly, so, what, I just use you?"

"Who says I'm not using you?" She retorts.

"You don't want that."

"Yeah, 'cause I'm a nice girl?" she licks her lips, her condescension clear.

"Maybe you aren't, but you aren't that girl either."

"Are you asking?"

"Did it sound like a question?"

"Jesus, we're going in circles here. Last night was—"

"Take one more step toward me, Serena—"

She steps up to me instantly, and I grip her arms, pinning them behind her back and bringing her flush to me. Pulse pounding, I issue my last warning.

"I'm no good for you."

"Do it, Thatch," she orders in challenge a second before I crush her mouth. Our kiss immediately goes inferno as she fights to free her hands, and I keep them idle, knowing her touch will be too much. It's when I pull away to release her that she refuses me. Palming my neck, she kisses me with just as much behind it as the one I just delivered. My protest dies on the tongue gliding against hers as I deepen it. Her frozen fingers start exploring as she feverishly sucks my tongue.

Hands roaming, she works a path beneath my shirt and runs them up my sweat-slicked skin. It's then I start thrusting my tongue into her mouth, like I would my cock, delving into every corner. Claiming and consuming while memorizing her taste. Embedding the curl of her reciprocal tongue into memory. She's so goddamned perfect, every inch of her.

But what's more perfect is the way she kisses me back. The way she seems to understand everything I'm refusing her. Hard, aggravated, and coming close to fucking her to within an inch of her life just yards from her father's back door, I rip myself away a second time.

It's her arresting eyes that recapture me again as I stare down at her. It's possessive need which prompts the question that spills, unchecked, from my lips. "How many men have you kissed that way?"

"I think you know how many—"

"Then tell me again that it's not that serious."

"You kiss me back the same way," running her palm back up my bare chest, she digs her nails into my skin, knowing full well what it's doing to me.

"Fucking brat," I utter as her lips lift in victory. "You want to 'have fun' with me, Serena, fine. But this probably isn't going to end well," I warn.

"Your worry, not mine. Tonight," she whispers in order and without hesitation as she scores her nails once more down my chest. I'm so fucking hard for her that my cock is weeping in my boxers. "And since we can't manage conversation, we don't have to talk."

"Stop," I demand as she digs her nails in a little deeper, and my dick strains against my fly.

"Make me, Handy Man," she chides before lifting and pressing her lips against mine again.

"Weak at best," I drawl of her kiss, allowing part of the depravity I've been repressing to take over. "You're going to have to give me a better reason to come back."

"Didn't I?"

"It's a matter of incentive," I challenge before she lifts, palms my neck, and kisses me ferociously, clawing my raging dick briefly before pulling away.

"See you tonight."

Fuck. Fuck.

Fuck.

Not long after, Allen approaches me, an envelope extended in his hand. Hesitantly, I take it. Thanking him before pocketing the money.

"That should do it, right?" He asks as guilt threatens to swallow me whole.

"Close, yes. Allen, listen, I can't thank you enough—"

"No, Thatch, you earned it. Every penny."

"I hate this. I wish things were different. I wish—"

"I would have paid three times as much for delivery of this wood." He eyes the growing pile. "You've overdone it."

I nod as a baited silence runs between us. "Allen, I need to talk to you about Serena—"

"Have you told her?"

I swallow. "No, Sir. I don't see the point—"

"You can't start out that way."

"There's nothing to start—"

"It's already started, son," he gives me a pointed look. "So let's not play ignorant."

"Why did you do it?" I ask. "You know that it can't last."

He shrugs. "Our daughter was coming home no matter what, and we both wanted you to meet her. Thatch, you know you're like family to us now, right?"

"And you really approve of this?" I ask as he tucks his fingers into the back of his jeans, his return stare intent as if he's asking himself the same.

"We made an introduction. That's all we did, but we had a feeling you two would get on well. Truth is, we hoped you would."

"But if—"

"Start with honesty, the way you did with my wife and me."

"We can't start, Allen, and you know why."

"You're lying to yourself and right now, to Serena. Just tell her."

"Or you will?" I ask, swallowing.

He pauses, no offense in his return gaze as he reads the hesitation all over me. Stepping forward, he palms my shoulder.

"We love you, Thatch," he releases so easily, a burning ball instantly lodges in my throat, my eyes stinging as sentiment mutes me. "You just don't believe it, but we wish you would."

Grabbing an armful of wood, he starts the short walk back to the house and pauses, glancing at me over his shoulder as the earth swallows the last of the daylight. "We trust you because you've earned it. But if I'm honest, I've trusted you since day one."

Eli, Brenden, and I congregate mutely at the kitchen table as every drop of alcohol we consumed seeps out of our collective pores. Being the saints they are, Ruby and Allen whisked the kids away to a local inn for breakfast. Something they started to do after the first girl's night. Sadly, they weren't so charitable today after seeing the state of the cabin this morning. Issuing orders to Eli and me to clean the place up before they make it back this afternoon.

Then, they stole mine and Brenden's trucks to fit our herd of little people in.

Seemed just.

Even more so as I glance around to see the living room littered with toys, various bags, and other items necessary for the day-to-day. Though there's only been the addition of one new grandchild in recent years, the family has grown larger with Eli. The cabin, though spacious, barely houses all of us at this point.

"I must hate myself," Brenden whines as we brood at the table while the women sleep it off upstairs. Though I could have sworn Serena started stirring when I got up not long ago. "Or my life," he carries on, "because I tried to die last night. Jesus, you guys weren't kidding about the level of hangover multiplying by every year after *forty*."

"Welcome to hell," I grin over the brim of my steaming coffee cup.

"One day you'll learn to listen to your elders," Eli chuckles, then frowns. "But, there was *something* in the air because you guys know I don't drink often, and even *I* got a wild hair last night."

"More like a *hairball*," I give him a pointed look before glancing out of the floor-to-ceiling cabin windows.

"Speaking of wild—" Brenden spouts, and I clear my throat loudly after catching all three of our wives descending the staircase in my peripheral. It's as they approach that I start to notice Erin can't look at Brenden, or rather is *avoiding* looking at him. And Whitney . . . is not walking right. Serena sniggers behind them, catching my eye and winking as all three women wordlessly head straight into the kitchen toward the coffee pot. As the quiet lengthens with no greetings exchanged, I begin to sense the start of a cold war. Glancing between Brenden and Eli, I see their posture tensing as their collective eyes lower.

"You dumb bastards," I say. "You let your egos win and busted yourselves."

"Let's hear you say *five minutes* now, *Bee*," Eli hisses, butchering his pet name for Whitney as his eyes trail his wife into the kitchen.

"Lack of *ball service* not a hot topic for you today, huh, *traitor*?" Brenden mutters after his own wife before looking between us. "Probably because she wrote them a fucking sonnet."

"We get it," Eli cuts in, "you got ball service last night."

"And you're a saint? Do you want to tell me why my sister is walking like a fucking baby goat this morning?"

Eli grins into his coffee mug as I issue a grave warning. "You don't get your wives back while they're drunk." As if in afterthought, they both look at me, fear quickly replacing their smug expressions. "You don't do that, boys. And you're about to learn the hard way as soon as they get caffeinated."

I draw the sign of the cross in the air over each of them as they both pale. As if on cue, ramblings sound from feet away before a sinking feeling filters through the air.

"Oh, Eliiiiiii," Whitney calls, mimicking 'Here's Johnny' from *The Shining*. A paling Eli turns to address her call just as Whitney pulls the butcher knife from the block. "Want to help me in the kitchen, honey?"

"I would," Eli audibly gulps, "but I-uh, already told Thatch I would chop the wood—"

"And make pantakes?" She laughs maniacally, probably from some inside joke they share, as Eli goes ghost white. Brenden's no better for wear as his jaw inches down. Glancing over, I catch Erin full-on glaring at him over the top of her coffee mug.

"Told you," I chuckle as both men turn to me. "I'm going to chop wood and leave you two to the house. But HAVE A NICE DAY!"

They both jump back, recoiling in horror as Whitney grabs the sharpener from the block and begins scraping the knife down it theatrically.

Glancing up, I give Serena the 'come hither finger' and head into the den. As I'm wrapping up, she meets me there, giggling. Both of us giddy, I lift a finger to my mouth and lift my chin in indication for her to turn back.

From our vantage point, we get the most epic view of the stare-off happening between the livid ladies in the kitchen versus the gents currently pissing their pants in fear at the table. The lingering silence hysterical before I open the sliding door and whisk Serena outside. She immediately starts to shiver as she rubs her hands together.

"Oh, this is too fucking good, Thatch!" Serena says. "And you know what, for once, I'm glad it's not us doing the bickering."

I pinch her chin. "We don't always bicker."

"Uh, yeah, we do," she counters instantly.

"Okay, we do, and yeah, this time it isn't us."

"Just let me revel in it," she says.

"Gotta admit, I love it when our code trumps other codes, and it works to our advantage. And I wouldn't change shit, Serena."

"Me neither, babe," she shivers again, and I warm her hands between my gloves. "Okay, I'm freezing, I'm going to head back in."

"Before you do, I just wanted to say," I run my gloved finger down her cheek before tracing the top of her pajama top, "I'm sorry I was a little too buzzed to *properly* thank you last night."

"The show was enough, honey," she rolls her eyes, and I chuckle. "Besides, I thought you were holding out?" She shivers again, and I lean in and take her lips soundly.

"There are *other ways* to thank you, Mrs. O'Neal."

"Hmm," she says.

"Babe, real quick, where did Gracie disappear to last night?"

"She was in the Raggedy Ann room, *reading*."

"Oh . . . reading?"

"A starter book. Good news is, she hasn't stopped. Without her phone, she's hooked."

Her confession has me pausing. "It's not like a *grapefruit-sugges-tive* book, right?"

"No, Thatch, no," she snaps. "What kind of mother do you think I am?"

"Sorry, I just . . . don't want her getting any ideas so young."

"It's a romance, but it's *age-appropriate*, thank you very much, and don't be so quick to judge *me*. I heard through the grapevine that you got kicked out of a four-year-old's club last night."

"Nothing is sacred. Nothing," I snap. "Bro code is a myth."

"Well, you sang like a canary," she grins, "and only got a little titty."

I drop my jaw. "Not nice, Brat."

"Yeah, well, maybe I'm not nice, *Handy Man*."

"Oof," I grin. "Someone is acting like they want to be punished."

"Nah," she drawls, giving me a quick once over, "you don't have it in you anymore."

In a flash, I'm gripping her messy bun and darting my tongue along her bottom lip. Her lips part as she chases my kiss, and I dodge her eager mouth. "I guess we'll see."

"You're an awful lot of *talk* lately, Thatcher O'Neal."

I tighten my hold a little and lean in, allowing her to see the multiple ways I plan on violating her before bending to whisper directly in her ear. "I'm still in week one," I whisper heatedly. "Remember *that*?"

She's nodding when I pull away before opening the door and smacking her ass. "Get in there. It's freezing, but," I rake my teeth suggestively, "plan on reminiscing a little later."

She shivers either due to the cold or the promises in my eyes, her gaze lingering on me a little longer after she steps in, and I slowly close the door.

CHAPTER TWELVE

Thatch

PIPING THE LAST OF THE ICING ONTO MY GINGERBREAD HOUSE, I rear back, eyeballing my handiwork. This year, I'm determined to be the one to get the first cup of snowman soup. Love to my brother-in-law, I'm the fucking architect—or close enough to one—and am destined to win the grand prize this year for the annual gingerbread house competition. The prize being the coveted first cup of snowman soup. Eli has been sipping the first mug every year since joining this family, and this Christmas, I'm determined to break his winning streak. Just as I add the last of the candy-swirled lamp posts, I spot my competitor descending the stairs in my peripheral.

"You don't have shit on me this year, bro," I call out to him. "Not a chance."

Peyton bristles next to me, eyeing my house with envy, his grudge for me still evident in his eyes as he utters a very diva-sounding "what*eva*."

Leaning over, I sniff my son's head. "Peyton, you stink. You need a bath and different clothes."

"I don't have any!" He shouts in exasperation as if it's been weighing heavy on his mind.

"Bet you're glad you packed all those toys instead of clothes, huh?" I taunt like a fellow toddler as he stabs at his gingerbread house with icing.

After a rough start after mystery Rudolph—including Peyton's meltdown, which led to an even rougher girl's and boy's night—once the matriarchs returned to their sparkling cabin, Allen demanded that his Christmas itinerary be put back into effect. No more deviations allowed.

With only two full days left before the main event and our typical Christmas prep cut short by the holiday falling midweek, we're now working double time to fit it all in. Starting with the gingerbread houses today, tree decorating is to commence tomorrow night. Followed by The Collins family karaoke before midnight mass on Christmas Eve.

Pausing the workings of my hands and ready to claim my prize, I glance over to the imposter who hasn't even begun to construct his house. Frowning when I see him frozen at the bottom of the stairs.

Looking utterly lost, he takes one giant step forward and pauses, palming the air as if it's helping his equilibrium before taking another. Laughter threatens as I stare on at him before noting something is fucking . . . *off.*

"Hey, Eli?" I call in concern, which has him jumping back in terror. His ice-blue eyes find mine before he darts them away and then slams them back into me.

What. In. The. Hell?

"What are you doing, Uncle Eli?" Peyton shouts as if his uncle has gone hard of hearing before glancing over to me, a nervous giggle leaving him. "Are you taking big, *big* steps? Is this a game?"

Forever in a bromance with his uncle, Peyton joins him in the hall, taking giant steps along with Eli as he continues to make his grand entrance.

"The hell?" Brenden asks from where he sits at the end of the table. Wyatt in his lap as he continually mushes their gingerbread house into a slobbery mix of goo in his hands. Their foundation never had a chance. *Amateurs.*

Completely unaffected that his son is an underachiever, a grin simpers on Brenden's lips as he, too, scrutinizes our brother.

"Getting your lunges in, bro?" Brenden asks through a chuckle, equally baffled.

"Baby?" Whitney prompts her husband from where she sits at the other end of the table, eating some leftover chicken spaghetti. Her fork stops midair as Eli takes one last giant leap for his kind before leaning against the wall as if exhausted.

"What. Is. Happening?" Brenden blurts before bursting into laughter.

"Peyton," Eli exhales in affection before kneeling in front of my son and pulling him in for a tight hug. "I love you so much, little guy."

"You acting weally weird, Uncle Eli, but you can be in my cwub."

Stab.

Tossing salt on the wound, the little shit looks back at me, *grinning* because he knows.

"Am I weird?" Eli jerks to standing. "Well, I'm," he looks over to where Whitney sits at the table, frowning at him. "You going to eat that?" He asks her where she sits, both frozen and terrified, her fork poised halfway to her mouth.

"Eat the food on my fork, babe?" She giggles nervously.

Eli stalks straight toward her and takes her bite of spaghetti, and she gapes at him.

"Savage, man," Brenden says. "I approve."

"Jesus for Christ!" Peyton exclaims.

"He's got my vote," Brenden jibes. "What is in the water this week?"

I glance over to see Ruby watching the interaction from where she's wiping down the counter in the kitchen. Her rag paused before a knowing smile upturns her lips.

"Mom," I call, and her eyes dart to mine, suspicion brewing in her expression. "What's going on?" I mouth.

"Beats me, kid, but then again," she lifts her chin toward Eli as if telling me to watch.

Eli gently pulls out a seat and slowly, so slowly, sits in front of Whitney as if introducing himself as a chess opponent before summoning another bite.

"Can I have more of that?" Eli asks, practically batting his eyelashes.

"Baby, there's a whole bowl of it in—hey! DUDE!" Eli, having snatched her fork, already has a third bite in his mouth before Whitney has a chance to fully object.

"So very savaaage," Brenden gushes in encouragement.

"Eli," I prompt, examining him closely. "What were you doing before you came downstairs?"

"I was cleaning," he animates in a way I've never seen, all his features twisting at once. "Toys everywhere, everywhere, I mean *everywhere*." He drops the fork suddenly and presses his forehead to Whitney's. "You're so fucking cute."

"Ohhhh," Wyatt says. "Bad word." I stare over at him, positive it's the only thing he's said since he's been here.

"Good on you," I tell him before flitting my attention back to Eli.

"Little ears, Eli," Whitney scolds even as she giggles at her husband's curious animation. "Mom, did Eli find your eggnog?"

"I will kill you," Brenden states. "If you drank it all, I'm taking your present back."

"Daddy!" Peyton draws out in a panic as Eli starts to kiss Whitney's hand and arm, leading it up to her lips.

"Eli," Brenden chuckles, "you have the Raggedy Ann room if you want to do disgusting things to my sister."

Whitney turns her head helplessly as Eli assaults her with crazed kisses while telling her she's adorable.

"Eli," I summon in fear, and he jerks back and stares over at me, his ice-blue eyes glazed, or rather *blazed*.

"Dude, did you get lost in the trees with Serena? Been cleaning the garage, man?" I ask, knowing he's well aware of our code.

"No, I *was cleaning!*" He insists before making puppy noises at Whitney for more spaghetti. "More, please? Please, baby, *please?*" Utterly terrified, she dips the fork into the spaghetti and gives him a bite.

"I love you," he coos, chewing slowly as Whitney looks back at us helplessly before narrowing her eyes. "Which one of you did this?"

Brenden and I immediately lift our palms in innocence as Allen's deep, vibrating snore reaches us from his recliner. His ears resting on the end table beside him. I can't help but think the man a genius as Whitney goes fast forward squirrel on our asses as we frantically plead our innocence. When Whitney gets no satisfaction from Brenden and me, she turns back to Eli and cups his jaw.

"Baby, you're acting really strange. Did you *take* something? Find something in the medicine cabinet?"

"No, but I feel . . ." Eli presses both his hands to his chest. "Different. My heart is beating really fast." He grabs her palm and presses it to his chest as Whitney starts to panic.

"Eli Welch, you need to tell me right now *exactly* what you did upstairs."

"I just told you, I cleaned," he drops his hands to shovel in another bite of spaghetti, "oh, and I ate some of those gumdrops in Gracie's purse."

Ruby instantly makes a beeline for the stairs as I freeze, and Brenden's eyes float to mine just as the doorbell rings.

My wife is the one to get to the peephole first, our entire world stopping when her fear-filled voice fills the chaotic cabin. "Oh my God, it's Aunt Gretchen."

"Gretchen, we weren't expecting you until *tomorrow*," Ruby greets from downstairs. Their mixed voices easily heard from where we are upstairs in the media room. Both of us perched on the carpet as

I sit next to Eli, who's lying on his back, his legs propped up against the wall, his hand white-knuckling mine. He's convinced he's having a heart attack and attempting to get the blood flowing back in the right direction. It took us a full five minutes of scrambling to finally answer the door. Half of which I wrestled Eli to get him upstairs, the other to get him in a comfortable position to have his freak out. Not only is he stoned for the very first time, but he's also fucking gummy stoned, which has hit him ten times harder.

"It's just a buzz, buddy," I assure him as he continually pales to a ghastly white.

"It's not a buzz, I'm dying. I can feel it coming, and it's getting dark in here," he taps his temple and turns to me, his face terror-stricken. I can only imagine the faces of those downstairs dealing with the nightmare that is Allen's sister. Otherwise known as Wretched Gretchen. Her annual presence always a looming dark fucking cloud and made worse with every visit. Whitney hit the nail on the head when she described her as Ursula the Sea Bitch. She looks almost exactly like her, sans the tentacles. No less formidable than she's been every single year, Eli has played buffer with her the last three Christmases. However, with this year's buffer now in my presence, I weigh my luck in dealing with him in this state or being down there to deal with Gretchen and quickly decide I'm better off. Though I do fear for my wife and children.

Whitney decided to stay downstairs and cater to her aunt in an attempt to get her fed and gone.

"Where is Eli?" Gretchen's voice trails up, and Eli's eyes bulge in response. Right before my eyes, he breaks out in a sheen of sweat, his upper lip coated as he stares over at me, eyes watering.

"She's come to drag me to hell."

"He's sleeping, Aunt Gretchen," Whitney answers, "he's not feeling well."

"He could, at the very least," Gretchen counters, "make an attempt to *greet me.*"

Eli furiously shakes his head as Whitney takes the possibility off the table.

"Could be Covid, so it's better not to take any chances.

Brilliant sister, no one fucks with that one!

Silence follows, *winning* silence until . . .

"I have Covid?" Eli says. "Oh, God, this is so bad." He pounds his feet against the wall, and I palm his calves to stop him.

"No, man, no, stop, you're good," I console.

"What was that racket?" Gretchen asks.

"Gretchen, how do you like the cheese ball?" Ruby prompts as I position Eli's legs down, and he kicks them right back up, shaking his head furiously back and forth while re-gripping my hands.

"Should I tell you my darkest secrets?" He offers, and I instantly open my mouth to stop him and stop myself instead.

Fuck it.

I'm going to hell anyway. I warned Serena I was bad news, and because she didn't listen, now we've bred demons. One of which poisoned him today, and so, it's only fitting that karma has battered us again. Determined to go down with some dirt on my squeaky-clean bro-in-law, I immediately speak the words of the devil, which is now firmly perched on my shoulder.

"Yes, if you want absolution, you absolutely should."

"I masturbate regularly," he immediately starts, "but not too often."

I cringe. "Let's skip the sexual debauchery for now."

"Oh . . . well, that's all I have to confess."

"That's all?"

"Yeah," he nods.

"Figures," I blow out a breath. Eli's a hard man for another not to try to measure up to. Over the years, I've found myself doing it more than I'm comfortable with. But it's his history that doesn't keep me envious. He's fought really hard to get to where he is in life. His path to Whitney tracked with loss, self-discovery, and a hell of a lot of fight. It's in thinking about that that I lean in, gripping him tighter to help him through the worst of this.

"Eli, I promise you, you're going to be fine, man. You're going to live a long, happy life with Whitney." He nods as I add, "and kid-free."

"We get sad sometimes . . . about the kids—or *no kids*," he admits, and my heart sinks. They both married just edged into their forties, and sadly, a part of their paths led to their inability to have children.

"Ever think about adopting?"

"No," he studies his hand, opening and closing it, "we decided not to because we have yours to shower with affection. We like the perk of giving them back. So don't keep them from us no more."

"I'm sorry, bro. I won't."

"It's cool, but, man. I love Peyton so much. I mean, don't get me wrong, I love Gracie, Wyatt, Conner, and Jameson too," he says. "Very much, but Peyton," he looks over to me. "Something about that kid gets me good."

The fact that he's speaking a lot more coherently is a good sign, and I decide to try and keep him engaged.

"I get it, and he is yours, too. In fact, take him home. Please take him with you."

"You say that, Thatch, but that kid is a daddy's boy." Eli takes a deep breath and holds it before pushing it out.

"Think so?"

"Are you kidding? I know so. All he asks for is play tools and hammers," he shakes his head at me as if it's obvious. "You think he's just into construction?" He squeezes my hand. "Thatch, you're a good dad," he dips, his tone low, "way better than Brenden."

"Anyone is better than Brenden," I chuckle before the guilt kicks in. "Okay, he's not that bad."

"I mean, he kind of is, but you? You're different."

"Not lately," I admit.

"Well, it's going to work out because it's you," he states.

"What do you mean?" I ask, most definitely fishing for compliments.

He turns to me, his ice-blue eyes sincere and a little dreamy. "Because it's *you*, Thatch. Everyone knows you've got your family, man. You've *always* got them."

The words don't even fully get a chance to leave Eli's mouth before Peyton's shriek fills the air. "Jesus for Christ!"

"Peyton!" Serena screeches next, a horrific gurgling sound coming from below. And just as a shatter reaches us, Eli full-on blanches white before he passes right the fuck out.

CHAPTER THIRTEEN

Thatch

"H EY, SWEETHEART, COME ON IN," RUBY GREETS, OPENING the door for me with a ready smile. "Dinner's almost ready." I step in, the smells from the kitchen and the feel of the house sinking into me. "Do you mind going to grab Serena?"

"No, ma'am," I say as music blasts down from the second floor.

"Tell her to turn that shit down if you don't mind," she tosses over her shoulder as I head up the stairs, a smile twisting my lips. Traveling down the hall toward the sound of the music, I place it as "Let Me Blow Ya Mind" by Eve and Gwen Stefanie. Knowing the girl playing it is probably in some sort of mood by the song choice, it's confirmed when I peek around the corner to see her shaking her pert little ass to it. Kicking back for the show just outside the doorway, I watch as Serena taps her hips perfectly to the beat, her long, silky hair dancing just inches from the top of her jeans. The camisole undershirt she's wearing hugging her palm-sized tits and tapering to her muscular, trim waist. She's slightly more bottom-heavy in the best imaginable way. A little thicker in the thighs, her heart-shaped ass everything I've ever wanted in a woman.

Everything about this girl turns me on.

Every. Fucking. Thing.

We've spent a lot of time in the last few days sparring, talking, and blistering each other's lips with kisses, and I can't fucking get enough. The gnawing in my chest as I watch her tells me I might not ever be able to. The girl is fire. Her eyes, her mouth, and what comes out of it. But she's got a softness, too. One I don't think many are privy to. One I fucking hope is reserved just for me. As much of a pain in the ass that I suspected she is—and is turning out to be—so far, I wouldn't change a thing.

If I had to change anything in this scenario, it would be me.

"Great, you look at her all googly-eyed too," Whitney huffs, passing me in the hall as Serena remains distracted. "I'll make sure to let her know."

"Little shit," I call after her as she giggles before making her way down the stairs. Serena, who somehow remained oblivious to our interaction, continues to flirt with her reflection. Brushing her hair, straightening her camisole, shaking her perfect ass, applying more gloss, I camp out for all of it. For as long as it takes for her to feel me watching her. Which isn't too much longer. When she spots me in her mirror, she instantly perks, no shits given about what she's been busted doing as she glances back.

"Hey," she greets, stalking over and pressing a kiss directly on my lips. I fold the arms lifting to wrap around me to her sides, widening my eyes.

"What in the hell are you doing?"

"Uh, kissing you, jackass. What are you doing?"

"We're not doing that in front of your parents," I exclaim.

"Really? You don't want them to see anything?"

"No," I bark.

"Oh, well then, you should probably shut the door," she says.

"Your mom sent me to get you to the dinner tab—put your fucking shirt back on!" I whisper-yell just as she loses her bra. My cock literally goes from chub to full-on salute as she gives me a pointed look.

"I told you to shut the door, Thatch."

"Jesus Christ," I rasp out, quickly shutting the door behind me, chest heaving as I palm it to keep it sealed. My temperamental opposite, she stands utterly unaffected at the foot of her bed. Bare from the waist up, tilting her head, her lips slowly curve up at my reaction.

Shit.

She could never draw this animation from me in the shed. There I'm controlled and in fucking control. Under Allen and Ruby's roof, I feel utterly helpless. Anger thrumming through me at Serena's advantage, I entertain rubbing the tip of my cock on her lips until it's soaked before bottoming out between her exposed tits. We haven't done anything more than heavy petting, but the sight of her has my mind spinning.

"What if your brother had walked by, Serena?"

"He's at a friends," she says.

"Your dad—"

"Never comes up here," still bare, she starts to stalk toward me, and I immediately start slapping the air like I'm in a bitch fight before gritting out my order.

"Put a shirt on, now, Serena."

Full-on laughing at me, she stops and shakes her head. "My God, do they not serve chill at the nunnery? I'm just changing shirts. And by the way, it's obvious my parents are aware there is something going on between us."

"It would be a monastery," I counter, like a complete douche, crossing my arms in an attempt to regain some control. This girl has me bottoming out at least once a day, and not always in a good way.

"Thatch, you don't like what you see?" She pushes her chest out before raking her lower lip.

"You keep fucking with me like this, and you won't like what happens."

She lifts her chin. "Pretty sure I will."

"Shirt, Serena, now."

She pulls on her sweater instantly, sans her bra, and I gape at her as she lifts her chin for me to open the door.

"Uh, bra," I order as she shakes her head and walks toward me. "That's not what you said, Thatch."

When she again goes to open her door, I shut it with my shoulder, *tempted to give in to the half a dozen scenarios I have for her. All in which she begs.*

"Brat," I snap, and her head whips toward me as I issue my warning. "Put on a bra right now, or I'm going to pay you back in a way you won't like."

"Bring it on, Handy Man," she states before playfully shoving me enough to slip out the door.

Eli lies comatose on the couch as Serena sweeps up Ruby's favorite candy dish, her eyes narrowing on Peyton as he offers his excuses.

"She tried to kiss me, Mommy!" He defends his actions, which were to shove his baby fist into Wretched Gretchen's mouth when she went in for some affection. This, in turn, leading to several adults leaping from their seats and one shattered candy dish.

"Can't really blame him," I utter low, and thanks to my wife's sonic mother hearing, she catches it, turning to laser my head off.

"Sorry, baby," I mutter, knowing that if Peyton heard it, I broke our deal not to undermine her. But if Wretched Gretchen tried to kiss me, I'd shove a fist up her ass. Feeling protective over Peyton for the first time in days, I walk over to usher my devil baby away as Ruby eyes the glass Serena is sweeping up.

"I'm so sorry," I issue to Ruby, knowing it was her mother's. Her deceased mothers. A memorable keepsake that she can't get back. Which no 'I'm sorry' is going to remedy.

"Can't deny I'm bummed, kid, but accepted."

"I'm sorry, Grammy," Peyton parrots, and it's obvious he means it. In return, she bends and presses a kiss to his forehead.

"Accepted."

When Serena's finished sweeping the glass, I charge Peyton to watch Uncle Eli sleep and tune him into the Grinch. Stalking behind her in the closet, she gapes at me when I close the door behind me.

"What?" She asks. "What did they do now?"

"They? Who is they?"

"The kids," she exhales.

"What kids?" I ask, fingering the hem of her hoodie.

"Thatch, right now, here? You can't be serious," she utters.

I lean in, running my palm up her stomach, molding one of her breasts until she's pressing into it before massaging the other. "Thirteen and a half years. If you think I'm going to wait that long to touch you again like this, you've lost your fucking mind, Brat."

Her bated exhale is all the fuel I need to clamp her neck between my teeth and flick her flimsy bra to the side. Running my finger over her nipple, I suck her neck lightly. Breaths start to pump out of her as she leans into me. The more pliant she becomes, the more I reward her. A system she's all too aware of.

"Should I fuck you right here?" I taunt, dipping my fingers into her leggings and teasing them over her clit. She instantly starts to buckle as my chuckle fills the dark closet.

"Thatch," she croaks as I lift her shirt and draw a nipple into my mouth, "oh my God, it's been so long."

"That's right, it has," I suckle her nipple in a way she's all too familiar with as I run my fingers over her panties once more. "Should I suck on this pussy tonight and make it remember me?"

"God, yes, please, yes."

Deciding to play hardball, I drive two fingers into her, and she grips my shoulders and bites my own to stifle her moan. Crazed with the need to take her, and knowing I've done what I've set out to, I pull away abruptly and click on the light.

Her mouth remains parted as she gapes at me, clothes fucked, eyes wide.

"Thatch, you can't do that."

"Remember the night you teased me at your parents?" I lean in. "No bra at the dinner table?"

"You can't be serious," she whispers.

"I warned you, baby. I warned you wouldn't like it—the payback."

"It's been twenty-two years," she cries.

"They say that revenge is a dish best served cold."

"Uh, yeah, no, you can't do this, I'm going to—"

"What?" I counter, "demand dick? How about meet me in the bedroom in a few hours, and I'll think about it."

"You son of a—" Serena starts as Whitney sounds before the door opens.

"What the hell is going on in here?"

Blink. Blink. Blink. Blink.

I chuckle and step out as Whitney looks between us.

"Uh . . . were y'all?" Her lips quirk up. "Did I just interrupt my sister about to get her swerve on?"

"Of course not," Serena snaps, frantically straightening her clothes. "Why would you think that?"

"Baby," I drawl, now standing next to Whitney as Serena's breaths come out like a bull who is about to rage in a China shop, eyes darting between the two of us.

"I was just in here putting up the broom and dustpan," she picks it up to prove her innocence, "up, and then *Thatch* came in here!" She points the plastic at me as both accusation prop and future weapon, "and—"

"Baby," I call a second time.

"What, Thatch. *What?*" She snaps, her cheeks reddening.

"You've got a hickey."

I barely dodge the dustpan.

CHAPTER FOURTEEN

Serena

THE LIGHTER'S HOT METAL BURNS MY THUMB, AND I FLINCH as I release the flame. Sucking it to soothe the burn, the last candle starts to cast a glow, filling the rest of the space with soft, amber light. Glancing around, pride swells at the result of my handy work. With a little lighting and some stolen Christmas décor, the dusty old shed has been transformed. Space heater set on high, the typical chill in here is absent, only making it more inviting. Nerves firing, I shed my coat just as the door creaks and turn in time to catch Thatch's reaction as he steps in. Though, I'm deprived of any reaction as his eyes remain zeroed in on me. Every bit of my ambience-altering efforts ignored as he stalks toward me, seeming like a man on a mission. He closes the space so rapidly that I damn near take a step back as he approaches. "Hey, I—"

Lifting me from my feet, he sits me on my father's workbench, nudging himself between my thighs before silencing the rest of my greeting with his ravenous kiss. Mouths molded, he thrusts his tongue in again and again until I'm dizzied and drunk. Kissing me past that until I'm wet and wanton. When he finally pulls away, he glances around and shakes his head. "You made this a date, Serena."

I shrug, unsure if he's upset by it. Though his eyes seem a little softer, I'm unsure about everything when it comes to him. After two weeks of meeting in the shed to make out or talk—mostly both—there's so much about him I don't know, yet he fascinates me. Though he refuses to get too personal, he's got a lot of opinions, refuses to talk bullshit, and won't at all allow me to back away from sharing my own take on things. He seems to be well-read and completely different from most guys I've dated in the past. Especially in the way he verbally spars with me. Never once backing down or giving an inch. Something I can't get enough of. Since our tiff the day he chopped wood, things have gotten a lot lighter between us. Even as our touches and kisses grow more intense and heated.

Much to my frustration, we haven't gone further than lengthy tongue tangles and heavy petting despite the threat he made that day. Sexually frustrated to the point of madness, tonight, I've decided to take matters into my own hands.

As I study the definition of his Adam's apple, he takes in the glowing candles, the lit garland, and pallet I made, which consists of throw pillows and a few comforters. Expression most definitely softening, he flits his focus back to me, his lush lips lifting. "You're so fucking hardheaded."

"Don't read too much into it."

"You've been with me every night since you got home. Aren't there friends you want to see while you're here?"

"I already told you I didn't keep pen pals, but as a matter of fact, I did hang out with one of them today at the mall when I got myself a Christmas present. Want to see what it is?"

"Shopping for yourself at Christmas, why doesn't that surprise me?" *He taunts.*

"Be nice. I was going to let you be the one to open it," *I tug on the bow, which sits tied in the middle of my present-themed sweater, and slowly release it. Taking his maddening time, he fingers both ribbons, which now lay limply against my chest, while shaking his head in amusement.*

"You're going to be the death of me."

"Nah, it's not that lethal, just a little lace," *I grip the hand he now* has molded to my hip and guide it under my sweater to cover the cup of my new bra. He instantly starts molding his hand around my breast, his touch tender as his eyes heat.

"We fuck around," he delivers, voice gravelly, "but you need to know you are beautiful, Serena. So fucking beautiful."

"So are you, Thatcher," I run my hands through his hair, loving the feel between my fingers. "Will you grow your hair out so I can see the curl?"

"God no," he answers. "Trust me, you don't want that, and I won't be—" he cuts himself off.

"Won't be what?"

He shakes his head. "Doesn't matter."

"Maybe if I ask nicely," I whisper, running one palm up his shirt as I run another to cover his cock. He's deliciously hard, and from what I can tell, there's a lot where that came from.

He backs away from my touch, pressing his forehead to mine. "Hey, stop."

"Please, let me touch you," I murmur, closing in to lick along his bottom lip as I run my hand up and down the raging bulge in his pants.

"God, help me," he rasps out, his delivery full of defeat.

Claiming my victory, I unbutton his jeans and free his cock from his briefs.

"Merry Christmas to me," I giggle before gawking at the perfection of what's in my hand. Thick, the perfect length, veiny, and a fat crown. I run my fingernail along the sensitive underside of his tip as we share a stunted breath.

"Serena," he exhales, "I'm cool with just messing around. You don't have to—"

"God, yes, I fucking do." Pushing at his chest to give myself the space, I hop off the workbench and turn him before slowly sinking to my knees.

"No," he jerks his head just as I surround him with my mouth.

"Fuck," he tries to pull away once more, and I palm his ass and take him in deeper, swallowing as I do. He exhales a string of curses as I swallow repeatedly, tightening my lips more and more with every pass.

"Damn you," he utters, gripping the hair at my crown between his fingers, his demeanor visibly shifting as his eyes start to pool into liquid jade. "Then suck my cock, Brat," he grunts as he starts to thrust his hips, his demeanor taking on the edge I've been desperate for as he issues another threat. "But you're going to swallow, and that's if you can even get me there."

The stretch is too much now for him to see my answering grin as I claw his ass and go feral. Sucking noisily as he begins to utter filthy words. His groans are so sexy that I feel it the second my panties flood.

Popping him out of my mouth, I look up at him and pump him vigorously. It's the sight that greets me that has me spinning out. Never in my life have I seen a sexier man. Eyes hooded, chest heaving, Thatch stares down at me as if I'm the sunrise, as well as the stars and a woman capable of hanging the moon. Capable of anything. No man I've ever been with has ever looked at me this way. As if . . . I'm the thing he needs, the thing he needs to see. To breathe.

"Thatch," I whisper as I stare at him, my whisper laced with the need I feel. "Be with me." Somehow unable to order him to 'fuck me.' The brazen, bold seductress gone due to the look in his eyes. Instead, I ask him again in the only way that feels right. "Please take me."

It's the closest I've ever come to uttering anything resembling 'make love to me.' Those words have more meaning but feel right. This feels intense and . . . important because of the way he stares at me—because of the way he makes me feel.

"Take me, Thatch," I order more forcefully.

"I can't," he murmurs mournfully, "but God, do I want to."

"Why? What in the hell is it?" I whisper, aggravated but unwilling to break the intimate bubble we're in, even as my frustration grows. I trace the head of his perfect dick with my tongue as he groans his approval. Darting it out again, I keep my gaze fixed on his as his eyes hood further. He's so beautiful, this infuriating man. Determined to prove it, I suck him in deeper, tracing every vein bulging along his perfect shaft with the tip of my tongue. I take my time, stroking him, savoring him, loving the look of him. His chest stops heaving altogether when I take him in as far as I can go before lengthening each pull. Pumping, licking, tracing every bit of his silky skin until he's gasping out my name. As he comes, I stroke him and suckle until I'm confident I've coaxed everything out of him. The instant I'm done, he lifts me easily to my feet.

"Proud of yourself?"

"Very," I muse as he walks me backward toward the bed I made for us before laying me down and kissing me until I'm fully wrapped around him. And minutes later, begging. Nestled between my thighs, he palms the floor and lifts, eyes intent as he lines us up and begins running his thick cock against me.

"Thatch," I gasp as he suckles my neck before inching lower, sucking the skin just below my shoulder, and latching on. So much so that I know he's left a mark as he rolls his perfect body against mine, hitting my clit where I need him to. My moans escalate as he keeps his eyes on mine and begins furiously grinding against me. In seconds, I begin to topple over as he kisses every inch of flesh. Just as I'm about to come, he pulls back.

"Show me that lace," he orders, his powerful arms keeping him hoisted above me. I pull the hem of my sweater up as he drops his gaze to the green lace.

"Perfect," he murmurs before lowering to trace the outline with his lips and tongue. Teasing, still teasing, always teasing. Frustrated and on the verge of losing my fucking mind, I bark out my one-word order.

"More."

"Then give me more," he counters, keeping his palms planted on the floor. "More, Serena,'" he commands when I don't react fast enough. The second I lower the lace, he's eagerly sucking my nipple into his mouth and moving more feverishly. My clit pulses as I rocket straight to the precipice of orgasm.

"I want to come with you inside me," I groan. "I'm on the pill."

"Fuck, baby. Fuck," he grits out as he thrusts again and again as if he's just as frustrated.

"I'm safe, Thatch," I assure as he grinds more urgently against me, the look in his eyes lethal, almost feral, until he shakes his head.

"You're anything but fucking safe for me."

"Please," I cry out hoarsely. "Please take me."

"I fucking can't," he rolls against me again as I pound against his chest, not wanting to go anywhere without the feeling of him. "Thatch, not this way, I want, ah," I topple over as the orgasm flushes through me.

He groans as he comes not long after and collapses, shuddering as he buries his face in my neck. I stroke the skin at his nape, staring at the ceiling of the shed, my chest thundering as my mind races with any reason I can think of for why he's refusing to go further.

"I want to," his words are muffled before he turns his head and presses his lips to sip the tiny tear of rejection I set free, thinking in no way would he catch it. Embarrassment threatens as he captures it with his lips and tongue.

"Serena—"

"Don't console me, Thatch. It's not that big of a deal."

"Fuck that," he forces me to face him, pinching my chin. "Believe me, I've never wanted a girl so much in my life."

"Yeah, well, it's obviously not enough to get past whatever is in your head."

"You're what's in my fucking head." His whisper is so faint, it's as if I've imagined it. "And you shouldn't give your body to just any man. Your attention. I don't deserve it. Not like this. We're in a filthy fucking shed, Serena."

"Thanks for the lecture," I state, pushing at his chest until he allows me to sit. "Do you think I'm some virginal princess that deserves white linens and a fairy tale setting?"

"Yes, I fucking do," he snaps. "I absolutely fucking do."

His response takes me by surprise, but I manage to counter. "Well, I'm not sure what world you live in."

"Not yours," he states before pulling away from me to stand.

"There are no princes, Thatch. That's what I've discovered since I left my castle, and I'm not really into the white knight thing anyway. I like sex. No, I love it, and I love to fuck," I spit venomously, "and to be fucked. I left dry humping behind in high scho—"

I'm cut off by his hand, which is now clamped around my throat, *his eyes flaring in warning from where he now kneels in front of me. His voice cutting through the air, tone lethal.*

"I'm hanging on by my last shred of decency. If you weren't Allen's daughter, I'd be balls deep in your perfect pussy right now while fingering your tight little ass. For the last fucking time, I'm not a nice guy, Serena. And I've never met or known a knight either because I'm a fucking gutter rat." He rakes his lip as he doles out more warning. "And we don't ask for permission. We take. You have no idea who you're inviting into your life and between your legs." He tilts his head. "But the more you run off at the mouth, the more I'm starting to think my influence on you is not what we need to be worrying about."

I can't help my grin as he releases his hold and finally frees me to speak. "So then, shut me up with some of that gutter."

He groans and drops his head. "Fucking Brat."

"What you thinking about sister?" Whitney asks as I eye Thatch as he drops the last of the decorations at the bottom of the tree. He smirks after hearing her question but doesn't look up.

"Nothing," I lie, trailing Thatch as he takes the stairs, two at a time, his lifting lips taunting me the entirety of the way up.

"I need to do some wrapping," I lie just as Kenny and Dolly start to sing 'I Believe in Santa Claus.'

"No Santa!" Peyton screeches in order to kill the music, though it's not enough to kill the vibe or my growing hunger.

"But we're decorating the tree," Whitney protests.

"Uh, it's just one present because it's a big surprise," I dig the shovel even further into my lie as I start to make my way down the ladder, "and I don't want it spoiled."

Truth is, I'm horny in a way I haven't been in *years*, and it's all thanks to my husband and the memories he's stirring up—with his whispers, subtle tongue flicks, and long looks. Over the last week, they've started to add up, and he's all but confessed his plans to seduce me. Oddly enough, and after decades together, it's working. Last

THE SLEIGHT BEFORE CHRISTMAS | 151

night we dry humped, and he refused to stop until I came, exactly like the night I just relived, now fresh in my memory.

Just after, wholly ready and prepared to fully reenact, Thatch tucked me into his arms in an attempt to force me to sleep. He was hard for an hour after because I was restless, and more than once ran my ass along his cock to try and tempt him. Only to be refused and further taunted by his infuriating chuckle. Rinse and repeat until I finally drifted off. With the memory warm both from that night and last night, I'm starting to feel the beat constantly. Clit pulsing now and thoroughly baited, I track Thatch up the stairs. In search of both the man and the friction, I deflate when I don't spot him in any of the rooms. Stepping into the Raggedy Ann room last, I spot Gracie on the bed, fully immersed in her book.

"They're decorating the tree," I tell her.

She nods absently, utterly ignoring me for the plot she's heavily into. Unable to help it, I grin and shut the door behind me. I was her age when I discovered reading and romance. In search of my chosen hero now, I deflate fully when I don't spot him in our cabin bedroom. Deciding he must have gone back down while I was talking to Gracie, I sigh in disappointment. Turning, I stop when I see Thatch behind me, slowly closing the door of the bedroom. His eyes travel slowly down my body as he lifts his chin, his expression smug as he secures me in his trap. "Looking for me?"

"Uh," oh my God, I'm nineteen again! "No," I say, just like a teen would. "I-was just—"

"Was just what?" He taunts as I narrow my eyes. This fool thinks he's getting the best of me after all these years? I cross my arms. Game On.

"Any more decorations?" I cock my hip, and he takes a step toward me, in an instant shifting our dynamic to tower over me.

"That's what you followed me up to ask me, wife?"

"Yes, what else would I ask?"

"Let me guess," he bends and bites the shell of my ear, and my eyes close. "Pussy pulsing baby? Need me to rub it out?"

"Uh, no, no," I utter pathetically, convincing neither of us.

"Sure?" His scent surrounds me, familiar, a comfort even as the air about him feels foreign. Running his hand beneath my hoodie and up the waist of my leggings, he dips his fingertips into them before playing with the hem.

"Thatch," I whisper. "Just—"

"I don't take orders, Brat. Have you forgotten?"

Commotion breaks out downstairs, and I decide unless the house is on fucking fire, I'm not leaving this room.

"Shit," he whispers, moving his hand as I grip it, opening my eyes.

"Don't you dare."

He grins, his expression heating at my outburst. "Okay, so let's try again. Someone's in need of . . . what?"

"Don't be a dick—"

"Well, dick was in there, but that didn't sound like an ask," hand still flirting at the top of my pants, he manages to turn me without losing his place and crab-walks me toward the closed door. Crowding me with his frame, he presses me against it while at the same time sliding his fingers into my panties.

"Jesus, fuck, you're so fucking wet," he utters, breaking his composure slightly due to the evidence of my desire.

"Thatch," I mewl as he recovers almost instantly with his reply. "Thatch *what?*"

He begins expertly rolling the pads of his fingers over my clit. Legs shaking, my release close, I sag against the door. In the next second, my mouth is clamped as his breath hits my nape.

"Shhhh, baby, little ears," he whispers as I come to, unrealizing I was getting loud. He rolls his fingers over my soaked, slippery center, his scent surrounding me, his powerful build at my back. "You're so fucking sensitive today," he murmurs. "Does my wife need me?"

I moan into the palm clamped over my mouth, the fire raging in me quickly burning out of control.

"You know, no matter how many times I soak this pussy, I always want to taste. Open, Brat."

I do and suck his waiting finger into my mouth, laving myself off him before turning my head. He immediately sucks my taste off my own tongue, his fingers increasing speed as I start to come apart against him.

"Already?" he utters, the bastard running his cock along my ass as he flicks his fingers once more and sets. Me. Off.

Moaning wildly and thankful his hand is back in place, I bite the flesh of it just as he bites into the back of my neck. The orgasm hits like a tidal wave, and I shudder uncontrollably. Miraculously, Thatch somehow manages to keep me upright. Long seconds pass as he continues to massage me until I'm whimpering. Just after, I go lax as he chuckles.

"Big one, huh?"

Turning in his arms, I attack his mouth, kissing his much too casual words quiet as I thrust my tongue against his, gripping his cock and clawing it through his jeans. When I feel I've delivered my message, I pull away, and his eyes light fire with satisfaction as he speaks. "There's my fucking girl."

"That's right, so bring the fucking gutter tonight," I demand.

He pinches my chin, eyebrows rising. "You sure about that?"

On fire, certain there is not a fucking thing in this world that can—

Knock. Knock.

"Mom? Dad? Peyton made Gramps piss his pants!"

CHAPTER FIFTEEN

Thatch

RUNNING A LINE THROUGH THE CARPET, SERENA STANDS idly by as my kids eyeball me, both of them lined up like they're reporting for duty as instructed. Irritation and fury rage for dominance within for a multitude of reasons. One, because I finally had Serena in a sweet spot. One that meant a hell of a good night for us, if not *the night*. Judging by her drawn-up posture now, all bets are off. Even more so that my kids struck again so soon after the last debacle. One in which we haven't even had a chance to deal with Gracie yet. Serena and I had wanted her good and scared before we addressed it. As things stand, our children still seem to be fearless.

"Sir," I clip out. "You will address me as Sir every single time you talk to me from here on out," I snap. "You will say please and thank you for everything. You will be polite and respectful when spoken to. *Respectful and Sir*, understood?"

"Yes, Sir," Gracie says immediately.

"Yes, Sir," Peyton parrots nervously, feeling the tension in the room.

"Gracie, you will feed your brother, bathe your brother, and not let him out of your sight until we leave this cabin. He is your responsibility until I say otherwise, and you will make sure he is cared for. Understood?"

"Yes, Sir," she utters.

"Peyton," I glower at him. "I don't even want to know how you managed to make your grandfather piss his pants."

He immediately opens his mouth to confess.

"I don't want to know!" I boom, and all three of them jump as I continue my rant, practically running in circles on the ancient, threadbare carpet of the Raggedy Ann and Andy attic. A room that I had taken my family to for some modicum of privacy to demand respect. "I'm fed up, and as of this moment, Rudolph has absolutely no reason to come here."

"Daddy!" Peyton shrieks as I stare down at him.

"Daddy, Sir," Peyton backtracks. "Yes, Sir," he finally says, eyes lowering.

"Tonight and tomorrow, that's all you have left. Tonight and tomorrow. If you want anything at all for Christmas, you will behave until then, understood?"

"Yes, Sir," they both say in perfect unison, but I'm not buying it.

"No more activities," I state as both their mouths drop. "Until karaoke. You read, and you," I point to Peyton. "No club."

"Yes, Sir," Peyton says, real panic in his eyes for the madman who has replaced his father.

"Peyton, go downstairs and stand next to Aunt Erin until we get to you. Gracie, you stay."

"Yes, Sir," Peyton says, looking toward his mother, his eyes saucer wide before he walks out.

The instant the door closes, Gracie begins to cry, and I cut my hand through the air. "Do you have any more drugs, Gracie? Anything else on you that we should know about? A loaded gun, perhaps?"

She shakes her head, her tears conveniently breaking free.

"Save them, Gracie. No one is buying them, especially when you can summon them on cue."

She reads my hostile gaze and sniffs.

"You scared the ever-loving shit out of your uncle, who's practically been sleeping for two days now—"

"Daddy, I—"

"You what?" I seethe, "what excuse could you possibly give me?"

"I didn't take any of them, I swear to God," she says, her real tears flowing. "A friend gave them to me last minute before we got out for break. I put them into my purse, and I was going to throw them away, but I forgot cause—"

"You got caught shoplifting?" I pose, and her cries come harder, these more fear-induced and far more convincing.

"I don't even recognize you," I dig in. "What were you thinking?"

"You and Mom smoke pot," she blurts, "I've smelled it."

I stop my footing as Serena whips her head up, her eyes searching my face helplessly as I glare over at my daughter.

Oh, karma, you angry, vengeful bastard. Absorbing the blow, I fire right back. "Are you eighteen years old?"

"No, Sir—"

"Do you pay your own way in this world?"

"No, Sir," Gracie barks back in utter fear, and I can only deduce it's from my demeanor.

"Until you do, until you are an adult who can make adult decisions, do not ever proceed to toss ours in our face, ever again, understood?"

"Yes, Sir."

"Pot is legal in a lot of states," Serena defends pathetically, but I hold up my hand. "Baby, I know what you're trying to do, but I know what our daughter is, too. Just like she knows exactly what she's doing."

Gracie cries harder as I burrow in.

"Don't you, Gracie? You know we're having a horrible week. That we're doubting our ability to parent and that you just made it ten times worse with your accusation. But the thing is, I know I'm responsible," my voice cracks as my mistakes eat away at me.

Regret instantly coats her voice as Gracie speaks up. "Daddy, I'm sorry."

Shaking her words away, I stop and level her with my gaze. "I've never put you in harm's way or endangered you, and neither has your mother, but what you just did was drive the knife further into both our hearts. But you *know that*, don't you?"

"Daddy, I'm sorry—" she pleads.

"No, you're not," I snap, "and until you are, I don't want to look at you or talk to you. Until you bottom out, and mean it, I don't want you anywhere near me."

I stalk out as Gracie's sobs follow me.

Walking downstairs, I hear Erin's scolding whisper and take the steps further down to see Brenden drawing a penis on Eli's face where he sleeps comatose on the couch. The head stopping just short of his gaping mouth. Peyton watches on, his eyes wide, his own mouth open in shock.

Serena stops at my back before bursting past me and stalking toward Brenden. Eyes widening, he immediately stops drawing, his voice low and cutting as Serena makes a beeline toward him, murder in her eyes. "Are you serious? My son is watching!"

"What? Isn't the theme of this Christmas adults behaving badly? Have I gotten the wrong memo?"

Peyton giggles as he watches Brenden quickly add the final touches, which include hair on the giant balls now marring Eli's face. Just as Serena is about to pounce, Ruby's voice cuts through the air and has us all stilling.

"I can't believe I have to parent my forty-something kids," she states as I take the remaining steps down, dread filling me.

Ruby gives us each a pointed look before ushering Allen in, or rather, coaxing him in. His eyes fill with fear as he surveys his family, and Ruby unleashes.

"Mere days in, and so far, we've had everything but a partridge in the most dysfunctional of pear trees." She spreads her glare between all of us. "This is not how we roll."

158 | KATE STEWART

"Way to go with the modern verbiage choice, Mom—shit, sorry," Brenden backtracks under her glare.

"Yeah," Ruby says, taking a menacing step toward him. "Let's start with *you*."

I wince at the delivery as Brenden points to himself, mouthing 'muah.'

"Get your ass to the store to pick up some alcohol to get that shit off your brother's face."

He frowns. "But we have some in the cabinet. I made sure."

"Oh, did you?"

"Yes, Mommy," he answers, and I'm not entirely sure it's sarcasm.

"Well, since you went to all that trouble of drawing a penis on your brother's face," I try to hide my smile. Really, I do, "I'm going to impose on a little more of your time."

"Understood," he nods, eyeing Erin, who lifts her brows unforgivingly. Her expression every bit 'I told you so.'

"And while you're at it, you can add this to your list," Ruby says, lifting a sheet of paper before it promptly rolls down three times its original size. Brenden's eyes widen at the length of her annual last-minute list. One she typically sends her most dependable kids to fetch. Not this year.

"Me?" Brenden squeaks like a pubescent boy.

"Last time I checked, you had two arms, two legs, and a wallet," she snaps. "And I swear to God, Son, you give me any more lip, you'll lose it."

"Yes, ma'am," he states, his ears turning a rare red. "Sorry, Mom," he adds genuinely before hauling ass to the hall tree to wrap up.

"You miss one thing on that list. You go right back," she snaps after him, refusing his olive branch so soon.

"Thatch, Serena," Ruby draws up next, and I walk further into the living room so she can address me, or rather, bitch me out.

"It's not working," she states, and I nod as she points to Allen. "Pants *pissed*!" She reminds us all as Allen hangs his head in shame.

"I'm on it, Mom," I relay as Gracie comes down the stairs, her face splotched, which is evidence enough, but apparently not for Grammy.

"Young lady," Ruby addresses her in her most serious tone. Gracie quickly scans the room in fear before facing her livid grandmother. "I don't care what you do in your own home—your parents can discipline you for that—but in this house, you will respect us. You will fall in line, do you hear me?"

"Yes, Sir," Peyton shouts as I palm my face.

"And you," she looks down to Peyton. "Take a damn bath, you *stink*."

"I going to Grammy! Daddy just told me."

"Good. Change your clothes, too, I'm sick of that shirt, and we don't take the Lord's name in vain in this house. No more 'Jesus for Christ,' understood?"

"Yes, Sir," he mumbles nervously.

"Erin, carry on, you're the only one who will be invited next year," Ruby says as Erin rocks Jameson in the recliner, grinning in response.

"Whitney," Ruby clips out, and Whitney shuffles in from the kitchen in her elf slippers, looking every bit like she's on the plank.

"When your husband wakes up from his coma, you two make dinner."

"Yes, ma'am."

"It's Sir, *yes Sir*, be spectful, Auntie Whit," Peyton whisper yells as Brenden slams the door closed, his laughter following him to his truck.

Ruby takes a patient breath, and it's then I spot the gumdrops in her closed fist. "I want a quiet night, and I mean *quiet*," she states. "Understood?"

We all nod as she turns on her heel and grabs Allen's hand, leading him down the hall toward their bedroom. "We need a miracle to save this Christmas, honey." We hear echo back as Serena meets my eyes, hers shadowed with the truth—we should have stayed home.

We ruined Christmas.

CHAPTER SIXTEEN

Serena

SHUTTING MYSELF INTO THE CAB OF THATCH'S TRUCK BEFORE
he has a chance to take off, he gapes over at me in surprise. His
complexion reddening just after in . . . embarrassment?

He ate quickly tonight, barely dropping his napkin on his plate with
a 'thank you' before making an excuse to take off. Even knowing we have
a standing date later, I followed him out just after, determined to delve
a little deeper into his life outside of our hideout. Knowing I'm crossing
a line he's continually drawn and made clear, it's evident in his reception
now that I'm flirting too close to it as he says as much. "What the fuck
are you doing, Serena?"

"Coming with you," I tell him, palming the space behind my right
shoulder in search of my seatbelt and coming up empty as he shakes his
head in refusal.

"No, you aren't. Go back inside. I'll see you later tonight."

"It's only fair. You've seen my room. So, now I want to see yours."

"That's a definite fuck no," he counters quickly and adamantly.

"Fine," I say, pulling out the gift card from my jacket pocket, "then
dessert is on me tonight."

He glares down at the card in my hand as I sink into my seat, knowing there's a good chance he might very well kick me out of his truck. In the last three weeks, we've gotten close. Really close. Closer than I thought possible in such a short time. Then again, we've spent endless hours together. Probably more than most couples when they start out. Our nights often ending just before sunrise. Neither of us wanting to part until we'd been forced away. But regardless of how close we've become, he still remains guarded. Too damned guarded. Especially about his situation with his family—or lack of. His history with them is the one thing I know he keeps closest to his chest. Refusing to let me fully in, it's clear now he has no intentions of breaking his stance as he treats my simple request as if I've just asked the impossible.

"It's a gift card, Thatch. Can you not take me to do something as simple as get a freaking dessert?"

His eyes blister me in warning as he palms his neck. "I mean," he glances toward my house, "I guess so, yeah."

"K," I flash him a grin, again blindly reaching for the buckle, "let's go."

"Your seatbelt is broken."

I shrug. "Okay, so don't wreck."

He shakes his head. "I don't like this."

"Please?" I palm his knee, and he glances out of his window before muttering a low curse. It's that curse that has me grinning again—in victory. Though I try to choose my battles, the suspense of what his life consists of outside our bubble is becoming too much. In thinking it, I take in my surroundings, or rather his. The dash is ripped, cracked by weather or age of the seventies, possibly early eighties model truck. Though the seats are a little ripped up as well, and it looks worse for wear, it's clean enough. What little possessions he has inside consist of folded jeans and shirts, which look freshly laundered and are stacked neatly on the floorboard between us. Just next to them sits a tiny bag holding a few personal items like deodorant, a toothbrush, and paste. His eyes remain glued to my profile as I purposely shift my footing so as not to disturb his things. After turning the key, the truck strains to catch for a few tense seconds before roaring to life. Thatch gives it some gas to warm it as I shiver where I sit.

"The heater doesn't work," he imparts warily, "and you're freezing."

I nod. "I'm good. Promise."

"Serena, we should take your car."

"I want to be in your truck," I tell him honestly.

"I don't even want to be in my fucking truck," he grumbles, his voice carrying the same edge it does every time we get too close to topics he refuses to delve further into. Aware I'm pushing him but too intent on some discovery, I speak up.

"Just fucking go, Thatch. Jesus, it's just dessert."

Blowing out a breath of irritation, he puts the truck into gear, and not long after, we're off. Mere minutes into the drive, I'm tucked at his hip, inhaling his scent. He'd reached for me just as I started inching over toward him, and I revel in the knowledge that we're rarely not touching in some way. Inhaling his fresh, woodsy scent, I close the last of any space between us, palming his chest as he drives with one hand on the wheel, his other on my hip, keeping me firmly pressed to his side.

"You know, I've always wanted to date a guy with a truck," I coo sarcastically. "We're truckin' now," I drawl cheerily, barely securing a lip twitch. Determined to curb whatever is ailing him, I go in again. "You smell good tonight, Thatchalamewl."

"Oh, Jesus," he sighs, but his lips lift fully just after.

"Ah ha! He smiles."

He shakes his head in annoyance. "I have to stop for gas really quick."

I frown before nodding toward his gauge. "It says full."

"Broken, too," he admits on exhale.

"Oh . . . so, where do you live? Close?"

"Serena—"

"On my side of town?"

"Sure," he lies as he pulls into a gas station and parks, tension again rolling off him when his truck backfires loudly just after he cuts it.

"Hey," I say, palming his jaw. "It's a cool truck, Thatch. A classic."

"Stop," he scolds gently, even as his eyes softly glitter on me.

"I like your truck, Thatchalamewl," I bat my lashes.

"Yeah, you're not getting away with that nickname," his grin comes a little more freely this time, and I take it as a good sign.

"We'll see about that. I'm going to go grab some gum, want anything?"

"No, but hold up," he says, pulling some cash from his pocket.

"I can get my gum," I tell him.

"I've got your fucking gum," he forcefully places a twenty in my palm. "Put the rest on this pump."

"Okay, Grinch," I mutter, getting out and heading in. After grabbing some spearmint, I put the rest of the cash on his pump number and head back out. Just outside the door, I'm stopped short when I see Thatch in a standoff with some guy on the small sidewalk patch of island between pumps. Posture-threatening, Thatch's hostile gaze flits toward me as I quickly approach.

"Come on, man. Don't be a dick," the guy he's squaring off with says. "It's been a long time."

Following Thatch's murderous gaze, when the guy catches sight of me, his grin morphs into something more sinister. The sight of it nauseates me, and I know instantly that the threat this guy is posing isn't at all physical. He's inches shorter and a lot less built, though dressed immaculately. His new Timberlands gleaming in comparison to Thatch's tattered black boots. It's clear he has history with the preppy douchebag taunting him, and it's not good. But it's the roll of the asshole's eyes over me which tells me all I need to know and has me hastening my steps to get to Thatch's side. "Ah, I see why you were trying to get rid of me so fast. Who's your girl?"

"What's going on?" I ask, hating Thatch's expression and the vibe coming from him.

"Get in the truck, Serena," Thatch orders without looking my way, positioning himself subtly in front of me.

"Or, you could stay out here, and Thatch could introduce us—"

"Shut the fuck up," Thatch delivers in a tone I've never heard, "and it's not like that."

"No," he taunts. "So, she's not yours?"

"Oh, I'm his," I hiss. "All his."

Thatch exhales a low curse as the guy's eyes light up. "Until next week, and you trade up, right, Snatch?" The asshole shakes his head at me as if I'm delusional. "Hate to break it to you, sweetheart, but my man here isn't the faithful type. He's fucked a lot of prime pussy in this city. Oh . . . wait, this is too good. You didn't know—"

"Shut the fuck up, Daniel. Serena, get in the truck."

"Yeah, Serena, get in the fucking death trap." Daniel drops all bull-shit pleasant pretense, his new demeanor downright hostile. "Tell me something, asshole, if you think you're so much better than me," he kicks Thatch's bumper. "Why do you drive this piece of shit when you could be riding like me again?"

"Fuck off, Daniel," Thatch warns again, and I can feel the tension rolling from him from the other side of the truck where I hesitate, hand on the handle. Unsure of what to do, I decide not to add to his stress. Just as I climb into the cab, Daniel swiftly situates himself in front of Thatch's driver's door, blocking him from getting in.

"Don't fucking take this there, man," Thatch hisses.

"I think you owe me an explanation, asshole. I think you owe us all one. So quick to fucking ghost us, but we were in this shit together. Aren't you going to at least say hi?" Daniel nods to the driver's side of his car—or rather his Porsche. Thatch briefly eyes the girl sitting in his passenger seat through the windshield, and I follow his gaze to see her eyes already glued to Thatch. A possessiveness starts to take hold, Daniel's words already searing me as Thatch looks away just as quickly.

"Don't remember your girl? Well, not much has changed. Pussy's still fucking good, but she's got a mouth on her," he imparts smugly as if she's disposable. "So, I'm thinking maybe you leveled up—or down," Daniel eyes me through Thatch's windshield where I sit with my door cracked, "yeah, no, she's no fucking model."

"Say one more word, and I break your jaw," Thatch delivers with so much venom and promise that I don't recognize his voice. "Say two more, and I take your nose."

Daniel lifts his palms in the air in feigned innocence, moving out of Thatch's way before stalking over to his driver's door. His last words drifting into the cabin as Thatch opens his to climb in.

"Well, I guess we all move on, partner. But then again, you know I'll be catching up with you sooner or later. I always do. See you, Snatch." His sickly grin finds me through the windshield. "And you too, 'all his' Serena."

Daniel's departing wink sickens me before he slams the door of his Porsche and tears out of the parking lot. Thatch follows suit, wordlessly starting his truck up to do the same. I don't bother to voice my objection, knowing it's futile, as Thatch barely acknowledges the traffic lights before pulling right back into my driveway.

My prompt to exit obvious, I ignore it, and instead, we idle for several tense seconds as fury continues to roll off him. The tension in the cabin stifling, I refuse to back down from the anger and the burn spreading through my chest.

"I'm trying really hard not to take the bait—"

"So don't," he snaps.

"But that was your girl?"

"Not really, no, and it was a long time ago."

"So I heard, Snatch."

His head whips toward me, his fury now directed to me. My own anger wins as I press in. "Tell me."

"You really don't want to know, Serena."

"Yes, I fucking do, and frankly I'm sick of begging for crumbs."

"Well, I'm not going to fucking tell you. Deal with it."

"Did you love her?"

"Love?" He scoffs. "Who in the fuck has time for that? Not me. . ." he runs his hand through his hair in exasperation before leveling me with his cutting jade eyes. A look I've never been on the receiving end of. One that singes me. "Jesus Christ, you can't be this oblivious—this clueless, and you aren't. It's exactly what it looks like. I'm exactly what you think I am."

"*You don't know what I*—"

"*Can't you fucking see I'm just trying to survive right now? I don't have time for this shit.*"

"*Thatch*—"

"*Just . . . go inside, Serena. This is done. We're over.*"

"*What?*"

"*This is over. Get inside,*" *he snaps.* "*I never should have laid a hand on you, and I won't again,*" *he shakes his head.* "*Just . . . go.*"

"*Thatch, don't*—"

"*Please, just get out,*" *he rasps, desperation lacing his words.*

"*Fine, fuck this,*" *I say, ramming my shoulder into the door. It's as I exit that panic seizes in my chest. Furious and fed up, for some reason, I turn back to look at him anyway, only to see him staring right at me. His expression muting any more angry words because, inside his green eyes, I see nothing but . . . pain. It's so clear that he doesn't want this to be over, but I can't allow myself to be humiliated anymore. Endless hours of kisses, of murmured words, of looks, and feelings I've only ever experienced with Thatch leave me aching, my words coming out raw as tears shimmer in my eyes.*

"*Please take care of yourself,*" *I whisper out of fear as his eyes frantically search my face.* "*You know,*" *I swallow as the first hot tear lands, trailing down my cheek. His eyes follow as I manage words around the hurt,* "*I really did want to be your girl, Thatch O'Neal.*"

His eyes close as I slam his door and stalk to the porch without looking back. He idles until I'm behind the front door, my face buried in my hands. It takes him only a minute, maybe less, to pull out of the driveway.

Chest stinging from the memory, I push my buggy down the lighting aisle. The air around the breakfast table this morning was tense, so I insisted we accompany Thatch to Lowe's when he said he wanted to pick up some last-minute things for something he was working on. Intent on giving my family a break and stinging from my mother's wrath, I bundled the kids up to give them all a much-needed reprieve.

When I had tried to press Thatch for what he was working on during the ride here, he'd grinned at me and told me I'd know soon enough. The rest of the way to town, I could feel the kids scattering their gazes between us until Thatch grabbed my hand. Kissing it, he'd given me a reassuring wink, one that told me this too shall pass. Once we got here, Gracie offered to take Peyton down the blow-up aisle to keep him occupied.

Thatch had left them both with a stern warning before leaving me with a kiss and a few more words of assurance. Feeling like a pariah and deciding on a little retail therapy, I've been perusing the luminaries in search of the right light for our half bath. Another perk of being a carpenter's wife is that he's added them to every room in the house. Making each room a little more inviting—cozier. My heart warms at the truth that no matter how many I've ordered or brought home, he's never bitched about installing them.

Just as I pile a few in my cart on clearance, I hear a woman's overly exaggerated laugh and pause when it's followed by the low rumble of my husband's voice.

Perked, with a ready glare, I quickly push my cart down and perch it between aisles. Peeking the next aisle over as covertly as I can, I see the hyena standing too close to my husband. So close that my blood immediately starts to boil. Well aware of just how appealing Thatch is, it's evident I'm not the only one who thinks so as she practically drapes herself in the space between them. Her eyes sweep him repeatedly as she pretends to be interested in what he's saying.

Did this hoochie approach my man?

To Thatch's credit, he seems to be keeping the conversation casual while subtly inching back from her as she practically presses herself against his cart.

The possessive fire I felt moments ago from reliving my memory kicks in full force, licking along my spine as I watch another woman ogle my husband. Furthermore, *watching him* for any sign that he's encouraging and indulging her evident flirtation. I'm not a girl who gets jealous often, but with the vibe we have going, the sexual tension, along with the hurt currently stinging my chest, I'm about ready to fuck shit up. The more I watch her—especially when a manicured hand lands on his forearm—I decide I might as well take it out on *Hyena-Harlot* on aisle *get-your-hand-the-fuck-off-my-man.*

Ready to pounce, but deciding to have some fun with this— even as Thatch backs further away—I go in guns blazing.

"Oh, Thatchalamewlllll," I snark, seeing him tense immediately as I fully take the corner with my buggy and begin aggressively closing the space toward them both. "There you are, honey! Oh, I see you made a little friend. Never have met a stranger, have you, Snatch?" I go low.

Thatch glances back at me, a ready glare in his eyes, which I decide is better than guilt or a 'busted' expression. It's at the sight of it that I decide to forgive him a little faster. But it's the memory of her hand on his forearm that fuels me.

"Oh, h-hi," the woman, who does have such an expression, starts to stutter while taking me in. "Your husband is just the best, he was helping me pick out some flooring."

"Is that so? Well, he's just the man for it," I pipe overenthusiastically. "He's *really good* at *installing*," I continue, stopping my cart so abruptly they both jump.

"Serena," Thatch utters low in warning as I shoot him a nasty side-eye before turning to deal with *all-hands Hannah.*

"Well, did you find what you were looking for?" I prompt. "Because I love my flooring. In fact, I think I'll have *my husband* install some more really soon."

Thatch's smile breaks through while *laughs-a-lot Laura's* fades because I'm so obvious now, I've made it uncomfortable. I have no issue with appreciation from afar, but Thatch never takes off his ring. And for all who do appreciate it, a wedding ring is a well-known shining symbol to honor the code and keep a respectful distance. And most definitely, keep their *hands* off. So, since she chose to ignore said ring—and my comfort—gloves off for making it fucking easier to get away with it.

"Well, I'll just be going," she proffers weakly, offering Thatch an even weaker "thanks for your help" before turning on her wheels and stalking away.

"Hey, *handsy*, you forgot to grab your flooring!" I call after her as she speeds up, going double-time before disappearing around the corner.

"Babe, you made your point," Thatch snaps, shaking his head.

"And why did I have to? She was too close," I hiss, "she was too fucking close, Thatch."

"She was a good two feet away, I have a two-foot rule," he assures.

"Oh, do you? Get hit on often, husband?"

His grin breaks through. "Damn baby, you're on fire today."

"I'm not shit and don't get all giddy. When she put her hand on you, you should have told her to fuck off."

His grin amplifies, his eyes roaming down me. "Message received."

"Whatever," I roll my eyes, "ha, hee, ha," I noisily imitate her giggle to further embarrass him as he crosses his arms, utterly unaffected.

He quirks a brow. "You done?"

"Yeah, I'm done," I snap before grabbing my purse. "Unless you want to find another donkey to entertain. I'll be in the truck."

"Maybe *you should* put yourself in a corner, Brat," he says, eyeing the luminaries in the buggy.

"Maybe you should grab a name tag, Mr. Helpful." I stalk off, "you could clean up in installation appointments."

"Babe, get back here."

"That would be a hell no," I snap, glancing back long enough to see my chosen lights in his hands. Score!

"I have wood," he calls.

"Well, good luck in getting that taken care of!"

Jesus, how long are these aisles?

"No, lunatic," he chuckles harder, "I have wood coming. I can't leave."

"Whatever, I'll meet you in the truck. Try not to pick up any more *husband-hugger-hussies* on your way out. I'll have our *children* with me."

"That's not an incentive," he taunts as I flip the bird before finally clearing the aisle, his rumbling laughter following me.

Without stopping, I crook a finger at Gracie, whose eyes bulge when she sees my expression before she ushers Peyton to follow. Gripping both their hands, I walk them out of the store and secure them both into Thatch's truck.

"Mommy's mad again?" Peyton asks Gracie.

"Quiet, Peyton," Gracie has the good sense to say, meeting my eyes in the visor mirror after I pull it down.

"Yes, Sir," Peyton answers as I tilt my head back on the rest and sigh.

Fuming for the whole ten minutes we wait for Thatch; when he finally opens his cab door, I catch his sparkling eyes and accompanying grin. Proof he's enjoying this all too much.

"Daddy, what did you do?" Gracie finally asks a few infuriating minutes into the ride—no doubt because of Thatch's taunting perma-smile.

"Your daddy made a friend in the store," he coos, "and Mommy got mad."

"Only because you like to boast about your installing skills!" I counter.

"Naw, baby," he squeezes my knee, "that was *all you*."

"Well, go back and set up an appointment for all I give a shit."

His jaw ticks. "I haven't made an appointment with another in over two decades."

"Could have fooled me," I snap.

"Gracie," Thatch says calmly, "do you know that I never had a girlfriend before I met your mom?"

I whip my head toward him.

"Refused to. Never dated a girl for longer than two months. Never wanted to. But the first time I saw your mother, I became a one-woman man."

When Gracie doesn't gag, I turn back to see her listening intently, her eyes darting between me and her father, a small smile curving her lips. Her reaction stuns me briefly.

No gag?

No fake puke?

No 'erm my gawd.'

Scrutinizing Gracie a little, his attempt to appease me misfires when his son pipes up from his car seat. "Daddy makes new friends *all the time*, Mommy," Peyton informs.

Thatch eyes his son in the rearview, uttering a low "demon" though his smirk deepens with every mile.

CHAPTER SEVENTEEN

Serena

S TILL FUMING AS I OPEN THE BATHROOM DOOR, I DON'T EVEN detect Thatch until he's pushed me back inside, shut it, and pinned me to the back of it. Chest to my back, he leans in on a heated whisper. "You proud of yourself, Brat? Like making a scene?"

"Let go of me right now, asshat." He only tightens his grip as heat that only makes me angrier starts to gather below. "I mean it, Thatch."

"I don't take orders, baby. Not in here."

Gripping my hip, he yanks it back, running his hard cock along my backside, his words heated as he continues to taunt me. "Threw a little fit, didn't you? Good and fucking proper, I'm thinking maybe you need to be fucked that way. Thinking maybe the vigilant, doting husband isn't quite doing it for you lately."

"You're thinking too much about me, and it's not reciprocal," I snap as he continually runs his cock along the flimsy material of my leggings which are doing little to nothing to barricade the feel of him. Shifting behind me, I'm pressed harder against the door as his zipper sounds. In the next second, my hand is snatched behind me and wrapped around the naked feel of him.

"It's going *somewhere*, Brat. In your fucking mouth, in your pussy, and I swear to God, Serena, if you put up much more of a fight, I'll take your ass, too."

"Thatch," I groan, my blood heating to level insanity as I feel it all—the rush of nostalgia but also the feel of him in the here and now—of his want of me in the here and now. Of my attraction for the man he is. Electricity plays at my fingertips as I jerk against him, resisting him while feeding into our long game.

"I believe you're the one who just pitched a bitch about the thought of another woman trying to take what's yours. Well, here I am, baby. Hard as I've ever fucking been. Isn't this what you wanted?"

My lips curl up, and I purposefully poke the beast within as I scoff, all too ready to play. "Don't flatter yourself. Been there, done that. I'm good."

"Yeah?" He quickly rids me of my hoodie, issuing more venom as he unhooks my bra and rips it from my arms, pinning me again with his cock alone against the door. "Let's see how *'done that'* wet you fucking are."

In an instant, my leggings and panties are peeled down to my thighs before he's running the fat head of his cock up and down my soaked slit. My palms against the door, heavy breasts heaving, I push back against him in offering, anxious for the overly full feel of him. Clit pulsing in anticipation as he wraps my hair into his fist, I angle my head slightly to view us in the mirror and lose my breath at the sight that greets me. His shirt is also absent. From this vantage point, Thatch is all hard lines, his profile drawn into a lethal mix. Both of us naked from the waist up, our pants down mid-thigh, his menacing posture alone spurs me on. His disposition distant but familiar. Absolutely everything about the sight of him sets me alight. Head tilted down, eyes fixed, he looks utterly consumed by the sight of himself—of us—as he continually teases me with the head of his cock, too distracted to notice I'm watching his every move. It's when he presses an inch into me, my hair now fisted as he covers one of my hands with his own on the door, that he starts his slow torture.

"Maybe I should fuck with you," he hisses, feeding me another inch, which is just enough to set me on edge as I feign all calm.

"Maybe you should try to prove whatever point you're trying to make, *Handy Man*."

"Nah," I catch his smirk in our reflection as he pulls out completely. "Not going to work today. You think I don't know what games you play?"

Knowing our time is limited, I shake my head as our reality sets in.

"Thatch, my parents—"

"I couldn't give a fuck less," he drives into me so hard that I cry out, "if the whole fucking house hears us."

"Oh . . . God, yes, but no, not really though, right? Because we're just playing, oh fuck!" Thrust, thrust, thrust, "T-thatch!"

"The only one playing right now," thrust. Thrust. Thrust. Thrust, "is you," he utters, his voice full of lust as he clamps a hand to muffle my increasing moans while tightening his grip on my hair. My clit pulses as he slows his pace to toy with me, sliding in just enough to penetrate without giving me the full feel I'm so desperate for.

"Thatch," I mewl against his palm.

"What's that?" He allows an inch of space for me to speak, loving my beg. It's everywhere on him. His beast on full display. The curve of his perfect ass mesmerizes me, as does the way he rolls himself into me. He's so damned beautiful, but all I can voice is my need.

"Touch me . . . f-fuck me, Thatch. Please."

"Need to be fucked, Brat? I thought you were all good?"

Sliding the palm on my mouth to my throat, he pulls me flush to his chest as he thrusts in deeper while still allowing me to keep my view.

"Yeah, I see you watching me fuck you. I see everything at all times, Mrs. O'Neal. Maybe you should keep that in mind for the future."

He drives in hard to punctuate each word, and I go boneless. Gripping my hip, he bottoms out with his next few thrusts to the point I see stars. I've always loved it hard and a little painful, and when my husband is in this rare mood, he delivers.

Every. Single. Time.

Anxious to feel him, for him to fully unleash, I savor every second of this version of my man, of the hostility in his posture. As much as we played lately, I finally got to him, like I used to—the payoff so incredibly worth it.

"Since you seem determined to send me to an early grave, I'm going down the way I want to." He fills me to the brim, thrusting so hard he practically lifts me from my toes as he muffles my groan. I sink against him, overfull and brimming, my fingers inching toward the pulse between my thighs. Missing nothing as stated, he swats my hand, hard.

"You think you can make yourself come better than I can?" Pushing me back down, he starts to pound into me, his palm firmly against my parted lips as I begin moaning uncontrollably.

"You're so full of shit, Serena. Walking around, putting on airs like you're some kind of nice girl with high standards, but I know better because you love being fucked by this gutter rat."

Thrust, thrust, thrust, thrust, thrust.

I watch him jackhammer into me, lost in sensation, in the movement of his hips, the flex of his ass, all of it as I start to climb.

"Getting close already. You can't fake that. I know this pussy so well. Because I claimed it a long time ago. Just like I know the girl. The girl who wants so badly for permission to act bad."

Thrust. Thrust. Thrust. Thrust.

He strokes me perfectly, to the point I start to climb and tighten around him, even as my pulsing clit begs for attention. Fully attuned, he shoves his fingers into my mouth. "Wet them thoroughly if you want that little clit to get the attention it needs."

Sucking his fingers deep, I soak them as he pumps into me with abandon, my legs shaking uncontrollably as I quickly start to come undone.

"Oh no, you're not getting off so easily." Stopping his hips, he turns his head, finding my eyes in our reflection as he issues his threat. "Maybe you're not getting off at all."

"Thatch," I beg, fucking beg, as he begins to pump into me again, the climb heightened by our connection.

"I know you," he whispers. "I know how fucking filthy your mind is. I know what this pussy wants," he reaches around and presses his fingers against my clit, massaging it so perfectly that I let out a loud moan. "Fuck, for a smart girl, you sure are being fucked stupid," he spits, eyes narrowing as a cry escapes me. "Now we're definitely going to get caught."

"Thatch, please, we don't have much—"

"I'm going to fuck my bitchy little wife for as long as I want," he counters, pounding into me with such force that I inch my lower half away, angling myself to get him deeper.

"Christ, you're so fucking dirty. You only wish you were half as nice as the girl you want to be. But it's your nature, baby. You want that pain, and we both know I can make it fucking hurt."

My answering moan fuels him as he unleashes briefly before slowing and stopping altogether. He shakes his head as if I'm daft to further insult me. "Someone can't handle their dick, so I guess we'll have to stop."

"No," I protest as he pulls out of me, and I turn on him, clawing his biceps.

"Don't you fucking dare," I say, sinking my nails into his skin—something I know turns him on. My husband is no stranger to the love of a little pain with his pleasure. This interlude, as hot as it is, is only half the level of freaky as we can sometimes get. But sadly, I know our time is running out.

"Thatch," I say in a one-word demand.

He lifts a skeptical brow as I peruse him. Covered in a sheen of sweat, his defined pecs heave with his chest as he schools his features expertly. "What'll you give me?"

"Oh, fuck you," I dig my nails in deeper as I dip my gaze to his cock. "I'm not the only one—"

"Nah, see, baby. I can go long stretches in this state. You made sure of that. So, I'll tell you what . . . you get on your knees and beg without words, and I'll think about it."

"You're serious," I gawk as his contempt-filled stare sets in with resignation.

"Knees on the floor now, or I pack this up," he threatens, stroking his perfect dick to the head and back down.

"I guess then, pack it up."

In an instant, I'm flattened to the counter, and he's driving into me. His palm on my crown, lifting my head and forcing me to watch as he palms my mouth again with the other. Fucking me at a furious pace, I'm just about to come when he pulls out.

"Damnit, Thatch," I snap, chest heaving, peaked nipples grazing the counter.

"On. Your. Knees. Brat," he spits as I turn and slowly sink to my knees on the bathmat.

"You know," I hiss, gripping his perfect cock tightly while wetting my lips, "you really shouldn't piss a girl off and then put her in a position that makes you so vulnerable." I bite his head lightly as his eyes flare with satisfaction.

"Why do you think I do it?" He taunts, tracing my lips with the head of his cock.

"Think I can't make it hurt?" I suck in his head and bite a little harder before licking his crown, just before he thrusts it past my open lips, forcing me to take some of his girth in.

"Less talk, more sucking, Serena. There's only one way I want to deal with your mouth today, and it's not for conversation." I take in a little more and smirking, he grips my face, thrusting in deep and gagging me.

"Better," he smarts sarcastically as I start to deep-throat him. Hollowing my cheeks, I go all in, swallowing and sucking while pulling on his sac.

"That's my girl," he murmurs, running his fingers around my lips, reveling in the sight of me, utterly turned on and submissive.

"Fuck, baby, looks like there's going to be a happy ending for *one* of us."

I pop him out of my mouth instantly, even as I stroke him. "Don't you dare—"

"Don't what?" He grips my upper arms, easily lifting me to stand. "Don't tease you to the point you're fucking losing your mind?" He places my hands on the lid of the toilet, so my ass is up in the air, purposely pushing me forward so I'm on my toes. Thighs burning, he lines himself up with me as we glare at each other in the mirror.

"Don't make promises with your mouth you won't back up? Now you know I never do that." Thrust. Thrust. Thrust. Thrust. "Take it, Brat."

He drives home for emphasis as we both go feral, our moans and grunts echoing through the small space as he brings me to fast orgasm, and I succumb, silencing myself just enough so we're not too obvious but loud enough that his eyes fire with victory.

"Once again, Serena, you learn the hard way," he taunts, thrusting into me furiously until I'm certain I'll feel him, feel this, for days to come.

"Come inside me, Thatch," I order, needing him, all of him. Wanting the pain, memorizing the look on his face—which is etched in ecstasy—as he quickens his thrusts to an unreal pace before he lets out a long groan, bordering growl, spilling into me. His orgasm tips me over into another, and his eyes fire in satisfaction as he milks it from me.

"Mmm," he utters, watching me so carefully in the mirror that I know he's marking this memory too. It's when he pulls out, watching his cum spill out appreciatively before pushing it back in, that I turn and snatch his neck, crushing our mouths together. Refusing that this stolen time is over along with me, Thatch's return kiss is just as fiery, just as full of need. When he pulls away, his lips turn up as he palms my face. "I fucking love you, Brat. Always."

I grip his hardening cock in my hand and waste no time spouting my order.

"You too, but I don't want conversation. On the mat, now, and once I suck you hard, don't you fucking dare hold back."

Within a minute or two, he's palming my thigh up on the floor and thrusting back into me. Not long after, we're both palming my mouth.

Wrapped in Thatch and sated sometime later, we stare at one another as if with fresh eyes. The film of the years between us seems to have cleared as we run our hands over one another's skin. I can't stop looking at him, my husband. It's like his presence is new, even if I sleep next to him every night. Years ago, we had this sort of re-connect, but this . . . feels different, and I say as much.

"Where did we go?" I ask.

"We grew up and became parents," he answers instantly, men-tally in the same place.

"I've taken you for granted," I admit, my heart speaking for me as he palms my back.

"Same, baby, same. I see you too, now. For who you are now, and I love what I see."

I palm his jaw and softly say his name to stop his wandering eyes and hands.

"I'm sorry," I tell him sincerely. "I'm sorry I let myself stray so far from the girl you met. Let myself get caught up in my ideas—"

"Fuck that, Serena, I'm falling madly in love with the woman you are now. Maybe that's a horrible thing to say because of what it implicates, but I don't mean it that way."

"No, baby, no. I completely get what you mean. I see you, too."

"We've changed probably half a dozen times in our marriage, and I've fallen in love with every single version of you, Serena . . . but we played those games back then to mask the truth."

"Thatch," my eyes water as I shake my head, refusing what's in his eyes. "I was just remembering getting kicked out of your truck because it wasn't like—"

"Shh baby, it's okay," he murmurs. "You know," he says thought-fully, "I made a decision a long time ago that changed everything. It was before I even laid eyes on you." He gently strokes my cheek with his thumb. "A decision that started me on the path to you. It was a split-second choice to listen to the voice in my head, to my gut, and I've never once regretted it. I've only ever been grateful for it. But even though it led me straight to you—to a life with you—I never truly felt I deserved you or like I belonged in this family. I always felt like I had to earn it. Earn my place with you—with your father at that table downstairs. I felt like an imposter for so long." He scrapes the tears running down my cheeks with gentle thumbs. "It's the one thing you could have used against me in a nasty fight that would have taken me out. Deep down, you've known that but have never used it."

"Because I don't fucking believe it, Thatch, and never will. You aren't your family, your parents."

"Yeah, well, you're the perfect combination of yours," he boasts, "mixed with the little devil I love, and thank fuck for that."

He gazes into my eyes, the inside of his screaming of devotion, of forever.

"But for whatever reason, you and your parents adamantly decided to *make me fit.* I feel it now, baby, my place with you all."

"Only now?" I gape at him. "I can't believe you're saying this. Thatch, you've always—"

He shakes his head gently. "But I didn't truly feel it. No matter how good your parents have been to me, it always felt like a mix of pity, too."

"I hate that," I refute, "I fucking hate it."

"No, baby. It was a mental barrier I could never break through—until now. It's taken me a long, long time, but it's so fucking sweet. Honestly, it feels good. The wait has been worth it," he flashes me a boyish grin. "I feel a little invincible."

I smirk at the fact he's growing hard beneath me. "Seems that way."

"Like I'm twenty again," he smirks as he shifts us, lifting me to straddle him.

"Oh my God, Thatch, we haven't—"

"Fucked three times within an hour in a decade?" His eyes pool as he adjusts himself on his back and lifts me to hover over him. "Yeah, well," he pumps his hips, lightly brushing against me, and I know I'm going to feel this for a week.

"You bring out the beast in me, baby. Always have. And it goes without saying that this," he thrusts up, filling me in one go, "is yours and only yours, but if you need me to prove it again and again," thrust, thrust, thrust. "I'm more than happy to. Any objections?"

I slowly shake my head as our eyes close at the connection. When I'm fully seated, I take control, riding him slowly as our tongues tangle and dance. Our words intertwine as our fingers explore, the diamond on my wedding ring glinting in the light of the bathroom as I glide it over his skin. The feeling of today surreal as I tip over and fall—right back in love with my husband as I have so many times before.

When we finally pull ourselves from the floor sometime later, knees red, backs aching, I bask in the love I feel for him—in the long road it took us to get here. Leaving behind the heartache and uncertainty of the girl I was.

Happily trading that scary time for the love and certainty we feel now versus back then. Our fall was scary in a way, and our road was unclear.

It's far different now. I used to miss the road, the uncertainty, the danger, and the intensity of the connection in the beginning, but all I feel now is grateful. Grateful for the fact we're more solid than we've ever been. Even more so for whatever split decision he made back then that led him to me.

CHAPTER EIGHTEEN

Thatch

AFTER SHOWERING, SERENA AND I MADE OUR WAY downstairs to a much calmer, much more communal atmosphere. The vibe more fitting of the Collins family's typical Christmas. It was almost like magic as we descended the stairs. Erin and Brenden seemed to have ended their cold war—or at least called a temporary truce. And on this blessed third day, Eli rose, but not at all like our messiah. Instead, more in the fashion of an old-school Dracula, sans the creepy arm placement. The faint remnants of a penis still outlined on his face and slightly bloated from the carbs he inhaled in between long naps, he came to, blinking rapidly as Brenden greeted him with a "welcome back brother."

Even Ruby seemed to have forgotten her grudge for us as she handed me my prize-winning cup of snowman soup, declaring me the winner.

"A day late, but you deserve it, Thatch. That house was one for the books." I drank the hell out of that hot chocolate, properly boasting as one should.

Shortly after, Brenden was summoned into the kitchen to learn how to make eggnog. Ruby's reasoning? They weren't going to live forever.

Surprisingly, that kept Brenden's whining to a minimum. Probably because Allen immediately saw fit just after to put Eli and me to work to set up for karaoke. The peace was maintained throughout the day as the girls stayed busy in the kitchen. And we did Allen's bidding, putting the pieces together and stringing lights for his ever-important 'backdrop.'

An Elvis fanatic and former competitor in impersonation, Allen was forced to box up the cabin's den a couple years back. Tears shimmering for days as he packed away endless amounts of memorabilia and trophies. Something he's never quite gotten over, and I swear, still glares at his wife for when she isn't looking.

I glance over at Allen now in remembrance of a different time. A time in which we worked side by side for months all those years ago—when he became the father I never had. When I was a scared shitless kid that had little to no faith in people in general, in the definition of family, or in myself. He allowed me to be his apprentice, into his life and, quickly after, his family. As if he's thinking the same, he glances over at me and shoots me a wink.

"How is business?" He asks.

"Booming, Dad, really. Almost to the point that it's too much sometimes, but I'm dealing."

"I'm thrilled to hear it, my boy. Just please, whatever you do, don't let it get in the way of family," he warns. "Pretty soon, you'll be an old man and won't be as useful."

His words have me pausing as Ruby snaps at Brenden in the kitchen, briefly stealing Allen's attention. My chest tightens painfully at the idea that he might feel more like an ornament in this family at this point.

"Allen," I say, and he waves me away, shaking away any comment I might make in reply. It's clear in his eyes as they flit over his family that he wishes he wouldn't have said anything. Unwilling to drop it, I stand firm in my decision to deliver my rebuttal in a unique way tomorrow morning. One I hope shows him just how much his damned presence means to me.

"Hey, Witchy Poo," Brenden says, bickering with Serena, "stop ratting me out to Mom, you damned buzz kill."

"It's already got enough liquor in it," she snaps, stalking over to grab the bottle he's continually draining into the fresh nog mix, "some of the rest of us would like to drink it, too. *Mom!*"

"Snitches get stitches," Brenden warns.

"Mom!" Serena calls again, knowing Ruby is the only way to stop him.

"I'm in the john," Ruby hollers back faintly.

"Alexa, shut my kids up," Allen says, his fascination with her a lot less than it was when he started his affair with her years ago. Not a second later, she answers from a nearby speaker. "*I'm not quite sure how to help you with that, Allen.*"

He grins over to me. "See? Even the smartest woman in existence has no idea how to raise kids."

I share his chuckle. "I'm glad we stopped at two. Don't know how you managed *three*," I pluck the electrical tape from the nearby bin.

"I didn't manage shit," he says, "it's a miracle they still have heads."

"Oh, you getting mad, sister?" Brenden taunts Serena, "are you so, *so mad?*" He continues, holding the bourbon bottle out of reach as she jumps for it.

"God, I can't stand you," she snaps, swiping one last time for it to no avail. When she turns in a huff to stalk out of the kitchen, Brenden quickly pulls a piece of paper towel off the holder, pinning the top corners of each side with his finger to each of her shoulders while shadowing her. The paper catches air, looking every bit like a little cape as she snaps back at him.

"The hell are you doing, idiot?"

"Now you're *super mad*," he snickers as Eli and I burst into laughter. Serena turns herself completely out of his hold, managing a cat swipe on his chin before her own laughter gets the best of her.

"Gah," she laughs, "you are the worst brother, fucking ever."

In response, Brenden surprisingly pulls her into him for a hug.

"Of that, I'm proud, but I vow to you I didn't add but a half a cup more, Witchy. I shall not ruin the nog. Let's stop the bitch fest, and get along today, for Mom, okay?" he proposes.

Serena, surprised by his gesture, hugs him back tightly and nods into his chest . . . just as Brenden angles them to give me and Eli a flash of the fingers he has crossed at his back. His smirk growing over the top of Serena's head, where she still hugs her brother.

Fucker.

God, how I love this family.

As I watch the two of them, I become convinced Peyton got some of his fuck all, devilish genes from his nightmare of an uncle. Briefly, I imagine and can only hope that Gracie and Peyton have a similar relationship as adults one day. Even if it's filled with sibling rivalry and a little bickering. Because at the heart of it, I know they'll have each other's backs when it really matters.

As the day winds down and delicious smells begin to fill the cabin, the Christmas spirit arrives. Not long after a thankfully uneventful but delicious dinner of Allen's 'roast beast,' we all huddle together in front of the stage for karaoke. Serena sits next to me, Jameson in her lap as Peyton watches on, seemingly a very jealous man. Allen surprises us all by kicking off the night with a rendition of "Lady" by Kenny Rogers rather than his typical Elvis tribute. His timbre and delivery are pure talent. So much so that even the kids watch on, stunned by it.

The song is old and most likely lost in most collector's archives, but it's significant to me because of the memory it stirs.

Probably as close to as significant for the man currently serenading his tearful wife. The memory brings one I hadn't got to recollect yet—of one of my favorite nights with Serena in our shed, or rather outside of it. Though Serena's remembrance has her past me in the timeline of our early days, I know I'm left behind in one of the sweetest spots. At least for me, because the very first time I heard this song was just after Christmas—before I lost my shit and kicked Serena out of my truck, ending what we started.

Already freaked out by her insistence that we take our relationship out of the safe space of the shed, the reality and fear that fueled me to end it after my run-in with Daniel drove the guttural truth home for me.

But before the night I almost lost the love of my life to utter fucking stupidity, there was the last push into my full-fledged fall.

"I'm hungry," Serena says, looking over to me. "Let's have a Honey Baked ham sandwich."

"What?"

"Ever had one?"

"No," I tell her. "What's Honey Baked ham?"

"Oh, baby, it's the fucking greatest," her endearment a first, it rocks me slightly as she continues. "The sweetest ham ever, but not too sweet. It's a place that specializes in ham. It's got a brown sugar crusty outer layer, and it's just, it's so good."

Serena knows ham is my favorite, and my mouth waters at the idea of it.

"It sounds good."

"Okay," she pulls away from me and straightens her clothes, looking thoroughly kissed and freshly sated. The sight of her like this is my favorite. Standing in front of me, she holds out her hand expectantly.

"I'm not going with you," I shake my head.

"Let's think through this logically, Thatch. You just fingered me to orgasm out here. Now weigh that," she lifts her hands to mimic a tipping scale, "against getting caught making a fucking ham sandwich with me in our kitchen. Which do you think would upset Allen more?"

"Good point," I say, standing.

She threads our fingers together and glances up at me. "They know we're together, Thatch."

"Serena—"

"Ah, fuck ya objections tonight, my gorgeous man," she lifts and plants one on me. "Let me be happy with you, okay?"

Biting my lip, I nod, loving every word she spoke even as my heart cracks at the fact that very soon, I'm going to strip every one of her notions about us away. Pissed at myself for not being honest with her the way Allen ordered me to, I squeeze her hand.

"Come on, baby, I'm starving."

"Because you just smoked two joints," I counter, counting two 'babies' and one 'gorgeous man'. I'm so fucked, and the thing is, I want to be. But I can't be. I can't fucking be here. I'm done. I'm a free man, and she's now standing in the way of it. I was supposed to tell her tonight, and I couldn't. I couldn't look at her and be honest, again.

"Will you ever smoke with me?" She asks as we make our way toward the house.

"I doubt it," I say honestly, the thought of driving away from Nashville now becoming less and less appealing. As we both cross the deck, hand in hand, music starts to filter through the air, gaining volume as we draw closer to the house. The arrival of it has me hesitating.

"Huh," she says, "well, they're definitely up."

Unease takes hold as she grips my hand more tightly and immediately ushers me through the back door so I can't object. Once inside, Kenny Rogers' voice fills the air, and the two of us sneak through the short hallway that leads between the kitchen and living room. Serena stops just short of the living room, her face quickly becoming covered in various shades of Christmas lights as her expression morphs into one of utter captivation. Studying her just as carefully as whatever she's surveying, I know that what she's seeing, she wants for herself. I'm only further convinced as her eyes water, and she looks over to me, nodding her head, encouraging me to peek in.

Moving to stand behind her, her crown resting just inches from my lips, I stare into the living room to see Ruby and Allen dancing next to their Christmas tree. The two of them tangled together, their posture intimate, their eyes locked. But it's the way they're looking at one another that briefly steals my breath. More specifically, the look in Serena's mother's eyes. A look that convinces me of what I'm starting to feel—believe. Because I've seen that same look in her daughter's eyes. More than once.

Love.

Swallowing, I slide my arm around Serena's waist, and she sinks back against me as we watch her parents dance. When the song ends, Journey's "Open Arms" begins to play, and I can't help my words.

"I love this song," I whisper to her temple as she sways in front of me.

"Me too," she says, stilling when I don't entertain her movement. She runs her fingers gently against my hand as I feel myself sinking deeper and deeper into the feelings threatening to puncture my skin, utterly incapable of uttering a single word to her to describe what she makes me feel. But for the first time in my life, wanting to. Fisting my free hand, Serena holding the other, securing her to me, she turns in my arm, giving me the very look Ruby is openly giving her husband.

She loves me.

Warring emotions strangle me mute as she looks up at me, her profile lit. This girl who doesn't see any of my mistakes or the glaring differences between us. Mistakes I've purposely kept her blind to. Concealed from her to steal more nights away and as many blistering kisses as we can before I'm forced to leave her.

"You know what else I love?" She asks.

I swallow and swallow again. It takes every bit of effort for me to slowly shake my head. Heart on fucking fire, I wait on bated breath for what's coming.

No part of me wants to run away if she gives me the words, but no part of me thinks she's anywhere near a place where she can align herself fully to them—align herself to a guy like me. She may love what we have hidden away from reality, but she would fucking hate ours if she knew what being with me consisted of—of the condemnation. The price and consequences that come with choosing me. But even as I think it, I'm swept in by the softness in her rich brown eyes, by her touch as she palms my jaw, and I close mine briefly. By her scent as she surrounds me in a warmth I never knew existed. Utterly fucking gone for this girl, I feel myself holding my breath as she leans in, and I close my eyes in anticipation.

"Ham. I love ham," she says, giggling as she rips all fucking hope from my chest and drags me into the kitchen.

Glancing over at her now, all these years later, I catch her eyes already on me. The same litter of colorful lights dance along her profile as she gazes back at me, and without a doubt in my mind, I know she's lost in the very same memory. This sweet spot, in the here and now, has my chest stretching, tightening with gratitude. Gratitude I felt then and still feel thanks to the crystal-clear love reflecting in her eyes as she mouths "I love you" just as the song finishes.

Serena and I remain in an eye lock as we both start to clap. Just after, I pass Wyatt off to his mother and stand. Serena frowns at my unreturned sentiment, and I feel her gaze on me as I walk over to where Whitney sits next to Eli, Peyton in her lap. Bending, I whisper my request to my wife's sister, and Whitney looks back at me, giving me a grin and a quick nod.

Minutes later, the opening notes of Open Arms start to play as Brenden fake gags before he's struck stupid by a Kleenex box, thanks to Ruby.

As Whitney, the most incredible of songbirds—her voice literally one of an angel—begins to rival Steve Perry's delivery, I catch my wife's eyes and walk over to offer my hand. Serena stares down at it, a rare blush warming her cheeks as she hands Jameson off to her brother before taking it. Ushering her from the couch, I walk her in front of the Christmas tree and pull her into my arms, and after twenty-two years, I dance with her.

We've probably danced twice in our entire marriage. Both times at our weddings, but I dance with her tonight not out of obligation or because it's expected but, in truth, because I fucking want to. Like I did all those years ago. Because when I saw Ruby and Allen dancing that night, Serena's want became my own. It became my hope for us, even if I was terrified to both want and admit it.

And so, as I stare into my wife's watering eyes, I gaze upon her with the same love in remembrance of the exact moment I knew I did. It's then that I find the words I couldn't back then and bend to whisper the return sentiment. The way I wish twenty-year-old me had the moment I felt it all those years ago. But I decide it's better late than never. And though I've said it a thousand times or more after that night, I make sure it rings clear for the time I felt it and failed to use the words.

"I love you, Serena Collins."

Sniffing, I feel her nod for not using our shared last name because she knows.

CHAPTER NINETEEN

Thatch

"MAY THE LORD BE WITH YOU," THE PRIEST FINISHES.
"And also with you," the congregation replies in unison as the music begins filtering in, concluding midnight mass. The crowd begins to disburse, and Gracie and Serena file out of the pew along with the rest of the family. Searching for my son, I find Peyton standing in the middle of the aisle, blocking traffic, staring at the priest who's greeting people before they start filing out of the church.

"Come on, Peyton," I usher as he keeps his eyes glued to the priest, his intrigue confusing me. He turns to me suddenly, wide green eyes earnest.

"Daddy, I need to speak to him," Peyton says. "Okay, Dad—er, Sir?"

I bite away my grin at the way he's addressing me as I look over to see the priest surrounded.

"I mean," I swallow, "He's pretty busy. So you might—"

Peyton turns as if on a mission, and I'm on his heels when he stops a good five feet away and turns back to me. "Daddy, is I respect you if I ask you not to come?"

"What?" I cringe at the idea of my four-year-old son approaching a Catholic priest, which starts to sound like an opening line for a joke, with a punchline I'm pretty sure will humiliate me.

"He's busy. Maybe I can help you?"

"No, no," Peyton shakes his head adamantly. "Can you twust me, Daddy?"

"Uh." *No, no, no, please, no, not in your house, God.*

But it's my son's shaky voice and wide eyes that have me hesitantly giving in. "Okay, but please mind your manners."

He's already turned again as he walks over, his voice nowhere near church level as he instantly starts to yank on the priest's robe.

"Excuse me, Sir. Please, Sir, are you Jesus's friend?" Peyton asks, glancing back at me to make sure I've kept my respective distance as I sink where I stand. My gut tells me to stop this as my son's eyes plead with me to let him go through with whatever exchange is about to happen.

Most of our family is already out of the cathedral, and I can feel Eli's eyes on the two of us—forever the protective, doting uncle, even from where he idles far enough away to give us this moment. As the church continues to empty, Peyton's voice carries more clearly back to me. Dressed in a suit that Eli got him as a present, I can't help but notice how adorable he looks. Eli even styled his hair tonight, slicking it back in a modern-day Pompadour. As I admire his dress, my nerves fire off as my heart starts to gnaw at me for the things I've done in the last week. The fear is real that I'm about to get in trouble in the house of the Lord if my kid rats me out. The feeling sucks, and maybe I deserve it. I don't have long to mull it over when the man is cut abruptly from his well wishes by the blunt and overly polite demands of my loud kid.

"Sir, excuse me. I respect you, Sir, but excuse me, I weally need to talk to you!"

The priest glances down at Peyton and smiles, his eyes drifting over to find his parent—me—before he diverts his attention back to Peyton. He looks a lot younger than the norm, and I note he's probably only a decade older than me, at most.

"Hello, young man," he bends down to make up their difference in height, "how can I help you?"

"I," Peyton dawdles as I move to intercept him, but the priest holds out his hand to let me know his patience isn't thinning. Swallowing, I gaze on at my boy with longing in my heart. It's then I realize I miss him. Just as much as I missed my wife's absence, and the sting becomes harder as it starts to lodge in my throat.

"I'm sorry, Sir. I don't know. Can I ask, are you Jesus bess friend?"

"I like to think I am," he replies, clearly entertained.

"Is it okay if Jesus comes to my Grammy's house tonight?"

"Sorry?"

"Rudolph's not coming," Peyton proclaims as if it's already a fact. It's the acceptance in his voice that has the ache increasing tenfold. I've convinced him, and nothing about that sits well with me.

"What makes you think that?"

"I've been bad. I'm on the naughty list," Peyton admits easily, ratting himself out as a lump grows unbearably while my curiosity grows at his request for a visit from the messiah himself.

"So, you want Jesus to come instead?"

"Jesus job is for miracles to work?"

"He's a miracle worker," he nods. "That's right."

Peyton leans in. "Grammy says we need a miracle to make Christmas better."

"What kind of miracle?" The priest asks as the burn in my throat spreads to my chest.

Peyton quickly glances over his shoulder before leaning in. "I need him to—" I strain to hear but to no avail. Frustrated, I take a step forward just as the gut punch is delivered by the way of the priest.

"Why would Jesus need to bring your daddy back to you? Is your father not behind you?"

"He's not my daddy anymore. He's not nice to me because I was too bad for too long, and he's over it."

I'm going to hell.

"I see. Well, Peyton, the truth is that Jesus is everywhere in spirit, so you can ask him anytime."

"Right there," Peyton says, pointing to the cross on the wall, one I know he's terrified of and purposely avoids looking at during service every year.

"Right here," the Priest fires, pressing his palm to Peyton's heart as my eyes burn with the sting. "But, from what I'm hearing you say, you are the one who can bring your daddy back."

"I dunno, Sir . . . am I respect you and be polite?"

"Very," the priest nods.

"I'm trying very hard!" Peyton declares in watery exasperation, that has my heart cracking dead center.

"Then that's all you can do." The priest shoots me a look, one of reassurance, as I softly call Peyton's name.

"You better run along, Peyton, but remember, you can talk to Jesus at any time if you want him to visit."

Peyton looks up at the graphic cross, thorns, and blood, and I see it the instant he makes his decision before he stalks toward the twelve-foot, bloodied messiah and bravely starts to shout at him. "Jesus, if I promise to be nice, can you please send my daddy back?!"

"Very good," The priest says, knowing his message didn't quite get received, but *mine did*. My son just had a figurative and literal come to Jesus moment—for me. Bursting at the seams and desperate to get my son in my arms, I stalk over and make it to him just as he turns to me, his eyes brimming with tears.

"I'm right here, buddy," I assure him.

"Not you," his lips quiver. "Not *you*," he cries, face twisted in anguish.

And with that, I crack clear in half. Scooping him into my arms, he cries loudly as I pass Eli, my eyes spilling over as reality sets in. I fucked up. Badly. I've scared my son, my boy, my baby. My behavior doing nothing but intimidating him into becoming an overly polite asshole.

"Peyton, I'm right here, buddy. I'm right here," I whisper hoarsely as he pushes at my chest to free himself of me as I continually break. I'm furious with myself for thinking there was any other way through this than plain old parenting. No shortcuts to fast results will do over patience, guidance, and example. There's no quick fix, and I was a fucking fool to think otherwise.

"Not you," he pushes at my chest again and again, adamantly trying to wiggle out of my arms. "My *other* daddy," he accuses as his palpable heartbreak sears my chest raw with a hellfire I've rarely felt. His cries cracking me wide open as I stalk down the aisle and push through the doors. Stepping outside into the brisk night, I glance toward the parking lot, lifting my finger to Serena and Gracie who sit in wait in the idling SUV.

Stalking out of the way of the passersby, I round the corner of the sidewalk.

"Peyton," I say, sitting him down to stand on the side of the church, the sight of his tiny wingtips rawing my heart out further as I take a knee in front of him. "Buddy, I'm sorry."

Peyton's face twists in anguish as he cries openly in front of all of the church traffic, and I find myself giving no shits who lays witness. I caused this and deserve whatever they hear.

"Daddy's been bad this week," I rasp out. "But he just wanted you to understand that all little boys don't get the things you get. My daddy didn't do the things I do for you. He wasn't my best friend, Son. He was really mean to me, and I just want you to know that, so you try to be nice to your mommy and daddy, who try so hard to be nice to you."

He cries a little longer, his words breaking as he finally speaks.

"So you s-say sorry, then we can be n-nice again to each odder, D-Daddy?" his voice drags with his soul-deep plea. "Please, Sir? If I promise to try really hard to be good every day?"

"Yes, that's all your Daddy wants. So much. Mommy does too, I swear," I say before he plasters himself to me, his little chest heaving. Feeling every bit the asshole I am, I try to soothe him with words of comfort, running my hand over his thick hair and down his back. "I'm sorry, buddy. I never wanted to be mean to you. I'm just trying to make you understand and I didn't do it the right way. Sometimes, daddies aren't good at their job, and I'll do better, too. I promise."

"I hated it when Rudolph stolded our tree," he airs his grievances in a shaky voice. "I hate it Mommy won't eat cereal with me. Mommy is so mad. You are so, so mad and distapointed. I don't want to be in trouble anymore, Daddy. Is that okay?" he sniffs, "Sir?" he whispers pointedly in my ear, which singes me to ashes.

"Peyton," I croak, holding him tightly, clutching my beautiful boy with my arms along with the whole of my heart. For the baby who stared right back at me just after making his entrance into the world. Seconds from his birth, capturing me utterly. "I'm so sorry for not being nice."

"It's okay, Daddy." He pats my shoulder, consoling me as I realize I'm crying just as hard as he is.

"I want you to listen to me and listen good, okay?"

He nods.

"Yes, you've been very naughty, and you've done some naughty things, but I love you so much, Peyton O'Neal. More than anything on this earth. And you might not be a good boy all the time, but you're *my boy*, and I'm proud of you. Mommy is too. No matter what, okay?"

"I'm proud of you, Daddy . . . Sir, oh my dawd," he laughs, palming his face nervously. A hint of fear in the gesture but a recognition of authority. Healthier fear and recognition than none at all. One that might have him stopping in the parking lot when I order him to do so. With that image forever in my mind, I try not to guilt myself over it. Whatever damage I've done with my fucking stunt, I'll do my best to rectify if need be. Peyton holds me for long seconds, well, longer than the usual three before I speak up.

"Can I tell you something?" I ask him.

"Uh huh," he whispers, his full focus on me.

"When you ran in the parking lot when Daddy told you not to, I've never been so scared in my life, Peyton." My vision blurs as the images resurface. "That truck almost hurt you," anguish fills me at the sight of the truck whizzing by a second, two at most, after I snatched him into my arms. A vision I've been trying to outrun since it happened. "I've never been so scared in my whole life. Daddy would never be okay if anything happened to you. Mommy would never be okay, either."

"I'm sorry, Daddy."

"I'm glad you are, but please, please don't ever do that again," I croak. "Don't ever run from me like that, okay? You're my whole world, my whole life. I can't do this without you, okay?"

"Okay, I won't ever run in a parking lot again." He holds out his tiny hand to keep his promise, and I swallow, doing my best to keep my shit together as I take it.

"Thank you." As we start to walk toward the SUV, I glance down at him and see his chest bounce as I whisper my assurances. "It was just a bad couple of weeks, buddy. Okay? That's all this was. We'll have more bad days and bad weeks—that's just the way it is, but if you want, we can start making it better right now."

"It's okay if Rudolph gives my toys away." He gives me his puppy dog eyes as he rambles on. "I really, really want that Rail Ride, but I duderstand I've been bad."

And there's my wide-eyed, manipulative boy. I can't help my grin at his arrival.

"Maybe Rudolph heard you apologize," I wink.

He nods, his little chest heaving from the strength of his cries. Unable to help myself, I scoop him up, kissing the tear lining his little cheek. "I love you. Big hug."

"Big hug," he parrots, squeezing me tight as I release a few relieved tears of my own, knowing I'll never be able to erase or outrun the image of my baby nearly losing his life. Seconds, mere seconds. When he pulls away and shoots me my own smile—my little replica—I melt, deciding if it's the last thing I do, I'm going to make his Christmas special. He's been put through the wringer and is starting to deserve it.

Fuck it, he's mine to spoil *and discipline*.

That's the job. Loving him is the easy part. Parenting is the rest.

"Let's go home and hurry to put some carrots out, okay?"

"Yes!" Peyton shouts. "We have to hurry, Daddy!"

"Let's go."

After I get him buckled in and take the wheel, I glance over to Serena, who sees my reddened eyes, splotched face, and tense. "Oh my God, baby. What is it?"

I open my mouth to speak when my little mouth piece explains for me.

"I runned in the parking lot and almost got hit, Mommy. Daddy cried and asked me never to do that again."

Serena grips my hand tightly in hers as I wordlessly beg her to forgive me. I told her about the scare, but I hadn't told her how much it fucked me up. But I allow her to see it now and let her fully in. The way I always have. In her return gaze, I see nothing but trust, understanding, and the love and strength I've come to rely on for half my life.

"Let's go home."

"Yes, all buckled, Daddy Sir. We have to get the carrots and hurry!" Peyton rings out as Serena's eyes widen, and she mouths a "wow."

I nod, leaning over to take her lips in a brief kiss. "I love you, Brat."

"Love you too, Handy Man," she whispers as we both wait for the comment that doesn't come and instead freeze when something else entirely does.

"Merry Christmas," Gracie whispers, and I glance back in the rearview to find her expression sheepish but sincere.

"Merry Christmas," Serena and I parrot, my wife's smile hidden from Gracie so as not to make her amusement too obvious. But

THE SLEIGHT BEFORE CHRISTMAS | 199

it's because I know my wife felt it, as I have—the slight shift in our family dynamic. Small or big as it might be, it's perceptible enough to have a little pride running through me. We're nowhere near perfect, but we're not where we were a week ago, and that's enough. Plenty.

"Merry Christmas," Peyton rings out last as I take in the sight of all three of them before putting the SUV into gear and pulling out of the church parking lot. Clicking on The Wiggles as we hit the mile mark, my son's joy is worth the torture, a balm to my stinging heart.

Not long after, with carrots on the fireplace, Serena and I usher Gracie onto the couch in the living room. I toss a few logs on the fire as Serena sits next to our daughter, whose eyes are darting between us as if she's waiting for her verdict.

"You're grounded for three months," I state before turning around. "There won't be a single exception for any reason. You'll go to school, come home, do your homework, and your chores. You'll be limited to internet and other things, but you won't be going *anywhere.*"

"No worries there, I don't think I'll ever be invited anywhere again," she says, her lips wobbling as she turns to Serena. "I'm sorry." She looks up at me. "I'm sorry, Dad. I know you don't believe me, but I really am. I just didn't want to be the only one without a basket. It's so stupid. And now, God, I'm so embarrassed. The way they looked at me after I got caught. I don't even want to go back to school," she palms her face and cries for a few seconds. We both stand by to let her process it before she pulls her hands away. "Daddy, I know this is the one thing that you can't forgive me for—"

"Not true. I come down on you hard and talk to you about theft often for good reason, Gracie."

"You hate thieves," she states. "You said it a million times that there's nothing you hate more than a thief—than someone who takes what others work for."

"It's the truth, but there's very little I won't forgive you for," I tell her honestly. "We all make mistakes and screw up, but your mother and my main concern right now is who you'll become if you continue to think you're owed everything. No one, not even your parents, owes you anything. But our love is free. There's a reason I hate thieves, Gracie, and I think it's time I tell you about the day I met your grandpa."

She looks up at me as my chest starts to burn. "It was one of the scariest days of my life, the worst and the best." I kneel down in front of her to make sure she doesn't miss a word. "You haven't asked too much over the years, but there's a reason you've never met my parents or my brother and never will. But you're old enough now to know the truth, and your mother and I think you need to." Serena stares at me, concern marring her features. Gracie does the same, her expression more of curiosity as I kick open a door I've long since shut.

CHAPTER TWENTY

Serena

ZIPPING MY LAST SUITCASE, I GLANCE OUT OF MY BEDROOM window to see the darkened shed. I haven't been out there once in the last four days. I haven't stalked it to see if he's been there. Been waiting, allowing my anger and hurt to overrule the urge. To protect me from suffering any more humiliation. I went out on a limb and actually fought for the time I stole with Thatch. Too much already to continue to respect myself if I do anything more without reciprocation. No matter how good it felt.

After carrying my bag down the stairs and placing it next to my luggage, the dread for the trip sets in—along with the knowledge that I'll be back at school tomorrow. Trepidation seeping in, briefly, I allow the ache to outweigh the anger, and it's then my feet move of their own accord. Within minutes, I'm stepping inside the shed.

Heartache seeps into every pore as I glance around the lifeless space. Sections of the darkened room being replaced by flickering amber light-laced memories. Some of the best of my life. A few of us talking while measuring our hand against the others. Others of him hovering above me, wordless but in the midst of discovery.

202 | KATE STEWART

The first night seeps in, that memory hitting the hardest. Where Thatch stood at the workbench and glanced back at me, and the words he spoke.

"Looking for something?"

I had. I'd been searching for some time for a connection like ours—even if it had turned out to be one-sided. What I felt with Thatch was unmatched. Even if it wasn't strong enough to hold him. He's never made a tenth of my effort, and despite his lash-out, it's the true reason I made peace with letting him go.

The connection was there, something that felt it could be lasting, but I'm done trying to make him see it. Done waiting for him to respect and care for it. Even if it seemed to come so fast. I wasn't alone in that—that I'm certain of.

He'd been warning us about it the whole time, and I've played ignorant, but I'm fully aware that what we had felt was rare, and if he refuses to catch hold of it, then it's time to let it go. On that front, I agree I deserve better.

Making peace with the heartache, I'm about to turn when I catch sight of a wooden box sitting in the middle of the workbench. Walking toward it, my breath catches as it comes into view. Standing eight inches tall, the wooden jewelry box calls me like a beacon, a glittering red bow atop it. In seconds, I'm trailing my fingers over the slightly tacky wood. The fact that it's newly painted has my heart skipping a beat. Built in the shape of a tiny armoire, the handles on the double doors are shaped into arched, carved branches. The wood sanded and highlighted by a light stain and gloss. It's painfully apparent he spent endless hours working on it. My heart knocks with surety that so much care went into making it. Just as I'm about to pull open one of the double doors, his voice sounds behind me.

"It's empty," he whispers through the space, directly to my pounding heart—a heart that starts to hammer at the sound of his voice. Pulling the door open, I see two drawers with similar branch handles lining the bottom, and I turn the rotating necklace hanger on the top.

"*You wear a lot of jewelry, but that's one thing I'm afraid I couldn't add to it.*"

"*It's beautiful, Thatch. Thank you.*"

"*You deserve jewelry, Serena. You deserve glittering things on your beautiful ears, laying on your neck, pushed on your fingers, and I'm not the man that can give them to you.*"

"*If you truly feel like that's what I want, then you don't know me. But the trouble is, you do know me.*"

"*I'm sorry for the other day. I just didn't fucking want that piece of shit to know what you meant to me. Because you know it hasn't been fun for me, Serena, but it can't be more.*"

"*Yeah,*" *I run my finger along the wood. "I heard you the first dozen times.*"

"*I'm leaving, too,*" *he states. "I'm leaving Nashville.*"

"*For how long?*" *I ask, tears filling my eyes.*

"*For good,*" *he delivers, and my chest starts to roar with protest. "I'm never coming back, and that's why I was hesitant to start this up.*"

"*Where?*" *I clip, unable to look back at him as my heart rages in my chest, begging me to look at its new owner. Because I know I'm half in love with him.*

"*I was thinking Alaska.*"

"*Thinking Alaska? What do you mean thinking Alaska?*"

"*There's no future for me here,*" *he states, his words like a sling blade to my heart. It's then I know I'm not halfway anything. This man who's moving to Siberia—America, is taking my fucking heart with him.*

"*Well, you did. You met me here every night, and you started something. I did give you an out, Thatch.*"

"*I know, but fuck, I didn't expect it to feel like this.*"

"*Yes, you did. We both did. You were there the first night. You felt it, too. And after. Once you kissed me, touched me, you knew. At least I can say I fought for it.*"

"*That's because you didn't know who you were fighting for, Serena.*"

"*The fuck I didn't,*" *I finally look back at him, done asking the questions. His stare intent as he approaches. His scent surrounds me,* weakening me as he holds me captive. It's then I fully drink him in. His expression bleak, he looks tired, exhausted, and utterly disheveled. The sight of him only makes my heart ache more because I know it's because of me—because of our fight and the distance in the last four days. His outsides match my insides as he rattles in front of me, warring on whether or not to release the words. I stand my ground, knowing if he's ending this, I deserve them, while terrified of finally knowing his reasons for continually pushing me away.

"I couldn't ask you out because I'm twenty years old and barely a step above homelessness. I sleep between a rundown motor inn and my truck and don't have a damned thing to offer you. I'm a high school dropout who stole a car because his dad ordered him to pitch in, or he would kick him out. See, once upon a time, I was good at it. I stole everything, and when I quit, my heart and head wasn't in it. So when I was ordered to do it, I got caught and went to fucking prison."

Shock paralyzes me mute as he carefully weighs my expression.

"Up until a week ago, I was still on probation, and that's why I didn't . . . couldn't smoke that weed. I was a fucking week away from being sent back for not paying my restitution on time when I got the job with Allen. Thanks to your father and his odd jobs, I've paid my way out. Now that I'm free, I want to dust this place, this fucking city, because everyone with the last name O'Neal is a reminder of the life I fled. But stealing was so much fucking easier. I've had to fight the inclination every fucking day since we met because I wanted to give you everything. But I fought harder because I don't want to be that gutter rat anymore."

"Thatch—"

He shakes his head incredulously. "I don't know what the hell Ruby and Allen were thinking. You're practically a debutante who comes from a well-off, somewhat affluent family, and I'm . . . half of the O'Neal's, my family, are convicted felons. The other half are wastes of human life. So do yourself a favor and pop any illusion bubble you might have about us. This was exactly as you said, fun. You're beautiful, and I'm crazy about you, but you deserve to know why." He whispers a thumb along my cheek. "You're going to make some man—"

I pop him good as my chest roars with the pain, and he doesn't so much as flinch.

"Some other guy happy, Thatch? Why not leave me with 'it's not you, it's me.' How about this isn't the right time? Want to quote a goddamn after-school special from the eighties, or how about a beer slogan? Jesus Christ, Thatch, give me a minute to try to understand the truth about you!"

The handprint on his face blisters my insides. "I'm so sorry I—" I cover the light handprint I left with my palm as tears spill over my cheeks. He didn't even flinch when I did it, which is all I need to know. He's been taking hits his whole life—physical and otherwise—and it's evident as he stares back at me, lifting his chin slightly as if he's ready for more. "I've never struck another human in my life. Not like that. I'm sorry." The tears come faster. "Why are you hurting me?"

"I'm doing you a favor, Serena. I swear I am. Just let me save you the trouble."

"Jesus, Thatch, can't I at least get a chance to make the decision?"

"No," he states before turning and stalking off, the sob that escapes me stopping him at the door of the shed. He stares back at me with little to no life in his eyes, but his voice shakes with his delivery. "I'm glad I met you. I'm glad I got to know you." He wavers slightly but maintains. "To kiss your beautiful face, touch you. But fucking you would ruin me, and so I didn't go there. I knew the second we got that intimate I wouldn't be able to walk away from you. I'm too into you to deal with that, and I'm too set on leaving to stay for a girl who will only see the light one day too late. I'm sorry, but this has to be classified as nothing but fun. Take care, Serena."

"You know what you have to offer me?" I snap, and he stops, keeping his back to me. "You. And that would be all I needed. Anything I want, I can work for and obtain my fucking self. All I want from you, Thatcher O'Neal, is you."

When he remains standing there, I feel my mother's gaze at that table as resignation sets in. To fight, for the first time in a very long time for an idea, a spark, the strongest inclination I've had in forever to seek the life I want.

"You know, when I got to school, I thought I would meet all these amazing, creative thinkers who would open my mind and intrigue me—make me look at the world differently. Expand my horizons and all that crap. But it was so obvious that I had just landed in an amplified version of high school. Same guys, fuckboys, only down for themselves. And girls who were only interested in the fuckboys. At the first party," I swallow, "I was miserable because the truth rang home as I looked around. And just before I walked out, I realized the worst feeling in the world is being surrounded by people and feeling completely and utterly alone."

I swallow and swallow again.

"All I could do to keep my shit together was look forward to Christmas break, and ironically, all I had to do was get here to meet the mind, the guy I thought I would find in college. Because you fascinate me, you intrigue me. You see through my bullshit and call me out on it. You rebuke the persona I've been ridding myself of since high school. You're the first person I've met since then that felt like the right company—fuck that, felt right for me. That sparked something inside me and made me feel like I wasn't alone."

"Serena—"

"So fuck you. I'm glad it was fun for you, Thatch, but I'm pretty sure you just broke my God damned heart because as crazy as this may sound, I'm in love with you. God," I shake my head, palming my burning cheeks as he snaps his head toward me, eyes glazed.

"Don't fuck with me."

"Fuck with you?" I scoff. "I'm not. You know I'm not, but it seems I'm the fool of the two of us. I mean, you warned me, but I guess I thought you couldn't walk away from this. I know I couldn't. So, I guess, make sure to drop us a postcard from fucking Alaska, jackass."

"Tell me again."

"That you what? That you're a dumb bastard who's walking out on a good woman? Nah, I'll spare myself since I'm the only one saying anything that actually means something."

Heartbeats pass as he stares at me, his expression guarded, his eyes glazing. He swallows and swallows again, fists at his sides. "What if I love you?"

"Well, if you're willing to walk out on me with that shitty kiss good-bye and nothing but a 'see ya,' your love can't be worth much."

His voice breaks on every word of his reply. "My dream has been to leave this place for ten fucking years, Serena. To escape my family. To leave it all behind."

"You already have, Thatch, just not mentally, and running to the Alaskan wilderness to do it isn't the fucking solution. Ever heard the saying, 'everywhere you go, there you are?' Same shit. You're too smart to believe otherwise," I state, unsure if my heart is still pumping because I knew the minute I saw Thatch O'Neal that he would mean something to me. The confirmation running with surety of what that something is now because I've fallen in love with an idiot.

"Well, then, go, my first heartbreak. I gotta admit, it stings like a bitch, but I'm sure I'll move on. Go to Alaska, Thatch. Your destiny awaits."

"Say it again, Serena."

"Leave!" I screech. "You've humiliated me, and I'm not a fan of that. Maybe you aren't so special."

"I can't," he swallows as if the words are hard to get out, "I can't imagine never touching you again," he rasps out hoarsely. "I can't imagine a future without you now, God damnit!" His expression shatters me, the hope in his eyes blinding me as our eyes bolt and hold. "I've done everything right since I met your dad, gone against every instinct drilled into me since I was a kid. To take, take, take what didn't belong to me. To steal what someone else has worked for. To take what someone else deserved. But if you say you're mine, you better fucking mean it."

"Look at me, Thatch," my chest heaves and shudders as I feel like I'm about to explode. Too many feelings, too damned soon. If this isn't love, then it's something really close. "Do I mean it? I feel like I'm dying, so do what you will with that," My chest bounces as tears stream down

my cheeks. "But if you take another step away from me, you will never get to know."

"Don't fuck with me," he repeats, his eyes shining. "Please don't fuck with me. I can't give you some fairy tale life. I'm not the fairy tale guy. I don't know how hard it will be with me. I'm a convicted felon and I'm . . . it will be hard."

"I don't care. My heart is set on you, Thatch."

He rushes me, pinning me to the workbench as he did the night we met, his expression one I've never seen. Unguarded, utterly and completely raw.

"If you tell me one more time that you're mine, I'll stay. I'll wait until you graduate, and I'll fucking ring your finger, Serena," he whispers. "I will earn you, and I'll fucking take you from the guy who deserves you. I'll steal you right now from the man who deserves your hand, your heart, your body, your future. I'll steal your fucking future because I want you that fucking much."

"Then take me, you stupid bastard," I rip at his hair as his lips brush mine, "but don't leave me."

We collide, our kiss hungry even as we exhale relieved gasps into each other's mouths.

"I love you," he croaks as my heart bursts into rhythm with relief. We rip at each other's clothes as he pushes my knees apart.

"I'm too pissed at you to return the sentiment."

"It's too late now, I'm not leaving you for anything. Not ever. I will marry you, Serena."

"Fine by me, jackass," I snap as he pulls my jeans and panties off, as I rip at the buttons on his fly. "But I expect a better proposal when the time comes."

"God, baby," he cups my face as I wrap around him, his length meeting my soaked middle. "You're really mine?"

"Been yours since we locked eyes, Thatcher O'Neal."

"Then fucking tell me," he demands as he runs his head along my soaked sex.

"I'm too pissed," I croak as he crushes me with his desperate kiss.

In seconds, he's lined up with me, pushing inside me inch by delicious inch.

"One day . . . you're going to have my baby," he declares with ferocity.

"One day," I whisper back, knowing he means it, feeling he means it as he claims the rest of me in one sure thrust. We both cry out at the feel of our connection as our desire runs rampant. The surreal feel of him, of us. Of our stinging hearts soothed now as he burns through me. I revel in the stretch as I claw his heated skin. My soul skyrockets as he rears back and thrusts in again and again, every single one claiming. Somewhere between fucking and making love, we collide over and over, becoming more solidified. On fire and utterly swept away, we make love all night. In the morning, we lay tangled in one another. Tangled in the hope of the words we spoke. Intertwined by the promises we made and determined by what's in our hearts to keep them.

"Young, stupid, and in love, but we kept them," I whisper, staring on at my husband, who breaks down boxes in clean up, his expression full of pride at his handiwork before he grins over at me. I cut the lights a second later to take in the view of both my husband and the snow drift falling in the cabin window behind him.

"What's that?" Thatch asks.

"I can't believe we're still together after all this time."

"What?" He asks, a little indignation in his tone.

"I mean, we fell in love *so fast* and decided on each other almost just as quickly. Made promises and then spent years seeing them through. You were under no obligation to stay in Tennessee when I went back to school. To marry me. Hell, we even waited a while after to have Gracie. We kept those promises because we truly did decide on each other that night. We knew, Thatch, and we meant it, but damn, the odds were stacked."

"It wasn't easy," he utters, seemingly just as reflective.

"Not at all. I powered through years of college. Our first apartment was a shithole thanks to your pride, but we did the damned thing, Thatch. I graduated, and we got married. I can't stop thinking about the night I stopped you from leaving . . ." Tears fill my eyes.

He nods. "I was just there on the ride home."

"I wonder why this year it's different, why we're looking back so much."

"So when they arrest us for our horrific parenting, we remember the good?" He chuckles.

Not ready to dismiss it, I continue to admire the man I married. "I wonder if you would have left if I hadn't stopped you."

"I probably would have," he says truthfully, and his words sear my heart, but I love that he's still so honest with me. "But I think I would have come back. I've never felt so much for anyone in my life. I knew—even though it scared me—I never would again. If you had let me go, I would have come back."

"You went from a hardened criminal to a boyfriend, an apprentice to a construction worker, to husband and father. Then, to master contractor and business owner. You're the epitome of self-made, Thatcher O'Neal. You underestimate yourself, but we didn't. I'm so proud of you. And you're right, you've really fucking come into yourself this year especially, and God do I love who you are." I relay as his eyes shine. "But with or without me, you would have become the man you are. I want you to know that."

"Doubtful," he whispers, his eyes shining. "You're so much of the reason I wanted to do better."

"No," I rake him. "No, Thatch. I love you for saying it, and maybe you believe that, but I know you would have done it. You'd already abandoned your worthless family and found your passion. Your aspirations were blooming. So, if it wasn't me, you would have found a woman to grow into yourself with. To believe in you and love you. To see you like I see you." My eyes water. "How lucky am I that it was *me*?"

His shimmering eyes spill over as he shakes his head. "Fuck, Serena."

"You need to hear this because though you just told our daughter the worst about your past, of what you're most ashamed of, I couldn't be more proud of the man I married. I'm so glad it was *me*."

"Baby, stop," he whispers, shaking his head in denial.

"In many ways, by comparison, you're almost a completely different man than the one I fell in love with in mere weeks, and somehow, you're still *my* favorite version of Thatcher O'Neal."

"Are you trying to kill me?" He utters in exasperation. "You can't bitch at me for twenty-two years and then say all these nice things at once. It's too much," he runs his knuckles on his chest. "Yep, I feel a heart attack coming."

"Stop joking, Thatch. I'm trying to make you realize that I understand now that we're the lucky ones. The kids and me. Have always been. We are the lucky ones—Gracie, Peyton, and me, and I'm sorry if I've ever made you feel differently."

He stalks over to me and kisses me softly, then deeply, and for a brief second, I'm the terrified nineteen-year-old holding her heart out for the first time to a boy, praying like hell he'll take it. In that kiss, he does, with every swipe of his tongue, his tender touch ringing out the same promises he made all those years ago. When we part, we touch foreheads. Pulling back, his eyes glitter down on me and, in those seconds, I feel it. The fleeting butterflies, the initial zing that bound us. But it's our lasting love and the life we made after that keeps us connected now. In keeping the promises we made so long ago, when we were far too young, too naïve, and had too much life to live to know if we would be able to keep them. But we did, and to this day, we do. Through it all, year after year.

"I'm just as proud to be your husband."

"Thank you, baby."

"Sometimes when I pull into the drive," he says, "I think about the road we've traveled," he states, reaching down and dipping into his jeans pocket, "and during every step, you made whatever house we had into a *real* home. Every single time." He takes my hand, opening it so my palm is up before depositing a locket into it, slowly piling a chain on top of it.

"Thatch, it's beautiful," I say, studying the uniqueness of it.

"Yeah, it's a pretty shiny thing, and I know how you like those, but it's what's inside that takes my breath away," he murmurs.

"My husband, the newborn romantic," I state. "I could really get used to this." I frown. "I hope it isn't a phase, like the faux hawk. I really love the damned faux hawk."

"Let me finish," he states.

"Sorry." Noting the O carved into the metal for our last name, I lift it so we can both admire it as he moves to stand closer to view my reaction.

"Baby, open it," he urges, his eyes alight as I press the tiny button on the side to release it, and it pops open. The hinge tight, I crack it wider and gasp when I see pictures of both Gracie and Peyton, and . . . me. Each of them in my arms, what looks like mere seconds after I gave birth. In both, I look an utter mess in my hospital gown, my hair plastered to my head, my eyes glued to the baby in my arms.

"Aside from the first time I laid eyes on you and the day you wore white and pranced down the aisle toward me—*smugly*," we share a smile.

"I totally pranced," I agree.

"These are the two images that stick out most in my memory. I mean, you looked like hell, let's be honest."

I glare at him, and he chuckles.

"But you still managed to be the most beautiful thing I'd ever seen. These images I've managed to memorize without needing a photo, but damn, am I glad I took them."

"When?" I study the photos that are so perfectly captured.

"Kicker is, I was obvious about it when I did, but you were too in love with our babies to notice. And baby," he draws my gaze to his with his tone, "that look in your eyes, the one you have for them right there, that's the way you look at me. How could I ever fuck-ing leave that?"

He hooks a finger under my chin, keeping my watering eyes to his. "We joke about you being my bitchy wife. Hell, I just made one, and over the years, I know you've felt guilty for the way you've spoken to me at times, Serena. But it's one of the reasons I fell for you. Even if my little masochistic kink has backfired here and there." He laughs as more tears spill over. "I didn't fall in love with you because you were a handful and expect you to at some point settle the fuck down. Let's face it, no amount of good dicking was ever going to tame you, Brat."

"Never mind, I'll never add romantic to your repertoire, Thatcher," I press my lips together before bursting into laughter. "You're the worst, but you have been so romantic this week. Is it over?"

"I hope not. But you and I both know we can promise one another to death and be a pathetic mess next week. I'm cool with whatever as long as it's forever," he declares.

"Me too."

"I mean it. That's why I want your family's motto right next to ours.

"What?"

He runs his finger down to the bottom of the locket and points at the inscription as I read it. "Chaos."

"And," he flips it over.

"Gravity. So cool, Thatch. I love it."

"Got to have one to appreciate the other, right?"

"You're awesome. And to think, all I got you was an *Elite* set of clubs."

His girly gasp follows me as I walk over to the coat closet and drag out the heavy bag that I donned with a giant bow as his jaw drops.

"Santa is real."

"Mep. You have a tee time set up at the country club for the first slot available—weather permitting—and a standing reservation every freaking week."

He frowns. "Baby, I can't play every week."

"You're taking it, Thatch. Daddy time. You time. Alone time.

Because what's the fucking point of being successful if you can't enjoy it?"

"Baby," he sets the clubs against the edge of the couch and scoops me beneath my ass, gazing up at me. "Damn, thank you. I know those were expensive as hell."

"You deserve them. Period. Merry Christmas, Thatchalamewl."

He rolls his eyes, his grin only amping. "Best one yet."

"I can think of another present to give you, Handy Man." I bounce my brows.

"I would be agreeable to that," he drops his voice, "but you're not really feeling that offer."

I gape at him.

"I know when my wife wants it, don't insult me. So . . . tops and bottoms tonight?"

"It's just, to be honest, I'm a little sore. I'm not as . . . flexible or quick to rebound as I used to be. If I'm brutal, my pussy feels like it got hit by a Mack truck. I. Am. Sore."

"I got a charley horse at the end," he admits sheepishly, "it totally almost fucked up my finish."

"Oh my God, I thought that was a new move!"

We both burst into laughter, and I shake my head. "What a life," I say on exhale. "Come on, baby, let's attempt some sleep. The kids will be up very soon."

We start to turn off the lights and toss all the remaining trash in the bag as I glance over at Thatch.

"You know, we've been dysfunctionally functioning for *twenty-two years*. Not that many couples can claim that. I'm proud of us. Hell, we even renewed our wedding vows."

"Like idiots," he jokes.

"Yeah, well, who's the idiot who *asked twice?*"

He gives me a lopsided grin. "And had two kids."

"You mean Gracie and the *Oops—*"

"Yeah, too bad we changed his name from Oops O'Neal. It suits him perfectly. They say you should always stick with your first instinct," I joke, tying off the trash bag as we both chuckle. "You think they talk shit about us like we do them?"

"Worse," he answers instantly, "and it is going to get worse. Think about how you, Whit, and Brenden talk about your parents."

"With the utmost respect," I defend.

His face screams skepticism. "Delusional."

After placing the trash just outside the front door, we glance back at the tree, the snow falling behind it as morning light threatens to break, a slightly purple hue filling the living room.

"Another all-nighter with my Handy Man," I say as he pulls me back to him, nuzzling me.

"Worth the loss of sleep," he murmurs.

"Yeah, but only for you and for our babies," I agree before we make our way upstairs. Not long after, my husband pulls his pajama top over my head before kissing me like he would his brat. Just after, tucking me into him. As he sleeps, I run my fingers through his hair with a thankful heart, sending a prayer up for twenty-two more years. Just after I doze off, Peyton knocks *twice*, announcing himself a split second before bursting through our door.

"Mommy! Daddy! Rudolph comed!!!"

EPILOGUE

Thatch

WRAPPING PAPER FLIES AS THE CHAMPAGNE CORK IS popped, a litany of glasses being poured as my son's voice sounds over it all.

"Oh my Dawd!" Peyton screeches. "Rudolph got my tickets, Daddy!" Peyton bursts with excitement from his designated unwrapping spot on the floor, where he sits next to his sister and cousins.

"Maybe if you're a good boy, you'll get to use them soon."

"Yes, Sir!" he sounds up, and I can't help but smile. His eyes linger on me for a few seconds before he suddenly pops up, running over to me full force where I sit on the couch. An "oof" escaping me as he rams into me before lifting his arms in instruction to help hoist him into my lap. I help his climb, his little elbows digging into me before he palms my jaw.

"I love you, Daddy, sooo much," he declares. Collective 'ahs' sounding around us before he closes his eyes and plants a slobbery, open-mouthed kiss right on mine. Chuckling, I wipe up his aftermath, my heart stinging because I know it's most likely one of the last of those kinds of kisses.

"I love you too, buddy, so very much." Holding onto the moment, I glance over to see our memory keeper, Whitney, with her phone raised, and I know she's captured it for me. I mouth a "thank you," to which she nods before Peyton rejoins the kids on the floor.

"I guess I'm mincemeat," Serena drawls playfully next to me, gripping my hand.

"You're anything but, baby," I whisper as she gives me a wink, no real offense taken.

"What's this?" Ruby asks, plucking the long tube I set in the corner last night from behind the tree. "For Mom and Dad?" She reads the tag. "Who is this from?"

"Me," I tell her as she beams over at me. Allen scrutinizes the tube, recognition lighting his features before a slow smile blooms on his face.

"What you up to, my boy?"

"Open it and see, Dad," I say. In seconds, Allen pulls the blueprints out and keeps his palms down to keep them open on the coffee table. The rest of the Collins crew gathers around them as Ruby looks on earnestly, and Allen raises his eyes to mine, emotion clogging his voice. "You want to expand the cabin?"

I nod as Ruby's eyes flick up and start to water. "Really?"

"I do, but I promise you, Mom, I will not mess up the integrity of this place. I just want to make a little more room for everyone. From what I've mapped, we have plenty of room to lengthen the back of the cabin. Enough for three more bedrooms and a Jack-and-Jill bath. This is only if you want it. No pressure. I just thought . . ." I swallow to tamp down the threatening emotions. "This place is special, and I want our children's children to enjoy it, too. What you've built. The family you, we made. It belongs here."

"You would really do that for us?" Ruby asks, tears shimmering.

"You should know I would do anything for you, Ruby," I tell her honestly, "but I would really love to do this."

"There's no deck?" Allen inquires in confusion.

"That, I thought we could redesign together and maybe build it out if I take some time off this summer?"

This time Allen's eyes water as I find the words.

"It was the scariest and best year of my life, and I really miss it."

"I have too," he whispers.

"Good, then it's a deal?"

Both of them stand, and I walk over and hug them individually. "This is incredible, Thatch. I'm so proud of you," Ruby whispers, "so proud. Thank you. I wholeheartedly trust you with this place and accept."

She pulls away as Allen tugs me into him, still a bear of a man. "You did good, Son. SO damned good."

"Thank you," I whisper, both as the terrified twenty-year-old he posed the decision to and the man that boy became. Allen gave me a chance where very few would, and for him, anything.

"What's this?" Serena asks, taking a round, wrapped package from the tree. "Oh, it's for *me*," she giggles before untying the bow and digging in.

Eli gives me a wink and lifts his glass to me, and I lift mine back as we both take a big sip of champagne, just as Serena speaks up.

"Pledge?" Serena balks, instantly offended. "Why would someone give me Pledge? What does this mean?"

Eli sprays the entire couch full of Collins' with the champagne in his mouth as Whitney's jaw drops, and she looks over to Ruby. "Oh my God, *Mom!*"

FALL
Twenty-Two Years Ago . . .

Exiting my rusted Silverado, I approach the bear of a man on the front porch of the house as his eyes roll over me. "Hey there, Thatcher?"

"It's Thatch," I say, extending my hand. "Good to meet you in person, Sir," I extend the welcome, shaking firmly while hoping he can't feel the sweat in my palm. Joshua's last call scared the fuck out of me. I can't go back to the life I barely escaped, nor a cell—not a second back in time. But if I don't land this job, I'll be stuck in my past, possibly for good.

With what this man's offering, I'll be able to pay up almost all of my restitution and get space from the dumpster fire I've been trapped in.

"Come on back," he says, walking down the short set of stairs to the backyard. "I'll show you what I'm thinking."

"Yessir," I say, trailing him.

"Allen," he states.

"Still Thatch," I joke, and I take his answering grin as a good sign.

"Smartass, huh? I speak it fluently, thanks to my kids."

Shit. Fuck!

"Shi—uh, I didn't mean it that way, Sir. Please take no offense."

He cuts his eyes back at me as I break out in a cold sweat. "None taken, Son, ease up. This isn't a desk job interview. If you have two hands, you're damned near qualified. I only have one other who answered the ad."

God, if you're there, it's me Thatch. Please. Just this job. I beg you. This job and I'll never ask for anything else.

"So, you do much carpentry?"

"I'll be honest, the minimum basics, but I take orders well. I only have to be told once, and I can haul every bit of this wood where you need it," I nod toward the gigantic stack of lumber.

"Well, what I have in mind is a bit complicated. This isn't a simple blueprint," he palms the back of his neck and looks over to me. "I'll be honest, it's pretty complex. This is a wrap-around, multi-level deck. Once we've poured cement and got the decking boards in, I might have us consult on more additions."

I nod as he grins over at me. "You don't have any idea what I'm talking about, do you?"

"No, Sir. I'm afraid I don't, but I will show up every day and do exactly as asked."

"I really could use an experienced hand," he delivers like a blow.

"I really could use this job, Sir. I'm quick on the uptake, I assure you."

"Where did you work before?"

"Odd jobs," I offer instantly.

He tucks his fingers in the back pockets of his jeans. "I see."

"You're not buying it," I swallow and swallow again.

"You're a little jumpy, Son, and frankly, you can't bullshit a bullshitter."

"I'm jumpy because I'm terrified of not getting this job," I state, and his warm eyes flit up to mine instantly.

"I'm sorry, Son, really. But I need someone with experience. This is a highly detailed project, and I was kind of hoping to find someone to help *guide me*."

"I understand, I really do. If I'm being honest, beginner was a stretch for me. Thank you so much for your time," I offer my hand, and he takes it, pumping it. Turning, I ignore the clog in my throat and the sting in my eyes, knowing that I just cost myself for lack of the right fucking words. My damned Achilles heel. My fucking father, my brother, they can both talk a nun out of their habits, but I can't get a fucking job as simple as a carpenter's hand. Can't keep my fucking cool enough to have a regular Joe view me as competent enough.

"Hey, Thatch," Allen calls behind me, and in a two-second stretch, I know I have to make the decision either to pretend not to hear him or try to come up with more words. I'm far enough away that his call could go unanswered, and he would know I'm ignoring him purposely to save face, but something, some whisper inside me, has me stopping in that yard and glancing back. Going with my gut, I stop my footing and face him, allowing him to see the tears rolling down my face as I run my wrist over them.

"You need this job that bad?"

Fucking humiliated, I nod, muted by the burn in my throat.

"Son," he exhales as if my expression pains him.

"Sorry," I croak. "See, this job c-could very well save my life,"

I gasp. "I'm sorry, I'm sorry, but it's the truth." I palm my forehead, breaking in front of a total stranger because I can't take another minute of the shitstorm that comes with being Christopher O'Neal's son. My levee threatens to full-on break as emotion seizes me, and I shake my head, warring with it to be able to speak my way into a different life. Forever screaming as I have been for the last ten years. For a chance to fight for myself.

Jesus, somebody, please fucking help me!

"Thatch," Allen gently coaxes, "can you try to talk to me about it?"

"I-I—" I glance back at my Silverado, my current home. One I've spent every night sleeping in for nearly nine months. Going from one apartment complex to the next and setting an alarm to jet before people start their morning commute—so they can't spot and get a chance to report me. People always assume sleeping in shopping center parking lots is the better way, but I've found apartments are the least likely to check—at least in my experience. But I'll take any night crammed up in that truck bench over a jail cell.

"I'm s-sorry, Sir. I'm fucking embarrassed."

"Need a minute?" He offers.

"N-no," the word comes out strangled as more humiliating tears roll down my cheeks. "I mean, yeah. Yes, please."

"Take as much as you need and meet me in the backyard."

I nod, palming my mouth, doing my best to try to get my shit together.

"Thatch?"

I look over to Allen, knowing my eyes are red-rimmed, and follow his gaze to see him staring at my truck as the truth of my situation sinks in on him. He glances back at me and holds my gaze.

"Take a minute, but don't go. Okay? And then come back and talk to me."

I nod, hating the fact that I can't control my emotions. Not once in lockup did I cry. I took every day on the chin and bore it. Not once in the years before did I show any of this weakness. Not even with my brother, who damn near fucking killed me with his endless

222 | KATE STEWART

antics. Not when my mother terrorized me with her fucked mind games. Not when my father congratulated me for getting away with my first car. From the beginning, I understood we weren't right—they weren't right. The cruelty of my reality and the fact that I didn't fit in at all and never really wanted to. I hated my family—still do, and now all I want is the space. Which is easier now with my father facing a sentence of twenty-five to life, my brother missing since I was in jail, and my mother having run off with some old friend of my father's. With their semi-permanent absence, I have this chance to finally free myself—to pay my restitution, finish probation, and leave Nashville. I gather my wits enough to fight again for my chance and stalk back to where Allen stands.

"Sorry about that," I say, my voice clear. "I won't bullshit you, Sir, but that means I risk losing this job. Even so, I won't lie to you, no matter how damning it sounds."

"Felon?" He asks.

"Yes, Sir. Grand Theft at seventeen, my juvenile record had me tried as an adult. I spent nine months in. I'm four months away from finishing probation, and I just need enough money to pay off restitution."

"Do you want to tell me why?"

"No, but I will. I come from a family full of criminals, and I followed suit. It wasn't expected, it was forced. The night I tried to escape it, my father pistol-whipped me to within an inch of my life. Two days later, I was arrested in a Maserati and was sentenced. I've broken all ties with my family and even offered them up for a plea."

"Christopher O'Neal."

"Notorious, I know. That's the damning part, and that's why I'm not getting any breaks and asking for any. I want to work my way out of this. I intend to get off probation and get the hell out of this state. Start over. Permanently."

"I have two daughters, Thatch, and a son I would move heaven and earth to protect."

"I'm cars only, and before that, I was petty theft. I can only give you my word that I would never harm you, as much as it might not mean. But I'm doing my best to try and make that word mean something. I can only prove myself over time. I just need the chance," I hear myself beg.

His eyes roam over me, and I see his reasoning kicking in, his expression not telling one way or another. "I'll need to talk to my wife about this. I'll have to get specific with her."

Deflating, I nod. "I can go."

"No, Thatch, stay, but I mean to tell her everything you relayed, Son. I do not lie to my wife. Ever. Well, at least about this, I did about the number of beers I drank two weeks ago."

We share a grin, and my chest heaves slightly with hope as I do all I can to keep my shit together.

"I'll work overtime for free, Allen. I just have to have a job to report to and get paid up. Pass my last few drug tests, and then I'm getting the hell out of here. I want no part of a future in Tennessee."

"I understand," he nods. "Sit tight and give me a minute. I'm making no promises, but if I go to bat for you with that woman, please don't fucking let me down."

"On my life, Sir, on everything, I will not let you down," the shake in my voice seems to pain him as he studies me for a long minute before he says three words to me I've never heard.

"I believe you." And then four more I never dreamed I'd hear. "I believe in you. I'll think you'll do exactly that, Thatch."

He turns abruptly as I jerk my head to the side, palming my face to keep my emotions from escaping. Pride battered beyond recognition, I vow that if I get this chance to escape the life I had, I'll take it with gratitude. Even if it means scraping by every fucking day on the wages of a convicted felon for the rest of my life, I'll do it straight, and I'll be fucking thankful. Any life over this one. Any life. Glancing around the house, I imagine what being on the other side would be like. To sleep within walls where people treat one another like they mean something and pitching in means taking out the trash. Doing laundry. Not hotwiring a fucking Jaguar in order to pay your own fucking way at eleven. Sinking into the grass of the peaceful house, I spot a blonde peeking her head out of the window. Terrified she heard Allen's confession, I give her a subtle wave and she waves back, a smile on her lips. She can't be more than sixteen, seventeen at most. In the next second, she disappears behind a curtain.

What seems like an eternity later, a woman's voice summons me. "Thatch?"

I stand abruptly and turn to see a beautiful woman standing at the back door. "Honey, do you like barbecue chicken?"

My eyes sting, and I feel the burst threatening, to the point that all I can do is nod.

"Well, come on then. Whitney's shucking corn in the kitchen. Let's get you washed up. You and me, we have some cooking to do."

"Yes, ma'am," I croak tearfully as she closes the door, giving me the space I need to collect myself. Palms on my thighs, I whisper out a "thank you, thank you" as guttural cries break from me. Once I've collected myself a second time, I begin making my way toward the back door. As I approach the house, I take notice of a wooden sign adhered to the glass at the top of the back door by little plastic suction cups. With every step I take, I'm able to make out another bolded letter—

G-R-A-V-I-T-Y.

The End

ABOUT THE AUTHOR

USA Today bestselling author and Texas native, Kate Stewart, lives in North Carolina with her husband, Nick. Nestled within the Blue Ridge Mountains, Kate pens messy, sexy, angst-filled contemporary romance, as well as romantic comedy and erotic suspense.

Kate's title, *Drive*, was named one of the best romances of 2017 by The New York Daily News and Huffington Post. *Drive* was also a finalist in the Goodreads Choice awards for best contemporary romance of 2017. The Ravenhood Trilogy, consisting of *Flock*, *Exodus*, and *The Finish Line*, has become an international bestseller and reader favorite. Her holiday release, *The Plight Before Christmas*, ranked #6 on Amazon's Top 100. Kate's works have been featured in *USA TODAY, BuzzFeed, The New York Daily News, Huffington Post* and translated into a dozen languages.

Kate is a lover of all things '80s and '90s, especially John Hughes films and rap. She dabbles a little in photography, can knit a simple stitch scarf for necessity, and on occasion, does very well at whiskey.

Other titles available now by Kate

Romantic Suspense

The Ravenhood Series
Flock
Exodus
The Finish Line

Lust & Lies Series
Sexual Awakenings
Excess
Predator and Prey
The Lust & Lies Box set: Sexual Awakenings, Excess, Predator and Prey

Contemporary Romance

In Reading Order

Room 212
Never Me (Companion to Room 212 and The Reluctant Romantic Series)
The Reluctant Romantics Series
The Fall
The Mind
The Heart
The Reluctant Romantics Box Set: The Fall, The Heart, The Mind
Loving the White Liar

The Bittersweet Symphony
Drive
Reverse

The Real
Someone Else's Ocean
Heartbreak Warfare
Method

Romantic Dramedy

Balls in Play Series
Anything but Minor
Major Love
Sweeping the Series Novella
Balls in play Box Set: Anything but Minor, Major Love, Sweeping the
Series, The Golden Sombrero

The Underdogs Series
The Guy on the Right
The Guy on the Left
The Guy in the Middle
The Underdogs Box Set: The Guy on The Right, The Guy on the Left,
The Guy in the Middle

The Plight Before Christmas

Let's stay in touch!

Facebook
www.facebook.com/authorkatestewart

Newsletter
www.katestewartwrites.com/contact-me.html

Twitter
twitter.com/authorklstewart

Instagram
www.instagram.com/authorkatestewart/?hl=en

Book Group
www.facebook.com/groups/793483714004942

Spotify
open.spotify.com/user/authorkatestewart

Sign up for the newsletter now and get a free eBook from
Kate's Library!

Newsletter signup
www.katestewartwrites.com/contact-me.html

Made in the USA
Las Vegas, NV
29 December 2024